D0015603

ZONE ONE

ALSO BY COLSON WHITEHEAD

The Intuitionist

John Henry Days

The Colossus of New York

Apex Hides the Hurt

Sag Harbor

COLSON WHITEHEAD

DOUBLEDAY

NEW YORK LONDON TORONTO SYDNEY AUCKLAND

This book is a work of fiction. Names, characters, businesses, organizations, places, events, and incidents either are the product of the author's imagination or are used fictitiously. Any resemblance to actual persons, living or dead, events, or locales is entirely coincidental.

 Published in the United States by Doubleday, a division of Random House, Inc., New York, and in Canada by Random House of Canada Limited, Toronto.

www.doubleday.com

DOUBLEDAY and the portrayal of an anchor with a dolphin are registered trademarks of Random House, Inc.

The epigraphs are by Walter Benjamin, Ezra Pound, and Public Enemy, respectively.

Book design by Pei Loi Koay
Jacket design by Rodrigo Corral Design

LIBRARY OF CONGRESS CATALOGING-IN-PUBLICATION DATA
Whitehead, Colson, 1969–
Zone one : a novel / Colson Whitehead. — 1st ed.
p. cm.
1. Zombies—Fiction. 2. Virus diseases—Fiction. I. Title.
PS3573.H4768Z36 2011
813'.54—dc22
2011008339

ISBN 978-0-385-52807-8

PRINTED IN THE UNITED STATES OF AMERICA

10 9 8 7 6 5 4 3 2 1

First Edition

TO BILL THOMAS

ZONE ONE

FRIDAY

"The gray layer of dust covering things has become their best part."

He always wanted to live in New York. His Uncle Lloyd lived downtown on Lafayette, and in the long stretches between visits he daydreamed about living in his apartment. When his mother and father dragged him to the city for that season's agreed-upon exhibit or good-for-you Broadway smash, they usually dropped in on Uncle Lloyd for a quick hello. These afternoons were preserved in a series of photographs taken by strangers. His parents were holdouts in an age of digital multiplicity, raking the soil in lonesome areas of resistance: a coffee machine that didn't tell time, dictionaries made out of paper, a camera that only took pictures. The family camera did not transmit their coordinates to an orbiting satellite. It did not allow them to book airfare to beach resorts with close access to rain forests via courtesy shuttle. There was no prospect of video, high-def or otherwise. The camera was so backward that every lurching specimen his father enlisted from the passersby was able to operate it sans hassle, no matter the depth of cow-eyed vacancy in their tourist faces or local wretchedness inverting their spines. His family posed on the museum steps or beneath the brilliant marquee with the poster screaming over their left shoulders, always the same composition. The boy stood in the middle, his parents' hands dead on his shoulders, year after year. He didn't smile in every picture, only that percentage culled for the photo album. Then it was in the cab to his uncle's and up the elevator once the doorman screened them. Uncle Lloyd dangled in the doorframe and greeted them with a louche "Welcome to my little bungalow."

As his parents were introduced to Uncle Lloyd's latest girlfriend, the boy was down the hall, giddy and squeaking on the leather of the cappuccino sectional and marveling over the latest permutations in home entertainment. He searched for the fresh arrival first thing. This visit it was the wireless speakers haunting the corners like spindly wraiths, the next he was on his knees before a squat blinking box that served as some species of multimedia brainstem. He dragged a finger down their dark surfaces and then huffed on them and wiped the marks with his polo shirt. The televisions were the newest, the biggest, levitating in space and pulsing with a host of extravagant functions diagrammed in the unopened owner's manuals. His uncle got every channel and maintained a mausoleum of remotes in the storage space inside the ottoman. The boy watched TV and loitered by the glass walls, looking out on the city through smoky anti-UV glass, nineteen stories up.

The reunions were terrific and rote, early tutelage in the recursive nature of human experience. "What are you watching?" the girlfriends asked as they padded in bearing boutique seltzer and chips, and he'd say "The buildings," feeling weird about the pull the skyline had on him. He was a mote cycling in the wheels of a giant clock. Millions of people tended to this magnificent contraption, they lived and sweated and toiled in it, serving the mechanism of metropolis and making it bigger, better, story by glorious story and idea by unlikely idea. How small he was, tumbling between the teeth. But the girlfriends were talking about the monster movies on TV, the women in the monster movies bolting through the woods or shriveling in the closet trying not to make a sound or vainly flagging down the pickup that might rescue them from the hillbilly slasher. The ones still standing at the credit roll made it through by dint of an obscure element in their character. "I can't stand these scary stories," the girlfriends said before returning to the grown-ups, attempting an auntly emanation as if they might be the first of their number promoted to that office. His father's younger brother was fastidious when it came to expiration dates.

He liked to watch monster movies and the city churning below. He fixed on odd details. The ancient water towers lurking atop obstinate old prewars and, higher up, the massive central-air units that hunkered and coiled on the striving high-rises, glistening like extruded guts. The tar-paper pates of tenements. He spotted the occasional out-of-season beach chair jackknifed on gravel, seemingly gusted up from the street below. Who was its owner? This person staked out corners of the city and made a domain. He squinted at the slogans cantering along stairwell entrances, the Day-Glo threats and pidgin manifestos, a.k.a.'s of impotent revolutionaries. Blinds and curtains were open, half open, shut, voids in a punch card decipherable only by defunct mainframes lodged in the crust of unmarked landfills. Pieces of citizens were on display in the windows, arranged by a curator with a taste for non sequitur: the splayed pinstriped legs of an urban golfer putting into a colander; half a lady's torso, wrapped in a turquoise blazer, as glimpsed through a trapezoid; a fist trembling on a titanium desk. A shadow bobbed behind a bathroom's bumpy glass, steam slithering through the slit.

He remembered how things used to be, the customs of the skyline. Up and down the island the buildings collided, they humiliated runts through verticality and ambition, sulked in one another's shadows. Inevitability was mayor, term after term. Yesterday's old masters, stately named and midwifed by once-famous architects, were insulted by the soot of combustion engines and by technological advances in construction. Time chiseled at elegant stonework, which swirled or plummeted to the sidewalk in dust and chips and chunks. Behind the façades their insides were butchered, reconfigured, rewired according to the next era's new theories of utility. Classic six into studio honeycomb, sweatshop killing floor into cordoned cubicle mill. In every neighborhood the imperfect in their fashion awaited the wrecking ball and their bones were melted down to help their replacements surpass them, steel into steel. The new buildings in wave upon wave drew themselves out of rubble, shaking off the past like immigrants. The addresses remained the same and so did the flawed philosophies. It wasn't anyplace else. It was New York City.

The boy was smitten. His family stopped by Uncle Lloyd's every couple of months. He drank the seltzer, he watched monster movies, he was a sentry at the window. The building was a totem sheathed in blue metal, a changeling in the nest of old walk-ups. The zoning commission had tucked the bribes into their coats, and now there he was, floating over the tapering island. There was a message there, if he could teach himself the language. On rainy-day visits the surfaces of the buildings were pitiless and blank, as they were this day, years later. With the sidewalks hidden from view, the boy conjured an uninhabited city, where no one lived behind all those miles and miles of glass, no one caught up with loved ones in living rooms filled with tasteful and affirming catalog furniture, and all the elevators hung like broken puppets at the end of long cables. The city as ghost ship on the last ocean at the rim of the world. It was a gorgeous and intricate delusion, Manhattan, and from crooked angles on overcast days you saw it disintegrate, were forced to consider this tenuous creature in its true nature.

If you'd asked him on any of those childhood afternoons

what he wanted to be when he grew up—tapping his shoulder as the family car inserted itself into the queue for the Midtown Tunnel or as they hummed toward their exit on the Long Island Expressway—he would have had nothing to offer with regards to profession or avocation. His father wanted to be an astronaut when he was a kid, but the boy had never been anything but earthbound, kicking pebbles. All he was truly sure of was that he wanted to live in a city gadget, something well-stocked and white-walled, equipped with rotating bosomy beauties. His uncle's apartment resembled the future, a brand of manhood waiting on the other side of the river. When his unit finally started sweeping beyond the wall—whenever that was—he knew he had to visit Uncle Lloyd's apartment, to sit on the sectional one last time and stare at the final, empty screen in the series. His uncle's building was only a few blocks past the barrier and he found himself squinting at it when it strode into view. He searched for the apartment, counting metallic blue stories and looking for movement. The dark glass relinquished nothing. He hadn't seen his uncle's name on any of the survivor rolls and prayed against a reunion, the slow steps coming down the hall.

If you'd asked him about his plans at the time of the ruin, the answer would have come easily: lawyering. He was bereft of attractive propositions, constitutionally unaccustomed to enthusiasm, and generally malleable when it came to his parents' wishes, adrift on that gentle upper-middle-class current that kept its charges cheerfully bobbing far from the shoals of responsibility. It was time to stop drifting. Hence, law. He was long past finding it ironic when his unit swept a building in that week's grid and they came upon a den of lawyers. They slogged through the blocks day after day and there had been too many firms in too many other buildings for it to have any novelty. But this day he paused. He slung his assault rifle over his shoulder and parted the blinds at the end of the corridor. All he wanted was a shred of uptown. He tried to orient himself: Was he looking north or south? It was like dragging a fork through gruel. The ash smeared the city's palette into a gray hush on the best of days, but introduce clouds and a little bit of precip and the city became an altar to obscurity. He was an insect exploring a gravestone: the words and names were crevasses to get lost in, looming and meaningless.

This was the fourth day of rain, Friday afternoon, and a conditioned part of him submitted to end-of-the-week lassitude, even if Fridays had lost their meaning. Hard to believe that reconstruction had progressed so far that clock-watching had returned, the slacker's code, the concept of weekend. It had been a humdrum couple of days, reaffirming his belief in reincarnation: everything was so boring that this could not be the first time he'd experienced it. A cheerful thought, in its way, given the catastrophe. We'll be back. He dropped his pack, switched off the torch in his helmet, and pushed his forehead to the glass as if he were at his uncle's, rearranging the architecture into a message. The towers emerged out of smudged charcoal, a collection of figments and notions of things. He was fifteen floors up, in the heart of Zone One, and shapes trudged like slaves higher and higher into midtown.

They called him Mark Spitz nowadays. He didn't mind.

Mark Spitz and the rest of Omega Unit were half done with 135 Duane Street, chugging down from the roof at a productive clip. All clear so far. Only a few signs of mayhem in the building. A ransacked petty cash drawer on eighteen, half-eaten takeout rotting on scattered desks: superannuated currency and the final lunches. As in most businesses they swept, the offices had shut their doors before things completely deteriorated. The chairs were snug at their desks, where they had been tucked by the maintenance crew on their last night of work, the last sane evening in the world, only a few askew and facing the doors in trample-exit disarray.

In the silence, Mark Spitz signed off on a rest period for himself. Who knew? If things had been otherwise, he might have taken a position in this very firm, once he completed the obstacles attendant to a law degree. He'd been taking prep classes when the curtain fell and hadn't worried about getting in somewhere, or graduating or getting some brand of job afterward. He'd never had trouble with the American checklist, having successfully executed all the hurdles of his life's stages, from preschool to junior high to college, with unwavering competence and nary a wobble into exceptionality or failure. He possessed a strange facility for the mandatory. Two days into kindergarten, for example, he attained the level of socialization deemed appropriate for those of his age and socioeconomic milieu (sharing, no biting, an almost soulful contemplation of instructions from people in authority) with a minimum of fuss. He nailed milestone after developmental milestone, as if every twitch were coached. Had they been aware of his location, child behaviorists would have cherished him, observing him through binoculars and scratching their ledgers as he confirmed their data and theories in his anonymous travails. He was their *typical*, he was their *most*, he was their *average*, receiving hearty thumbs-ups from the gents in the black van parked a discreet distance across the street. In this world, however, his reward was that void attending most human endeavor, with which all are well acquainted. His accomplishments, such as they were, gathered on the heap of the unsung.

Mark Spitz kept his eyes open and watched his environment for cues, a survivalist even at a tender age. There was a code in every interaction, and he tuned in. He adjusted easily to the introduction of letter grades, that first measure of one's facility with arbitrary contests. He staked out the B or the B chose him: it was his native land, and in high school and college he did not stray over the county line. At any rate his lot was irrevocable. He was not made team captain, nor was he the last one picked. He sidestepped detention and honor rolls with equal aplomb. Mark Spitz's high school had abolished the yearbook practice of nominating students the Most Likely to Do This or That, in the spirit of universal self-esteem following a host of acrimonious parent-teacher summits, but his most appropriate designation would have been Most Likely Not to Be Named the Most Likely Anything, and this was not a category. His aptitude lay in the well-executed muddle, never shining, never flunking, but gathering himself for what it took to progress past life's next random obstacle. It was his solemn expertise.

Got him this far.

He burped up some of that morning's breakfast paste, which had been concocted, according to the minuscule promises on the side of the tube, to replicate a nutritionist's concept of how mama's flapjacks topped with fresh blueberries tasted. His hand leaped to his mouth before he remembered he was alone. The attorneys had leased four floors, a sleek warren, and hadn't been doing too bad for themselves from the extent of their renovation. The floors above were chopped up into drab and modest suites, with dreary watercolors hooked into the spongy drywall of the waiting rooms and the same scuffed puke-pink tiles underfoot. Amenable leases made for a varied group of tenants, as motley as the collection found in the average rush-hour subway car. His unit swept consulting firms with fleet and efficient-sounding names, they poked through the supply rooms of prosthetics dealers and mail-order seed companies. They swept travel agencies nearly extinct in an internet age, the exhortations and invitations on the posters hitting shrill and desperate registers. On nineteen, they walked in formation through the soundproofed rooms of a movie-production house that specialized in straight-to-video martial arts flicks and in the gloom mistook a cardboard cutout of an action hero for a hostile. They were in the same kind of places day after day. Keys for the communal bathrooms down the hall hung on His and Hers hooks in Reception, affixed to broad plastic tongues. Recycled paper stretched expectantly across tables in doctors' examination rooms like a smear of oatmeal and the magazines in the waiting rooms described an exuberant age now remote and hard to reconcile. It was impossible to find a gossip magazine or newsweekly that had been published beyond a certain date. There was no more gossip and no more news.

When they stepped into the lawyers' suite they stumbled into a sophisticated grotto, as if the floors had been dealt into the building from some more upscale deck. In the waiting room, their helmet lights roved over the perplexing geometric forms in the carpet that they sullied with their combat boots, the broad panels of dark zebra wood covering the walls with elegant surety, and the low, sleek furniture that promised bruises yet, when tested, compressed one's body according to newly discovered principles of somatic harmony. Their three lights converged on the portrait of a man with flinty eyes and the narrowed mouth of a peckish fox—one of the founding fathers keeping watch from the great beyond. After a pause their lights diverged again, groping for movement in the corners and dark places.

Mark Spitz felt it the instant they pushed in the glass doors and saw the firm's name hovering in grim steel letters over the receptionist's desk: these guys will crush you. Tradition and hard deals, inviolable fine print that would outlast its framers. He didn't know the nature of their practice. Perhaps they only represented charities and nonprofits, but in that case he was sure their clients out-healed, out-helping-handed, overall out-charitied their competing charities, if it can be said that charities competed with one another. But of course they must, he thought. Even angels are animals.

Once inside, the unit split up and he swept solo through the workstations. The office furniture was hypermodern and toylike, fit for an app garage or a graphic-design firm keen on sketching the future. The surfaces of the desks were thick and transparent, hacked out of plastic and elevating the curvilinear monitors and keyboards in dioramas of productivity. The empty ergonomic chairs posed like amiable spiders, whispering a multiplicity of comfort and lumbar massage. He saw himself aloft on the webbing of the seat, wearing the suspenders and cuff links of his tribe, releasing wisps of unctuous cologne whenever he moved his body. Bring me the file, please. He goosed a leprechaun bobblehead with his assault rifle and sent it wiggling on its spring. Per his custom, he avoided looking at the family pictures.

He interpreted: We are studied in the old ways, and acolytes of what's to come. A fine home for a promising young lawyer. For all that had transpired outside this building in the great unraveling, the pure industry of this place still persisted. Insisting on itself. He felt it in his skin even though the people were gone and all the soft stuff was dead. Moldering lumps shot out tendrils in the common-area fridges, and the vicinities of the dry watercoolers were devoid of shit-shooting idlers, but the ferns and yuccas were still green because they were plastic, the awards and citations remained secure on the walls, and the portraits of the bigwigs preserved one afternoon's calculated poses. These things remained.

He heard three shots from the other end of the floor, in familiar staccato—Gary shooting open a door. Fort Wonton warned them repeatedly about brutalizing, vandalizing, or even extending the odd negative vibe toward the properties whenever possible, for obvious reasons. For convenience's sake, Buffalo printed up No-No Cards—laminated instruction squares that the sweepers were supposed to keep on their persons at all times. The broken window with the red circle and diagonal line across it was at the top of the deck. Gary couldn't restrain himself, however, future tenants and the grand design be damned. Why use the doorknob when you could light it up? "They can fix it when they move in," Gary said, as the smoke cleared from the C-4 he'd used to vaporize the door of an Italian restaurant's walk-in freezer. His crazy grin. As if cleaning up after semiautomatic fire were the same as touching up dings in the plaster where the previous tenants had hung their black-and-white landscapes. Gary dematerialized the half-closed curtains of department-store dressing rooms, converted expensive Japanese room dividers into twisting confetti, and woe to bathroom stalls with sticky hinges.

"Coulda been one of them in there trying to remember how to take a piss," Gary explained.

"Never heard of such a case," Kaitlyn said.

"This is New York City, man."

Kaitlyn rationed him to one unnecessary act of carnage per floor and Gary made the appropriate adjustments, even applying timeworn principles of suspense to when he attacked his targets. They never knew when he'd strike next. He had just made his selection for the fifteenth floor.

Mark Spitz got in gear. Gary was close and he wanted to look busy in order to head off any wisecracks about his work ethic. He turned from the window and briefly caught an edge of last night's dream—he was in the country, undulating farmland, perhaps at Happy Acres—before it squirmed away. He shook it off. He kicked in the door to Human Resources, thought "Maybe I'll come back and ask for a job when this is all over," and saw his error.

The door was not the issue. After all this time in the Zone, he knew the right place to slam these keypad doors so that they popped open, presto. The mistake lay in succumbing to the prevailing delusions. Giving in to that pandemic of pheenie optimism that was inescapable nowadays and made it hard to breathe, a contagion in its own right. They were on him in an instant.

They had been there since the beginning, the four of them. Perhaps one had been attacked down on the pavement by "some nut," that colorful metropolitan euphemism, and was sent home after getting a few stitches at the local underfunded ER—Do you have your insurance card handy?—before they understood the nature of the disaster. Then she turned feral and one lucky coworker made it out in time, locked the door, and left her cubicle-mates to fend for themselves. Some variation on that story. No one came back to help because they were overcome by their own situations.

He was the first live human being the dead had seen since the start, and the former ladies of HR were starving. After all this time, they were a thin membrane of meat stretched over bone. Their skirts were bunched on the floor, having slid off their shrunken hips long ago, and the dark jackets of their sensible dress suits were made darker still, and stiffened, by jagged arterial splashes and kernels of gore. Two of them had lost their high heels at some point during the long years of bumping around the room looking for an exit. One of them wore the same brand of panties his last two girlfriends had favored, with the distinctive frilled red edges. They were grimed and torn. He couldn't help but notice the thong, current demands on his attention aside. He'd made a host of necessary recalibrations but the old self made noises from time to time. Then that new self stepped in. He had to put them down.

The youngest one wore its hair in a style popularized by a sitcom that took as its subject three roommates of seemingly immiscible temperaments and their attempts to make their fortune in this contusing city. A crotchety super and a flamboyant neighbor rounded out the ensemble, and it was still appointment television, a top-ten show, at the time of the disaster. The hairdo was called a Marge, after Margaret Halstead, the charmingly klutzy actress who'd trademarked it in the old days of red carpets and flirty tête-à-têtes on late-night chat shows. She hadn't done anything for Mark Spitz—too skinny—but the legions of young ladies who fled their stunted towns and municipalities to reinvent themselves in the Big City recognized something in her flailings, and fetishized this piece of her. They had been reeled in by the old lie of making a name for oneself in the city; now they had to figure out how to survive. Hunt-and-gather rent money, forage ramen. In this week's written-up clubs and small-plate eateries, loose flocks of Marges were invariably underfoot, sipping cinnamon-rimmed novelty cocktails and laughing too eagerly.

The Marge nabbed Mark Spitz first, snatching his left bicep and taking it in its teeth. It never looked at his face, ferocious on the mesh of his fatigues and aware exclusively of the meat it knew was underneath. He'd forgotten how much it hurt when a skel tried to get a good chomp going; it had been some time since one had gotten this close. The Marge couldn't penetrate the intricate blend of plastic fibers—only an idiot cast aspersions on the new miracle fabric, born of plague-era necessity—but each rabid sally sent him howling. The rest of Omega would be here soon, tromping down the halls. He heard the sound of teeth splintering. The sweepers were supposed to stay together, the Lieutenant was firm about that, to prevent this very situation. But the last few grids had been so quiet, they hadn't stuck to orders.

The Marge was occupied for the moment—it took time for their diminished perceptions to catch on to the futility of the enterprise—so he directed his attention to the skel charging from two o'clock.

The bushy eyebrows, the whisper of a mustache—it was hard to avoid recognizing in this one his sixth-grade English teacher, Miss Alcott, who had diagrammed sentences in a soupy Bronx accent and fancied old-style torpedo bras. She smelled of jasmine when she passed his desk, plucking vocab quizzes. He'd always had a soft spot for Miss Alcott.

This one was probably the first infected. Everything below its eyes was a dark, gory muzzle, the telltale smear produced when a face burrowed deep into live flesh. Just another day at the office when she gets bit by some New York whacko while loading up on spring mix at the corner deli's Salad Lounge. Full of plague but unaware. That night the shivers came, and the legendary bad dreams everyone had heard about and prayed against—the harbingers, the nightmares that were the subconscious rummaging through a lifetime for some kind of answer to or escape from this trap. With those early strains, you might last a whole day without flipping. She returns to her cubicle the next day because she hadn't taken a sick day in years. Then transformation.

It happened every so often that he recognized something in these monsters, they looked like someone he had known or loved. Eighth-grade lab partner or lanky cashier at the mini-mart, college girlfriend spring semester junior year. Uncle. He lost time as his brain buzzed on itself. He had learned to get on with the business at hand, but on occasion Mark Spitz fixed on eyes or a mouth that belonged to someone lost, actively seeking concordance. He hadn't decided if conjuring an acquaintance or loved one into these creatures was an advantage or not. A "successful adaptation," as the Lieutenant put it. When Mark Spitz thought about it—when they were bivouacked at night in some rich fuck's loft or up to their chins in their sleeping bags on the floor of a Wall Street conference room—perhaps these recognitions ennobled his mission: He was performing an act of mercy. These things might have been people he knew, not-quites and almost-could-be's, they were somebody's family and they deserved release from their blood sentence. He was an angel of death ushering these things on their stalled journey from this sphere. Not a mere exterminator eliminating pests. He shot Miss Alcott in the face, converting resemblance to red mist, and then all the air was wrung from his chest and he was on the carpet.

The one in the candy-pink dress suit had tackled him—the Marge wrenched him off-balance with her aggressive pursuit, and he couldn't right himself once this new one rammed him. It straddled him and he felt the rifle grind into his back; he'd slung it over his shoulder during his pit stop by the window. He looked into the skel's spiderweb of gray hair. The jutting pins, the dumb thought: How long did it take for its wig to fall off? (Time slowed down in situations like this, to grant dread a bigger stage.) The thing on top of him clawed into his neck with its seven remaining fingers. The other fingers had been bitten off at the knuckle and likely jostled about in the belly of one of its former coworkers. He realized he'd dropped his pistol in the fall.

Surely this one possessed the determination befitting a true denizen of Human Resources, endowed by nature and shaped by nurture into its worthy avatar. The plague's recalibration of its faculties only honed the underlying qualities. Mark Spitz's first office job had involved rattling a mail cart down the corridors of a payroll company located in a Hempstead office park not too far from his house. As a child he'd decided the complex was some sort of clearinghouse for military intelligence, mistaking its impassive façades for clandestine power. The veil was lifted the first day. The other guys in the mail room were his age and when his boss shut the door to his office they got a splendid doofus chorus going. The only downer was the ogre head of Human Resources, who'd been relentless about Mark Spitz's paperwork, downright insidious about his W-this, W-that, the proper credentials. She served the places where human beings were paraphrased into numbers, components of bundled data to be shot out through fiber-optic cable toward meaning.

"Your check can't be processed without complete paperwork." How was he supposed to know where his Social Security card was? His bedroom was a dig. He needed special excavating tools to find socks. "You're not in the system. You might as well not exist." Where was The System now, after the calamity? It had been an invisible fist floating above them for so long and now the fingers were open, disjoined, and everything slipped through, everything escaped. By August he'd scurried back to the service industry, doling out pomegranate martinis on Ladies' Wednesdays. He tried to heave Human Resources off him. The skel's eyes dipped to the soft meat of his face. It went in for a bite.

Like most of the grunts in the sweeper units, he declined to wear his faceplate, despite the regulations, No-No Card, and all the times he'd witnessed that decision turn out poorly. You couldn't hump forty pounds of equipment up a New York City high-rise while fogging up a plastic faceplate. Supply lines were still a broken mess all around, and the sweepers were the lowest priority in everything except when it came to bullets. Everybody had enough bullets, from the Northeast Corridor to Omaha to Zone One, now that Buffalo had Barnes up and running, the former homemakers and chronic asthmatics and assorted old biddies on the assembly lines cranking out ammo day and night. Nowadays, Rosie the Riveter was a former soccer mom who had just opened her own catering business when Last Night came down and her husband and kids were eaten by a parking attendant at the local megamall's discount-appliance emporium.

Priorities: First Buffalo got what they needed, then the military, then civilian population, and finally the sweepers. Which meant Mark Spitz didn't have proper face gear, one of those fancy marine numbers with the lightweight impenetrable wire, proper ventilation, and neck sheathing. He'd seen one sad sack who patrolled in a goalie's mask—an affectation, really, because it was too easy for one of the skels to rip it off. Some of the guys in the other units had taken to drilling air holes into the thick plastic faceplate, and he made a note to try that last trick if he made it out of this mess. Face gear or no, however, you never wanted to get pinned.

First time he saw someone get pinned by a group of them was in the early days, must have been, because he was still trying to get out of his neighborhood. An invisible barrier surrounded his zip code, each opportunity for escape was undermined by his certainty that things were about to go back to normal, that this savage new reality could not hold. He was wending to the strip mall half a mile from his house—civilization's nearest representative consisted of the 24-7 gas-and-cigarette vendor, the famously grim pizza-and-sub place, and a moribund dry cleaner, that reliable exacerbator of stains. Mark Spitz had spent the night up in the arms of an oak, the first of many tree-limb slumber parties to come. It occurred to him that if anyone was equipped for this "new situation," it was Mr. Provenzano and the reputed arsenal he had stashed in the basement of the pizza shop. The basement weapons stash was a sturdy and beloved topic of speculation among mayhem-adoring kids and insinuating grown-ups alike, fed by rumors of mob-induction ceremonies and a robust lore centered around the meat grinder.

Mark Spitz didn't know if the pizza shop was accessible, but it was a better prospect than the silenced lanes of New Grove, the subdivision his parents had moved to thirty years before, their wedding gifts sitting in the foyer when they returned from their honeymoon. He waited for daylight and beat his numb legs and arms to get the blood into them. Then he cut through the clutch backyards, the hardwired shortcuts from his kid days, and crept and scrambled around the half-finished mini-mansion on Claremont trying to get the lay of the street before making a break for the main road. The construction company had lost liquidity the year before and his parents complained about the eyesore as if under contractual obligation. The plastic sheets rippling where there should have been walls, the great mounds of orange dirt that seeped out in defeat after every rain. It was a breeding ground for mosquitoes, his parents fussed. They spread sickness.

The old man came jogging down the asphalt. A gray cardigan flapped over his bare chest, and green plaid pants cut off a comical length above his slippers, which were secured to his feet with black electrical tape. Six of the devils congregated on the lawn of a mock Tudor halfway down the street, and they turned at the sound of him. The old man ran faster, veering to arc around them, but he didn't make it. Dark aviator glasses covered his eyes and he had a wireless rig stuck in his ear, into which he narrated his progress. Was the old man actually talking to someone? The phones were dead, all the stalwart and dependable networks had ceased to be, but maybe the authorities were fixing things out there, Mark Spitz remembered thinking, the government was getting control. Authority laying on hands. Two of them got the old man down and then all of them were on him like ants who received a chemical telegram about a lollipop on the sidewalk. There was no way the old man could get up. It was quick. They each grabbed a limb or convenient point of purchase while he screamed. They began to eat him, and his screaming brought more of them teetering down the street. All over the world this was happening: a group of them hears food at the same time and they twist their bodies in unison, that dumb choreography. A cord of blood zipped up out of their huddle, hanging—that's how he always recalled it, that's what he saw as he ducked down behind the cinder blocks and watched. A length of red string pinned briefly to the air, until the wind knocked it away. They didn't fight over the old man. They each got a piece. Of course there couldn't have been anyone at the other end of the call because the phones never came back on. The old man had been barking into the void.

Let them pin you and you were dead. Let them pin you and there was no way to stop them from ripping off whatever pitiful armor you'd wrapped yourself in, stuck your hopes to. They'd get you. He had wafted through damp summer afternoons at Long Beach, amid the chewy scent of fried clams. Cartoon lobster on the thin plastic bib, the stupefying melody of the predatory ice-cream truck. (Yes, time slowed down to give those competing factions in him room to rumble, the dark and the light.) They'd wrestle Mark Spitz out of his fatigues the way he'd pried meat out of claws, tails, shells. They were a legion of teeth and fingers. He grabbed Human Resources' wispy hair and yanked its head out of its advance toward his nose. He didn't have a free hand to grab his knife, but he pinpointed the place in its skull where he would have stuck it. He looked after his pistol. It lay near his waist. The Marge was on its knees, creeping down his arm to the gap between the mesh sleeve and glove. The light was such that he saw his face reflected in Human Resources' milky eyes, fixed in that mindless void. Then he felt the fourth skel grab his leg and he lost himself.

He had the forbidden thought.

He woke. He bucked Human Resources off his chest and it tumbled onto the Marge. Mark Spitz grabbed his pistol and shot it in the forehead.

The fourth one tried to grit down on his leg and was thwarted by his fatigues. Most of the meat in its face had been chewed away. (He'd seen, in that first week, a Samaritan administer chest compresses to a stricken fellow citizen, lean down to give mouth-to-mouth, and have his nose ripped off.) Thin, wide loops of gold dangled from its earlobes, chiming against each other as it scuttled up his body, and he aimed at a place at the top of its skull and put it down.

Gary said, "I got you." Gary kicked the Marge off him and held its shoulder down with his boot.

Mark Spitz turned his face to avoid the spray, squeezing his lips into a crack. He heard two shots. All four were down.

"Mark Spitz, Mark Spitz," Gary said. "We didn't know you liked the older ladies."

. . .

They started calling him Mark Spitz after they finally found their way back to camp after the incident on I-95. The name stuck. No harm. Affront was a luxury, like shampoo and affection.

He rolled away from the bodies toward the paper shredder and tried to catch his breath. He heaved, sweat riveting his brow. The faceless skel's foot swished back and forth like the tail of an animal dozing on concrete in a zoo. Then it stopped at the end of a circuit and did not stir.

Mark Spitz said, "Thank you."

"Mazel tov," Gary said.

In the last few weeks Gary had started employing the vocab of the polyglot city, as it had been transmitted through popular culture: the eponymous sitcoms of Jewish comedians; the pay-cable Dominican gangster show; the rat-a-tat verses of totemic hip-hop singles. He didn't always get the meanings right, but he had the delivery down, the correct intonations reinforced by countless exposures.

In the aftermath of the engagement, Gary's body withdrew into its customary scarecrow posture. In his mastery of technique, the man was an exemplar of the new civilian recruits, memorizing and then implementing the correct assault-rifle and blade technique, and melding his homegrown survival skills with crash-coursed military lore. Mark Spitz was lucky to serve in his unit. But he looked horrible. Each morning when they woke, Mark Spitz marveled anew at how his comrade was scarcely in better shape than the creatures they were sent to eradicate. (Discounting the ones missing body parts, of course.) Gary had a granite complexion, gray and pitted skin. Mark Spitz couldn't help but think that something bad roosted deep in his bones, uncatalogued and undiagnosable. His eye sockets were permanently sooted, his cheeks scooped out. His preferred gait was a controlled slouch, with which he slunk around corners and across rooms, the world's last junkie. Like everyone, he'd skipped plenty of meals over the last few years, though on Gary the weight loss registered not as the result of scarcity but as the slow creep of a subcutaneous harrowing. Mark Spitz was disabused of this theory when Gary showed him a picture taken at his sixth birthday party, the same ill demeanor evident even then.

Whatever the sickness, whether it was biological or metaphysical, its discharge leaked out of his hands, more specifically his fingernails, which were seemingly constructed of grime. As if he had clawed out of a coffin. Their first week at Fort Wonton, there had existed a certain Sergeant Weller who rode Gary about the disreputable state of his fingernails, bringing up pre-plague regs of military comportment etc. and threatening to "rain hell" on him if he didn't shape up, but Weller got his throat ripped out during a recon trip in a Newark railway station, and that was the end of that. The other officers' priorities did not include persecuting volunteers over dead standards. For his part, Gary didn't understand the fuss. Before the world broke, he'd dropped out of school to crank bolts full-time in his father's garage with his brothers, and he stood by this explanation for his appearance even though it had been years since he'd worked on a car or truck. Which left Mark Spitz to opine that what they were seeing was the *original* grime, the very grime of Gary's youth preserved as a token of home. It was what he'd scraped off the past and carried with him.

Gary prodded the Marge with his rifle. "No one told me it was Casual Friday," he said. Whether or not you agreed that Gary looked worse than your standard-issue plague-shriveled skel, it was indisputable that he had worse manners.

Kaitlyn materialized, running in from the hall and then slowing down and shaking her head as she took in the mess. She asked Mark Spitz if he was okay and surveyed the office. "Four of them and five desks," she said. She padded over to the supply closet. Any creature trapped inside would be making a racket at the commotion, but Kaitlyn was a stickler. From her stories, she'd been a grade-grubber before the disaster, and Mark Spitz had watched her maintain a grade-grubbing continuum in the throes of reconstruction, rubbing her thumbs over the No-No Cards and applying a yellow highlighter to the typo-ridden manuals from Buffalo. If she survived, she'd doubtless continue to be a grade-grubber in that coming, reborn world they crawled toward, paying her bills in a timely fashion once goods and vital services and autopay reappeared, first in line to pull the lever, if not manning the polling booths, once they could again afford the indulgence of democracy.

The Lieutenant put her in charge of Omega Unit for her constancy, although given his other two choices it didn't rank among his more visionary commands.

She mumbled "Sit-rep, sit-rep" under her breath as she opened the door. Inside the supply closet, cartons and stacks of adhesive notepaper, tax forms, and incomprehensible health-plan packets awaited Business as Usual. No lunging adversary waited inside among the paper plates and Styro cups cached for the miserable office birthday parties and farewell get-togethers. Kaitlyn sat on the edge of a desk. She grimaced at the bodies, distressed by the number and the reminder that she'd let her unit stray from procedure. "Thought it was too quiet," she said.

The owner of the desk had been drinking a diet cola and reading a best-selling romance/thriller Mark Spitz remembered from bus advertisements. Which one had it been, Mark Spitz speculated: Faceless over there? He corrected himself. There were five desks and four bodies. One of them had made it out. Not everyone perished. Perhaps the owner of the desk was doing chores at that very moment in one of the settlement camps, Happy Acres or Sunny Days, replacing the toilet paper in one of the chemical lavatories, eliminating dented cans of beets from the larders, and sipping whatever regional favorite diet cola the scouting teams had scrounged. The insipid slogan popped up in his head, insistent as malware—"We Make Tomorrow!"—and he flinched as he pictured the camp's administrative assistant handing out the buttons, which were then obediently pinned to scavenged clothing one size too big or too small. Resist. He had to get all that crap out of his head or else it would turn out bad for him. To bolster this argument he made a glum appraisal of the bodies on the floor.

"We got here just in time." Gary lit a cigarette. He'd rescued a carton of sponsor cigarettes from a bodega the day before and had acquitted himself nicely so far. They were an economy brand that hadn't been advertised in thirty years; it sufficed that parents and grandparents had exhaled its smoke into cribs, and the acrid scent of the blend and the cherry-red packaging were imprinted early, reminding its aficionados years later of a happier, less complicated time. "Had him on the ground about to give him a nose job," Gary added, using the tone he reserved for recounting particularly grisly and epic ways in which he'd seen people expire—he was an almanac of this field of study—and for deriding Mark Spitz's so-called survival tactics. Despite their friendship, the mechanic was not reluctant in sharing his bafflement that Mark Spitz hadn't been cut down that first week, when the great hordes of unadaptables had been exterminated or infected, too ill-equipped to deal with the realignment of the universe.

Gary didn't have much sympathy for the dead, a.k.a. the "squares," the "suckers," and the "saps." When using the word "dead," most survivors signaled to the listener, through inflection and context, whether they were talking about those who had been killed in the disaster or those who had been turned into vehicles of the plague. Gary made no such distinction; with few exceptions, they were equally detestable. The dead had paid their mortgages on time, and placed the well-promoted breakfast cereals on the table when the offspring leaped out of bed in their fire-resistant jammies. The dead had graduated with admirable GPAs, configured monthly contributions to worthy causes, judiciously apportioned their 401(k)s across diverse sectors according to the wisdom of their dead licensed financial advisers, and superimposed the borders of the good school districts on mental maps of their neighborhoods, which were often included on the long list when magazines ranked cities with the Best Quality of Life. In short, they had been honed and trained so thoroughly by that extinguished world that they were doomed in this new one. Gary was unmoved. From the man's description of his life before, the portrait Mark Spitz gathered was of a misfit befuddled and banished by the signs and systems of straight life. Then came Last Night, transforming them all. In Gary's case, latent talents announced themselves. He prided himself on how effortlessly he had grasped and mastered the new rules, as if he had waited for the introduction of hell his whole life. Mark Spitz's knack for last-minute escapes and improbable getaways was an insult.

"I got distracted," Mark Spitz said. He didn't feel the need to defend himself beyond that. He gave himself his usual B. Would he have bested his attackers if Gary hadn't arrived in time? Of course. He always did.

Mark Spitz believed he had successfully banished thoughts of the future. He wasn't like the rest of them, the other sweepers, the soldiers up the island, or those haggard clans in the camps and caves, all the far-flung remnants behind their barricades, wherever people struggled and waited for victory or oblivion. The faint residue of humanity stuck to the sides of the world. You never heard Mark Spitz say "When this is all over" or "Once things get back to normal" or other sentiments of that brand, because he refused them. When it was all done, truly and finally done, you could talk about what you were going to do. See if your house still stood, enjoy a few rounds of How Many Neighbors Made It Through. Figure out how much of your life from before still remained and how much you had lost. This is what he had learned: If you weren't concentrating on how to survive the next five minutes, you wouldn't survive them. The recent reversals in the campaign had not swayed him to optimism, nor the T-shirts and buttons and the latest hope-delivery system sent down from Buffalo. He scolded himself for succumbing to a reverie, no matter how brief. All that pheenie bullshit had clouded his mind. The tranquillity of 135 Duane Street, however, and a vision of what might be made him slip.

"The man gets distracted," Gary drawled.

Kaitlyn's standard op directed her to ignore their razzing and bickering. She came over and inspected Mark Spitz. She got on her knees and gently pushed on the underside of his jaw, which still throbbed. He shook her away. She told him to knock it off. He had been trembling; he stopped as soon as she touched him.

Her fingertips brought him back to playground mishaps—tumbling off a swing, launching from a seesaw—where the teacher scampered forth to check the damage and make sure the school wouldn't get sued. Teachers—why did he think of that? The skel on the floor that resembled Miss Alcott. He took a deep breath and fixed his attention on a dark slab beyond the window: a building that had been swept clean or had yet to be swept, full of shapes moving or not moving in the darkness. That steadfast binary. Kaitlyn looked for broken skin. He waited.

Finally she nodded and reached into her breast pocket for an adhesive bandage. A tiny scratch wasn't going to give the plague an entry, but conditions in the Zone gave Kaitlyn license to worry about the old run-of-the-mill bugs and infections. The familiar face of the popular cartoon armadillo grinned maniacally on the adhesive strip. "There."

Gary opened the blinds some more and gray particles twisted through the air. The smoke from the gunfire was perfume hiding the stench of the dead, reassuring Mark Spitz as it hovered in a dreamy layer. These aspects of the mundane, the simple physics of the world, always meant that the latest engagement was over. Safe until the next eruption.

"No indication they were in here?" Kaitlyn asked.

He doubted himself for a second and then told her no. He'd been foolish and let himself daydream, but he hadn't been that sloppy. You rarely got surprised by a group of them penned in like that—a jumble of file cabinets pushed up against a conference-room door or a busted-up table nailed to the kitchen door had a way of tipping you off. Little things like that. A barricade was a welcome mat these days: you knew what kind of reception you were going to get. There had been no barrier.

He stepped over the Marge and examined the lock. He hadn't noticed it was smashed when he kicked it in. Some quick thinker had busted it after locking the four of them in. The dead could turn a doorknob, hit a light switch—the plague didn't erase muscle memory. Cognition was out, though, once it overwrote the data of self. These creatures had been stymied for years by the broken lock. Bumping into each other and ricocheting around the desk and chairs and cabinets, losing wigs, rings, and watches as they grew more and more emaciated. Pratfalling over their accessories and then rising again like the mechanical entities they had become.

Kaitlyn pulled out her notebook. "Not trying to get on your case."

"For the Incident Report," Mark Spitz said.

"Gotta make sure the paperwork is right," Gary said.

"What's she, fifty?" she asked, scrutinizing Human Resources and scribbling. "Fifty-five? Can you look for IDs, Gary?"

The info-gathering directives came down from Buffalo a week after they were deployed to the island. The ten sweeper units were crowded into a dumpling joint on Baxter Street, the restaurant the Lieutenant staked out for his briefings. All the COs had annexed Chinatown turf for briefings and strategy sessions, spreading out from Wonton Main at Broadway and Canal according to their disparate appetites. General Summers, for example, claimed an elegant and cavernous dim sum palace on Bowery, rescuing it from the enlisted men's amusements. For months, the establishment had been used as a drag-racing track, the dim sum carts caroming across the linoleum. Friday nights became quite bleak when Summers put a stop to the competitions, until the marines relocated their arena to the roller rink. (Mark Spitz came across the roller rink's gigantic disco ball at random intersections as it made its journey through the metropolis, their scapegoat tumbleweed, kicked and shoved and rolled around the streets by the inebriated soldiers, shedding squares like mirrored tears.) Corporal Brent of the U.S. Army Corps, for his part, conducted his daily planning sessions at a noodle house, addressing his men and women from behind the counter as if serving up strands of udon instead of baroque strategies of city planning (or, more accurately, reconfiguration). The officers spread out, homesteading. Manhattan was empty except for soldiers and legions of the damned, Mark Spitz noted, and already gentrification had resumed.

The signage was in Chinese save for the Health Department regulations hectoring beneath the pictograms. His mother's logic held that a strong congruency between patron and cuisine signaled an "authentic place" and that they must serve up primo Chinese, Greek, or Lithuanian cuisine, what have you. Which had never made sense to Mark Spitz: Plenty of American restaurants with a majority-American clientele served crap American fare. Perhaps the emphasis was on the authenticity of its mediocrity.

In their meager bid at becoming regulars, Mark Spitz and Kaitlyn returned to the table they'd occupied at the previous briefing. Gary joined them in the coming weeks, but at that point they'd only been together for one grid, a bland residential stretch on Water Street. Omega hadn't clicked yet, hoisting their own personal three-person foxhole around wherever they went. That afternoon, Gary squeezed in with some guys he'd served with in Stamford securing abandoned gasworks. The majority of those in the sweeper units had been stationed in the Northeast doing infrastructure work, cleaning out the Corridor as Mark Spitz had been, or doing recon in the key metro areas and industrial clusters, which had been Gary's previous posting. Mark Spitz arrived at the island without a crew, the only one from the I-95 detail to transfer to the sweep.

The dumpling joint was prepped for service when they shuffled in for their first briefing, but the soldiers knocked the settings into incremental disarray week by week, as if across a single, slow-motion lunch shift. There were thirty of them, teenagers and men and women in their twenties, with exceptions in the form of characters like Metz. Metz looked fifty-something, but of course the late miseries had aged them so Mark Spitz couldn't say for sure. He had what Mark Spitz had come to call the Wasteland Stare. On special ops, the sweepers were equipped with night-vision goggles that featured gecko protuberances allowing them to see into different spectra; Metz and his brethren were equipped with additional lenses, and through them they gaped at stumps, shreds of structures, a blasted plain, as if through a visor of devastation. Whatever Mark Spitz saw—a typical downtown slop joint, fly strips twisting in the corners—Metz gazed upon an entirely different and cruel landscape. Given the vast galaxy of survivor dysfunction—PASD in its sundry tics, fugues, and existential fevers—the Wastelanders' particular corner of pathology was, Mark Spitz decided, unremarkable. Everyone was fucked up in their own way; as before, it was a mark of one's individuality.

Steady raids had depleted the back room of sponsored energy drinks, but there was good word of mouth about the medicinal properties of an enigmatic foreign beverage, bright emerald cans of which were piled in formidable stacks in the kitchen. The sweepers settled at the tables and crammed into the banquettes, sliding across bloodred vinyl. The menagerie of the Chinese zodiac pursued itself on the place mats beneath glass tabletops. Mark Spitz saw it was the Year of the Monkey. Attributes: Fun-Loving Witty Entertaining. Dead fish bobbed in a chunky murk in the tank by the entrance.

The Lieutenant took his roost at the host's station and informed them that from now on they had to fill out Incident Reports on every engagement. The decor flashed in his aviator glasses in sparks of crimson and gold. Considering the Lieutenant's nightly bourbon flights, the sunglasses were precious cover for his sensitive retinas, even in the half-light of the restaurant.

Buffalo, he explained, wanted information on the general outline of each engagement, but in particular they were keen for the sweepers to record demographic data: the ages of the targets, the density at the specific location, structure type, number of floors. Fabio, the Lieutenant's second, had rummaged Canal Street after special equipment for this very purpose. Fabio handed his boss the carton of kiddie notebooks, and the Lieutenant brandished it over his head, pointing out that they were equipped with convenient loops that held tiny pencils. The plastic-covered notebooks were candy-colored and palm-size, brimming with the characters and arcana of a prosperous and long-standing children's entertainment combine. The creation myth of the product line concerned the adventures of a clever, effeminate armadillo and his cohort of resourceful desert critters. Although the parent company was one of reconstruction's first official sponsors, until now Buffalo had found little use for their tie-in merchandise, apart from the well-branded adhesive bandages. "Doubtless you will appreciate this example of superior Japanese engineering," the Lieutenant said, sliding the pencil back and forth.

The sweepers groaned and dislodged belches redolent of the mysterious Far East beverage, smudging the air with ginger. The Lieutenant tendered his regrets over the hassle, in his custom. The Lieutenant preferred a light touch, ditching protocol when it served his purposes. Casting himself as the hip young teacher in the high school was part of his strategy for keeping them alive, Mark Spitz theorized. The Lieutenant's sweepers were a nontraditional brigade to say the least, volunteers from civilian pop. and untutored in the routine malevolence of military code. The training courses and drills of their boot camp had been the split-second decisions and pure, indifferent chance that had permitted them to survive to this moment. (Although it should be added that most of them had received a crash course in basic gun use since the advent of the plague.) Soldiers of the new circumstance. What did it serve to hold them to strict military standards when they were such an unlikely lot: unemployable man-children, erstwhile cheerleaders, salesmen of luxury boats, gym teachers, food bloggers, patent clerks, cafeteria lunch ladies, dispatchers from international delivery companies. People like Mark Spitz, seemingly unsnuffable human cockroaches protected by carapaces of good luck. The Lieutenant's first priority was keeping their limbs and assorted parts attached to their bodies, free of teeth; then came the trickled-down objectives; and, finally, servitude to the obsolete directives of an obsolete world.

The Lieutenant's casual attitude was facilitated by the fact that the sweepers' primary targets were stragglers. Compared to what the marines encountered in Manhattan during that initial, mammoth sweep, those assembled in the dumpling joint had it easy. Mark Spitz wouldn't have signed up for the island had it been otherwise, New York homesickness or no.

"Buffalo, as ever, has great plans for you guys," the Lieutenant said. He tossed the box of notebooks to the mule-eyed hulk slouching at the closest table, a man who went by the handle of the Professor, an appellation that contradicted his dumbfounded mien. He'd been a mate on a sport-fishing boat in sunnier times, steering rum-addled vacationers to schools of snapper via sonar. The Lieutenant motioned for him to pass the box around. "I know what you're going to say—we need boots and they talk to us about numbers."

Actually they had boots, and most of the sweepers had raided sneaker stores for more comfortable designer footwear after a round of death marches up high-rise stairwells; fortunately for them, the sneaker sponsor had manufactured several product lines for different ages, aesthetic appetites, and athletic inclinations. It was comforting, in the recesses of buildings, to see your buddy's heel blink from the tiny red LEDs in a novelty running shoe, although Mark Spitz did not partake because of the obvious ankle-exposure issue. *Boots* was the Lieutenant's catchall term for truly clutch materiel, the elusive, the vital. Mark Spitz heard the others shifting in boredom at the reference. What did boots symbolize for the man? Order. Sturdy rules. His trove of bygones. All survivors had them, the pet names and metonyms they used to refer to their pasts. Bagel, java, baseball cap, the object that was all objects, the furnishings of the good old days. Why couldn't the Lieutenant maintain his shrine? Everyone else did.

Mark Spitz flipped through the pad. Faint pink-and-purple cacti sprouted in the margins. He recognized the sense of Buffalo's plan. With the assembled data, their supply of eggheads could start projecting how many of the dead they'd find in your typical twenty-two-story corporate flagship, five-floor tenement, fifteen-story apartment complex, what have you. Every structure sheltered its likely trajectories and scenarios; they'd figured that out early. Take residential buildings, for example. Walk into one of the wizened tenements of downtown Manhattan and you could bet on finding at least one citizen who'd barricaded himself inside, turned, and then couldn't get out. In the first wave, people got infected, barely making it home ahead of collapse. Then the plague wiped and reformatted their brains and they were trapped in their abodes, the most pathetic kind of city shut-in, their hands eventually groping their way toward expensive security locks but incapable of reaching them for the passel of splendid contemporary furniture they'd piled against it. Mark Spitz cursed his luck when he realized they were going to have to remove the door and get all that shit out of the way before they could put the skel down: the particle-board media centers laden with layaway plasmas, limited-issue replicas of Danish-modern wardrobes, the beloved go-to recliners grimed at the armrests from summers of sweat. These specimens were your average skels, not harmless stragglers but a reliable if small percentage of what you'd find in Zone One, so you had to stay frosty.

By now, Mark Spitz could look at a building and know what kind of weather was brewing inside. Office towers were the least populated. The nine-to-fivers had stopped coming to work when it went down, and most of the rabid skels were lured out by the marines, which left stragglers. (Perhaps, he thought, there will be a study of the farthest a straggler had traveled to its haunting grounds—across streams! quicksand! perilous canyons!—but that was far in the future.) A building like 135 Duane, with its panoply of enterprises, had its idiosyncrasies but nonetheless conformed to the prevailing narrative. Department stores, multinational coffee chains, half-constructed condos. Churches and banh mi shops. Although every address, every new chunk of the grid assigned to them, contributed its special embroideries, the story never changed.

2.4 stragglers per floor in this type of structure and .05 there. Numbers permitted Buffalo to extrapolate the whole city from Zone One, speculate about how long it will take *X* amount of three-man sweeper units to clear the island zone by zone, north to south and river to river. Then on to other cities. There was no other entity like New York City, but the silent downtowns bided across the country with their micropopulations, acolytes of the principles of the grid. The truths of the grid's rectilinear logic, its consequences, of how people moved and lived inside boundaries, had already been applied to cities across the country through the decades, anywhere human activity and desire needed to be tamed and made compliant. Gangs of high-rises in Southwest municipalities flush with internet money, sterile pedestrian malls in Midwest cities of a certain size, run-down waterfront districts of fabricated historical import that had been tarted up into tourist mills. Sure, there was the problem of scale, but Manhattan was the biggest version of everywhere.

The city bragged of an endless unraveling, a grid without limit; of course it was bound and stymied by rivers, curtailed by geographical circumstance. It could be subdued and understood. Soon sweeper teams would roam the rural areas on an identical mission to that of the metro sweepers, concocting the equations of the countryside, putting numbers to nascent theories about skel dispersal patterns, and in time these numbers would deliver end dates and progress and the return to life before. As he sat in the restaurant, Mark Spitz pictured the Lieutenant's box of tiny notebooks, overflowing with half-legible sweeper scribbling, being off-loaded from a military helicopter upstate and rushed by a harried private into an underground chamber at Buffalo HQ. Like it was someone's liver being delicately transported to the waning recipient. He'd never been to Buffalo, and now it was the exalted foundry of the future. The Nile, the Cradle of Reconstruction. All the best and brightest (and, most important, still breathing) had been flown up to Buffalo, where they got the best grub, reveled in 24-7 generators and uncurtailed hot showers on command. In turn, they had to rewind catastrophe. Rumor was they had two of the last Nobel laureates working on things up there—useful ones, none of that Peace Prize or Literature stuff—chowing down on hearty brain-fortifying grub, scavenged fish oil and whatnot. If they could reboot Manhattan, why not the entire country? These were the contours of the new optimism.

After describing the kind of data that Buffalo expected of them and shooing questions of various pertinence ("No, Josh, we don't need their weight unless it is something truly spectacular," "Home addresses? What are you going to do, forward their mail?"), the Lieutenant shifted to his favorite pastime, the delivery of the Nightly News. He held that morning's feed to the light. It was all positive, in line with the trend of late. To wit: "Organic-food fans will rejoice that Happy Acres claims this year will bring their biggest harvest yet—"

Grateful noises filled the dumpling house, for who among them could forget the return of fresh corn last year? Never in human history had so many delighted in removing a bit of kernel from between canines and bicuspids. Mark Spitz stumbled upon the Happy Acres crops his first night in camp. He'd ditched the mess hall for some air, dizzy from the laughter of the army guys and the other new recruits. It was in those dwindling days before the looting regs went into effect and scavenger crews had routed a den of bandits who had taken over one of the mega-drugstores. Half the bandits died in the gunfight and the other half eagerly took oaths of loyalty to the provisional government upon surrender. They returned with three trucks' worth of medicine. Needless to say everyone took their cut, filling their utility vests and packs with booty, the favorite anti-tartar toothpaste and allergy tablets, travel size if possible. These products had kept them running in the old world, if only by placebo effect. The soldiers availed.

After they finished trading glory stories over their personal hauls, the conversation turned to speculation about the cigarette-salvage possibilities of Manhattan. A lot of people had taken up smoking lately. News of a potential NYC operation was starting to get out, and that morning's couriers from Buffalo disseminated gossip about the latest operation down South, a hydroelectric plant brought online. Then one of the snipers—Gibson was his name—told a story about a skel bonfire gone awry, which broke everybody up. The skel on top had been neutralized, but a chunk of his brain was still sending orders, apparently. The fire activated the creature so that it looked like the skel was "break dancing" in the flames. Mark Spitz had been laughing with the rest of them, more on account of Gibson's deadpan delivery than the anecdote, when his head was suddenly encased in lead and his vision went on the fritz. It was as if he'd been hit on the head with a pipe—he'd actually been hit in the head with a lead pipe in college, when a gang of townies had invaded the Spring Concert looking for trouble. In retrospect, this drowning sensation was the first indication that something started to go wrong with him when he came in from the wasteland.

He needed air. Mark Spitz ducked through the plastic tent flaps and lost himself in the rows of cabins, staggering between the red-and-yellow nylon tents containing the new arrivals who were also spending their first night at Happy Acres. He sensed them stiffening at his slow footfalls, which made him sound like one of the dead. They poked a head out, then calmed themselves and withdrew. He wandered toward the line of sodium lights at the far edge of camp. There they were, behind the fence, lit up, regimented, droopy with promise: the holy stalks, up to his chest and disappearing into the darkness. He'd been eating three squares a day, listening to actual jokes, seeing whole ragamuffin gangs of kids—when was the last time he saw more than one kid at a time? And now, fresh corn. The miracles turned routine. They pushed up like weeds.

"Back away from the fucking corn, dude." The two guards pointed their weapons at his head, at two of the five recommended skel-dropping points. The sentries couldn't have been older than sixteen. He didn't begrudge them their duty. The crops were important. The crops separated today's iteration of humanity from last year's. He waved the rifles away and gaped. It was funny: up against the gate, shivering in the slight wind, they were almost an army of skels approaching the camp's delicious signs of human life. Half the stuff was probably going to Buffalo, but that didn't matter. It was still a wonder. Mark Spitz backed away from the fucking corn.

The Lieutenant said, "And again, please ignore the scuttlebutt about what they use for fertilizer. What else, my young friends, what else? Supposedly the new incinerator is going run double our capacity, so you know what that means—"

"Ash Wednesday!" yelled someone in the back.

"And Thursday and Friday." The Lieutenant consulted the feed and informed them that a senior board member of that juggernaut clothing empire had turned up at Victory's Sword and magnanimously pledged his company's goods to the effort. The Lieutenant allowed his troops a minute, and then told them to simmer down. It would be difficult to describe their enthusiasm as unwarranted. The company cultivated four product lines: an upscale boutique providing sophisticated apparel fit for a day at the office or an evening out on the town; a mass-market suite of sensible, everyday basics; modestly priced designs for the cost-conscious consumer; and a recently acquired purveyor of plus-size lingerie that had fallen on hard times but had been turned around by the smart management of their new parent company. All the clothes were well crafted regardless of their price point; the company kept abreast of the latest fronts in cheap child labor. "The entire corporate family is open for business," the Lieutenant said, "for any item with a retail price of under thirty dollars. Check the price tags, fellas! If you need new skivvies or a sweatshirt or something."

"Can't get no sweatshirt under thirty dollars!"

Someone in the back, at one of the undesirable tables by the toilets, countered that it was easy enough to acquire a sweatshirt for less than that sum at the bargain store. Another seconded this assertion.

"Gary's getting some big-lady teddies," yelled one of Gary's old cronies.

"We think it feels good under the mesh—you should try it," Gary said, baring his gray teeth in a line. Everyone who worked with Gary quickly adjusted to the man's habit of referring to himself with the first-person plural. He was a triplet, one of three brothers. The other two perished on Last Night, but Gary continued to speak for their collective, maintaining what Mark Spitz assumed was a lifelong practice of presenting a united fraternal front to all who did not share their precise genetic makeup. It was a disturbing vision, Gary and his other versions standing in their mobile home's kitchen demanding sweets or more cartoons, much more disturbing than hearing a man in combat fatigues relate the enthusiasms of ghosts. PASD had as many faces as there were uninfected, and, as was the case with the Wasteland Starers, you took someone else's particular symptoms as harmless foibles. Simple courtesy, lest they take objection to yours.

Mark Spitz resolved to pick up some new socks. Now that the anti-looting regs were in effect, everyone—soldier and civilian and sweeper alike—was prohibited from foraging goods and materials belonging to anyone other than an official sponsor, whether it was Southern whiskey or all-natural depilatories. Food was exempt—

juice boxes were still legal tender in some parts of the country—but for the most part, no more stealing, people. There had been laws once; to abide by their faint murmuring, despite the interregnum, was to believe in their return. To believe in reconstruction.

The prohibitions were hard to enforce, however, for obvious reasons. The civilians in the camps could be policed, as most never left the perimeter, but untold Americans still walked the great out there, beyond order's embrace, like slaves who didn't know they'd been emancipated. The sanctioned salvage teams were largely unsupervised and the soldiers had personal needs that escaped the classifications on requisition forms, did not have ID numbers. Officers confiscated contraband when it was flaunted in their faces—designer sunglasses and the robust leathers favored by motorcycle fans of both serious and dilettante persuasion—but they had better things to do than babysit. Kaitlyn, in deference to the hall-monitor part of her disposition, kept watch on the two men under her supervision, Gary especially, and for good reason. He'd been a master bandit before the rise of the camps and, in addition, rather enjoyed Kaitlyn's shrill intonation when she used her discipline voice.

Buffalo created an entire division dedicated to pursuing official sponsors whenever a representative turned up, in exchange for tax breaks once the reaper laid down his scythe and things were up and running again. (Additional goodies the public would never find out about weeviled the fine print.) There were understandable difficulties in tracking down survivors in positions of authority over, say, the biggest national pharmaceutical chain or bicycle manufacturer, but they strolled into camp from time to time, with the typical scars but eager to contribute. They generally put a price cap on their goods or specified a particular product in their brand family, one not too dear, but their sacrifices were appreciated nonetheless. Pledge all your tiny cartons of children's applesauce, in all the nation's far-flung groceries and convenience stores? It was a no-brainer: they were expired anyway. The civilians out in the wild, unaware of the regulations, would be welcomed into the system in time, and they would obey.

Socks. Yes, socks. The prospect of a nice new three-pack of athletic socks never failed to hearten Mark Spitz.

The Lieutenant said, "An irritating number of you have been bugging me from the field for updates, even though I keep telling you to keep the comm channels clear, so here's the deal: The Tromanhauser Triplets are out of ICU."

Everyone applauded. Kaitlyn thanked God. Mark Spitz had walked in on her praying their first night in the Zone. She had stopped to talk to her God in the middle of flossing, the minty white thread looped around her index finger. Kaitlyn was embarrassed, although most people had started praying, or increased the frequency of their prayers, for obvious reasons. Religion had been a taboo subject in former times, but now impromptu proselytizing sessions broke out in besieged department-store stockrooms, in the attics of crumbling Midwest Victorians, as the holed-up survivors swapped deities and afterlife hypotheses. It passed the time until morning and the resumption of the gauntlet. Kaitlyn apologized, saying "I just want them to be safe," and he knew she was talking about the Triplets. Even Gary expressed concern in their progress, as they were fellow, natural multiples in an age where such a thing had been "cheapened by that IVF crap," as he put it. "They're gonna know what we know," Gary said, "how it is for our kind."

Mark Spitz clapped his hands desultorily. Doris Tromanhauser whiled away the ruination holed up in the Trenton branch of a respectable international bank, as part of a bunkered-down ensemble who'd given their fealty to an easily fortified brass-studded front door and impressive stone construction, both holdovers from a time when customers preferred impenetrability over glass-walled transparency in their neighborhood reserve. (Current events put an end to that debate for good.) The plucky band dwindled as they were forced to make the inevitable forays outside; all those present in the dumpling house were versed in this scenario, the relentless subtractions. Finally it was just Doris and one of the men who could have been the Triplets' father, until in due course he, too, ventured out for supplies. (A sequence of ménages made paternity impossible to establish, and a DNA test was, alas, impossible.) He never came back. The familiar story. After six months on her lonesome, surviving on who knows what, high-fiber deposit slips and credit-card brochures, she was rescued by a Bubbling Brooks recon unit. She did not survive the delivery, and the Triplets were in a bad way, bank literature being devoid of nutrients essential to prenatal development.

New life in the midst of devastation. Corn, babies. Word of the Tromanhausers spread through the Northeast settlements quicker than any uplifting news of this or that reconstruction effort, or contact with some faraway country that had been written off long ago. The babies even diverted survivors from delight in the discovery of the latest kill field, that phenomenon encountered with increasing regularity, the mystery that pointed to an ebbing of the plague. Did you hear that Finn opened his eyes, that Cheyenne is still unresponsive, they're not sure but they suspect that something may be amiss with Dylan's heart, a hole or a bump? Mark Spitz was pulling for them, rooting for them, or whatever it was that one did when the world was ending and a statistically meaningless fraction of the planet's extant population encountered a slightly larger daily portion of misfortune. He didn't want to get too invested. He was a firm believer, in the absence of any traditionally recognized faith, or even nontraditional and gaining traction in these murderous days, in the reserve tank. It was important to maintain a reserve tank of feeling topped off in case of emergency. Mark Spitz was not going to spare any for these cubs. A year ago, in the middle of the collapse, these babies would have been another miserable footnote, too small an item on the list of atrocities to merit more than a sad shake of your tragedy-boggled head. (And a footnote to what, for that matter. No one was writing this book. All the writers were busy pouring jugs of kerosene on the heaps of the dead, pitching in for a change.) But now things were different. To pheenies, these babies were localized hope, and they needed the Triplets to pull through. Buffalo could announce a vaccine tomorrow, or a process for reversing the tortures of the plague, and they'd still be talking Tromanhauser Triplets.

"We're all glad to hear this news, I'm sure," the Lieutenant said in a monotone. "If you want to donate part of your rations to their care, put your X on the sign-up sheet before you head out." He pressed his fingers to his temples and started rubbing in slow, assuaging circles. "Last but not least in this bona fide gusher of good tidings, your heavy loads be lightened by the news that USS *Endeavor* embarked safely and is en route to the summit."

The *Endeavor* was a nuclear sub. After what happened on Air Force One, it was the only way His Excellency would make the journey, and who could blame him.

"Get 'em, Gina!" Gary howled, earning guffaws. Gina Spens was Italy's emissary to the summit. Before the catastrophe, she had been a pornographic-film star of nimble and well-documented prowess, a Top 25 search string on adult sites across three hemispheres. She had her fans. Her comeback as it were, for she had retired from the business, was occasioned by the End of the World As We Know It, that epic saga to which all were audience and supporting cast. Still shooting, rewritten on the fly on account of the discouraging dailies. Gina performed her own stunts in a series of action sequences throughout Italy's contest against the dead—the Encounter at Horror Gorge and the legendary Ambush of the Wretches, among other credulity-testing adversities. Her feats trickled out with the reestablishment of communications with the European powers, and for her exertions she had become a player in her homeland's provisional government. Provisional governments were really big these days, an international fad in the grand old style.

A society manufactures the heroes it requires. Gina was that new species of celebrity emerging from the calamity, elevated by the altered definitions of valor and ingenuity. They walked among us, on every continent, in the territories of every depleted nation. What American had not thrilled to the inspiring story of Dave Peters, who spent six months drifting in a catamaran in a Michigan lake, living off a carton of cashews and paddling away whenever he drifted too close to shore, which teemed with the dead. Everyone thrilled to the story of Wilhelmina Godiva and her grain-silo fortress, how she'd battled her way to the Maryland settlements armed with nothing but her famous rusty pitchfork, which was now enshrined over the front gate of Camp Victory's Sword. Her mind was gone, sure, but she made it through, and her followers took care of her, wiping spittle from her lips as she murmured her prophecies into her digital recorder. Across the ocean, Gina Spens masterminded search-and-destroy missions in southern Italy and became a worldwide sensation, whispered about in the dancing glow of scavenged antimosquito candles. The more unlikely the tale of survival, the absurd extremity of one's circumstances in a world of extreme circumstance, the greater one's fame. Gina had made some spectacular kills. Yes, she had her fans.

"I'll keep you posted on how that goes, natch," the Lieutenant said. It was their last bulletin from beyond the island until next week. He distributed their new grid assignments. He closed with his standard "Now run along like good little pheenies," his sardonic pronunciation of the slang drawing grins. The Lieutenant's strategic informalities comforted his troops when they were out in the field. One of them worked on reconstruction, a real fucking human being among the abstractions doling out pronouncements and paradigms in Buffalo.

They were dismissed. On their own. "We ain't doing no homework," Gary said as Omega walked out of the dumpling house. He said it loud enough for the guys in his old unit to hear, Mark Spitz noticed, to show them that he was the same man, even though he was saddling up with characters of questionable mettle, the kind of saps they used to rob for rice in the dismal days of the interregnum.

"I'll do it," Kaitlyn said. "I was elected Secretary of the Student Council twice." Mark Spitz shuddered as if bitten: to admit such a thing without a smidgen of self-consciousness. To say it with pride. Who on the planet had put those words together in that sequence since the outbreak: Secretary of the Student Council? It was a half-recalled lullaby overheard on the street, cooed by some young mom bent over her kid in the summer glare, rekindling innocence: Secretary of the Student Council. The effect was abetted by a rare appearance of the sun, slumping out from the gray. Not too much ash in the sky even though they were only a few blocks from the wall.

He had been here before. It wasn't the Chinatown of old, but in the corners of his perception the pixels resolved themselves and reduced to zero the distance between Old Chinatown and New Chinatown. The crooked streets had been cleared to give the military vehicles access and soldiers walked slowly on their rounds, making jokes, cracking wise over a shop sign's mangled English, debating the attractiveness of the lady corporal who had arrived on that morning's transport. This section of Zone One contained the busiest streets in the city now. (Or the busiest streets where the people were still people—he retreated from the shadow that crept up, of uptown corners where the uncounted hordes gallivanted mindlessly.) The grunts and commissioned officers, the sweepers and the engineers, were nattily decked out in fresh, unblemished fatigues, in the new puncture- and tear- and abrasion-proof mesh, totally deluxe, they wore utility vests and carried weapons held in place by an assortment of snaps, buckles, and holsters, but they were doing what people did in a city: catching a breath between errands. And that was life.

As a kid, Mark Spitz executed Chinatown runs for fireworks

and bootlegs, and the congestion had always overwhelmed him, the way it had many sons and daughters of Nassau County. Grow up on Long Island living off one of the spiral arms of the expressway, and nothing kicked up the vertigo more than a visit to Chinatown, with its discordant and jostling multitudes. It was the stereotype of fast-talking, fast-walking, eagerly lacerating New York distilled into a potent half mile. You do not belong. You will be devoured by this monster. Outside the dumpling house, in this resettled northern edge of Zone One, the tiny chaos—the sudden shock of a supply truck's horn or a jeep backfiring—was the sound of promise, of a civilization stepping clear of the charnel house. The welter of Chinatown had been the larger hustle of the entire city condensed, and now the echo of that noise in this handful of streets spoke of a vanished order that might reassert itself. If you believed in the mission. The neighborhood would never be that roiling and exuberant again—at least in Mark Spitz's lifetime. They needed Tromanhauser Triplets and their ilk, the repopulating engine of babies, the unborn. But for a second, Mark Spitz glimpsed something of the new city they had been sent to build.

Omega walked downtown to their next assignment: Grid 98, Chambers x West Broadway, Mixed Residential/Business. "Here's to it's all walk-ups," Mark Spitz said.

"We wouldn't mind some more parking lots," Gary said.

"Or a big gas station," Kaitlyn said.

Parking lots were freebies. No one ever knocked a gigantic parking lot, snug in the bosom of that week's grid.

"It's about one and a half clicks," Gary said.

"Twenty blocks," Mark Spitz corrected.

"Clicks."

"Blocks."

"Clicks," Gary said as they marched toward West Broadway. Adding, "We hate that armadillo. Creeped us out since the crib."

Kaitlyn didn't mind the ludicrous notebook and in fact relished the opportunity to divert her companions down her nostalgia's alley. "I used to have all that stuff, I had everything," she said, proceeding to deep-caption the plushies, posters, and plastic statuary on display in her childhood's museum, the manifold tie-in merch of the effeminate armadillo's brand family. Gary smuggled his distinct bit of home under his fingernails, and their unit leader carried hers in the errant conversational tidbit or dimpled inflection that made it possible to pretend the three of them had been whisked away from the dead city and were riding in her family minivan, bouncing in the bright and splendid past, en route to the mall to meet up with the gang by the fountain in the middle of the food court, or queue up for the latest 3-D smash.

Kaitlyn's native herd had grazed on the sweet berries of gentility. Mark Spitz didn't have a complete dossier on Kaitlyn that day, but he was working on it. She had been bioengineered in the birthing vats of a sanctified midwestern principality, an upper-middle-class Kingdom of Bruiselessness. Here she was, long curls peeking out of her helmet, head cocked as she double-checked orders over the comm and absentmindedly wiped gore from her knife, when she should have been braiding the hair of one of her fellow sorority pledges, in her favorite pad-around-the-dorm sweatpants, sexually ambiguous pop avatar crooning from the computer speakers. Of course she had been elected Secretary of the Student Council twice: Who would make up such a thing?

Their unit might be standing before a line of hair dryers in a tony hair salon, nigh shod in jellyfish clumps of brains, and Kaitlyn would perkily chatter on about how she'd spent summers at her grandparents' cabin "doing the usual stuff, you know, riding horses and lifeguarding," or earning cosmetics money at the ice-cream store with her "Best Friends Forever Amy and Jordan." You don't say? Mark Spitz saw it clearly: Kaitlyn's implacable march through a series of imaginative and considered birthday parties—her parents were so thoughtful, here was a blessing bestowed from one generation to the next—each birthday party transcending the last and approaching a kind of birthday-party perfection that once accomplished would usher in an exquisite new age of bourgeois utopia. They strove, they plotted, they got the e-mail of that new magician in town, with his nouveau prestidigitations. Maybe, he thought one night, it wasn't utopia that they had worked toward after all, and it was Kaitlyn herself who had summoned the plague: as she cut into the first slice of cake at her final, perfect birthday party, history had come to an end. She had blown out the candles on the old era, blotted out the dinosaurs' heavens, sent the great ice sheet scraping forth, the blood counts zooming up into madness.

Working the island with Kaitlyn, Mark Spitz received steady dispatches from the extinguished world, weathered but still legible. That place lived on and persisted in her, in the minuscule tumult of Chinatown, and as long as she breathed, and others like her, perhaps it might return. When Omega wound down at night after their shift, Kaitlyn fired up the transporter and materialized these pristine artifacts of normalcy into their bivouac. "One time at Model UN, we pulled the fire alarm after hours because there were these cute boys from Michigan and we wanted to see them in their pj's." Gary and Mark Spitz traded incredulous glances: After all they had witnessed, whole realms of the peculiar had been held in reserve.

She had made it through. Just as Gary couldn't picture how in the hell a galoot like Mark Spitz bumbled through the host of menaces unscathed, so was Kaitlyn's journey impossible to imagine. No one at Fort Wonton, man or woman, failed to experience an episode of cognitive dissonance on meeting Kaitlyn, being subjected to her buoyant giggle. But she had done the same things they all had been forced to do. She had been hunted, and she had escaped. She had killed and had watched as the cast of her anecdotes was cut down, her former fellow pledges and debate partners. Her parents, who had obviously trained her in more than just the ways of a sunny disposition for her to have made it this far. She had survived, and that's why she was here in Zone One. No matter what her life had been before.

The scientists wanted the sweeper data to superimpose it on their map of the smithereens and generate prophecies. Kaitlyn and her stories of the past were another stencil to lay over the disaster, to remind them of the former shape of the world. In their separate warrens, these different parties toiled over the future with their instruments: "We Make Tomorrow!" Why else were they in Manhattan but to transport the old ways across the violent passage of the calamity to the safety of the other side? If you don't believe that, Mark Spitz asked himself, why are you here?

. . .

Omega finished the operation in Human Resources. It was a larger and messier cleanup than usual for a single room in an office building. Four rabid infected in one room, that was a blip in a straggler mission, especially after the marines' monstrous cull. Nothing Mark Spitz couldn't handle, but he cursed the idea that months of dropping stragglers had attenuated his skills.

There were your standard-issue skels, and then there were the stragglers. Most skels, they moved. They came to eat you—not all of you, but a nice chomp here or there, enough to pass on the plague. Cut off their feet, chop off their legs, and they'd gnash the air as they heaved themselves forward by their splintered fingernails, looking for some ankle action. The marines had eliminated most of this variety before the sweepers arrived.

The stragglers, on the other hand, did not move, and that's what made them a suitable objective for civilian units. They were a succession of imponderable tableaux, the malfunctioning stragglers and the places they chose to haunt throughout the Zone and beyond. An army of mannequins, limbs adjusted by an inscrutable hand. The former shrink, plague-blind, sat in her requisite lounge chair, feet up on the ottoman, blank attentive face waiting for the patient who was late, ever late, and unpacking the reasons for this would consume a large portion of a session that would never occur. The patient failed to arrive, was quite tardy, was dead, was running through a swamp with a hatchet, pursued by monsters. The pock-faced assistant manager of the shoe store crouched before the foot-measuring instrument, frozen, sans customers, the left shoes of his bountiful stock on display along the walls of the shop on miniature plastic ledges. The vitamin-store clerk stalled out among the aisles, depleted among the plenty, the tiny bottles containing gel-capped ancient remedies and placebos. The owner of the plant store dipped her fingers into the soil of a pot earmarked for a city plant, one hearty in the way the shop's customers were hearty, for wasn't every citizen on the grand island a sort of sturdy indoor variety that didn't need much sunlight. A man wrapped in the colors of the Jamaican flag loitered over the new bongs, the crème de la crème of head-shop apparatus, rainbow bulbs perforated according to the latest notions about air circulation, intake, draw. No smoke, no fire. In the desolate consumer-electronics showroom, the up-selling floor salesman halted mid-pitch, as if psychoanalyzing a skeptical rube who was simply, ever and always, not in the room, not in the market for purchases big-ticket or otherwise. A man bent before a mirror that perched on the glass counter of a sunglasses store, his fingers holding on the arms of invisible shades. A woman cradled a wedding dress in the dressing room's murk, reenacting without end a primal moment of expectation. A man lifted the hood of a copy machine. They did not move when you happened on them. They didn't know you were there. They kept watching their movies.

One morning Mark Spitz stumbled on some brain-wiped wretch standing at the fry station of the big hamburger chain and had to shoot him on general principles. Out of the abundance of a life, to choose fry duty.

They were safe in their houses. In front of the televisions, of course, a host of this type biding their time until the electricity came back on, the problem was solved, and the program resumed where it had stopped. All the time in the world. Their lives had been an interminable loop of repeated gestures; now their existences were winnowed to this discrete and eternal moment. In the bath, fully clothed before the nippled showerhead and its multiple-flow settings. Tilting a fluted vacuum attachment toward the scrunched curtains and their legendary hard-to-reach places. Underneath blankets and duvets whose number and thickness referred to a different season, a previous winter of mysterious significance. Slipping a disc into the game machine. Crotch-down on the yoga mat. Spooning bran from a bowl. Surfing the dead web. Yawning. Stretching. Flossing. Wound down and alone in their habitat.

For Omega's purposes, their habitat was Zone One.

In Human Resources, Gary corralled purses and read out the ages of the dead. He didn't bother with the names. No one cared about the names, not them, not the higher-ups. Since they hadn't maintained records of the dead starting Last Night, there was no point: easier to keep records of the living. Fewer numbers to work with, for one thing, and unimpeachable given the ascension of the survivor rolls to the status of holy register. They endured setbacks—supply lines broke down and refuges were overrun, not so much now, but in the interregnum everyone had been forced to flee a hideout or ill-considered shelter multiple times. No matter the daily advances and reversals, however, the names of the survivors maintained their willful stream into the zones of stability, over the comm, scrawled on paper, recited from memory by the weary emissary of a band coming in from the cold: These are the living.

Kaitlyn assigned Gary to ID collection, having picked up on Mark Spitz's aversion grids ago. He recoiled at going into people's wallets, pawing through their purses. Too much of the dead world floating in there. The detritus that passed for identity, the particulate remains of twenty-first-century existence, fluttered down to settle at the bottoms of wallets and clutches and messenger bags. The indicators of their brief appearance on the planet waited for Mark Spitz: the flavored gums and lip balms that would never again be manufactured, the despised driver's license photos that were the only proof that they'd had faces, the snaps of the kids and collies and boyfriends, the just-in-case tampons. All those keys to empty apartments now painted in blood, where lovers decomposed on the wall-to-wall. The fossil evidence that there had once been other types of people besides survivors.

Touching these artifacts nauseated him now, in the latest manifestation of his PASD. The first time he got sick, the unit had completed a sweep of a party-supply store, a narrow nook on Reade that had been washed off Broadway into a low-rent eddy. Dusty costumes hung from the ceiling as if on meat hooks: cowboys and robots from chart-busting sci-fi trilogies, ethnically obscure kiddie-show mascots, jungle beasts with long tails intended for the flirty tickling of faces. Kingdoms' worth of princesses and their plastic accoutrements, stamped out on the royal assembly line, and the requisite Naughty Nurse suspended in the dead air, tilting in her rounds. Do Not Expose to Open Flame. For Amusement Only. The masks had been made in Korea, delivering back to the West the faces they had given the rest of the globe: presidents, screen stars, and mass murderers. The rubber filament inevitably snapped from the staple after five minutes. The graft wouldn't take.

Gary crouched on the floor of the party-supply store and slit open the belly of a goat-shaped piñata with his blade. "We didn't know they made this candy anymore."

Mark Spitz removed his glove and rolled some bonbons in his hand. They were flavor combos of fruit he'd never heard of, the habitués of a jungle on another damp hemisphere. "That stuff has been in there since before you were born," he said.

Kaitlyn gently removed the piñata from Gary's hands. "It's tiresome, babysitting."

Gary proposed that the human body required sugar after periods of extended exertion, and was rebuffed. Kaitlyn pulled out her notebook. "Mark Spitz?"

He went looking for the creature's ID. The general theory contended that stragglers haunted what they knew. The where was obvious: You were standing in it. But the why was always somewhere else. This skel they'd discovered by the row of helium tanks, her hand dangling on a valve. She was wearing a gorilla costume. The costume draped off her shoulders, deflated on her shrunken form. She wasn't wearing the head, which was nowhere in sight.

He was exhausted—they'd hit two res high-rises back-to-back, and there had been a lot of dead pets to lug down—but he couldn't help sleuthing. Why did this cipher stake out this store, and this particular spot? On the wall by the register, next to the taped-up first-day-of-business good-luck dollar bills, a photograph captured a burly man surrounded by smiling children who nipped at the bag of candy he held an inch out of reach. The owner, let's say. Mark Spitz glimpsed no family resemblance before he eliminated the straggler's face. Was she the spouse, an employee or former employee, and if so, what about this place shouldered its way into her mentality, past the plague, summoning her here? Then there was the suit. Had she been infected while wearing the gorilla outfit, or put it on as she got sicker and sicker with the disease, and if this was the case, what made her select it as her shroud? Before the plague, the sight of someone walking the street in that costume wouldn't have raised an eyebrow—Manhattan was Manhattan—and in its aftermath, such a vision added only a small portion of the prevailing macabre. Why her post by the helium tank, the paw on the valve that complicated the mystery? When Mark Spitz shot her in the head she brought down the tank with her. The gong of the thing hitting the floor was the loudest sound they'd heard in weeks, in that silent city. They jumped.

Mark Spitz unzipped the suit to check for a wallet. The skel was nude, her body mottled with brown plague spots. An apple-size chunk of meat was missing from her forearm. Perhaps the explanation of her outfit and how she made it to this spot was plausible in the context of her former life. But there was no one to tell her story. Mark Spitz's bullet had transformed everything above her neck into globules of toxic fluid, gristle, and shards of bone.

Kaitlyn suggested Mark Spitz take a look-see in the back for an ID. He went into the recesses of the store. No light seeped from the street. He switched on his torch. The office conformed to the familiar disarray of small downtown businesses. Management had piled invoices, overstock, and decades of tax returns into a fortification of clutter that might protect them from extinction. The light from his helmet traveled over the file cabinets and boxes of seasonal merchandise, the lifeblood plastic Easter eggs and jack-o'-lantern streamers. He didn't find her clothes, or any clues, and the next moment he was weeping, fingers curled into a nautilus across his face and snot seeping into his mouth, sweetly.

The next time they needed to fill out an Incident Report, Mark Spitz begged off, and eventually Kaitlyn took note and removed him from the detail. He had nerve damage: input could not penetrate. The world stalled out at his edges. Sometimes he had trouble speaking to other people, rummaging for language, and it seemed to him that an invisible layer divided him from the rest of the world, a membrane of emotional surface tension. He was not alone. "Survivors are slow or incapable of forming new attachments," or so the latest diagnoses droned, although a cynic might identify this as a feature of modern life merely intensified or fine-tuned with the introduction of the plague.

Buzzwords had returned, and what greater proof of the rejuvenation of the world, the return to Eden, than a new buzzword emerging from the dirt to tilt its petals to the zeitgeist. In the recent calm, experts of sundry persuasion reconnected with their professions, hoping to get out of custodial duty and earn a ticket to Buffalo with the rest of the royalty. One canny psychotherapist—Dr. Neil Herkimer, who'd made a fortune in the days before the flood with a line of self-help books imparting "The Herkimer Solution to Human Unhappiness"—delivered the big buzzword of the moment: PASD, or Post-Apocalyptic Stress Disorder. Dr. Neil Herkimer climbed aboard a Buffalo-bound chopper soon after his diagnosis. As the chopper disappeared into the sky, he could be seen through the tiny window giving his buddies at Camp El Dorado a vigorous thumbs-up. Mark Spitz heard people jabbering about it over pea soup in the mess tents, or as he handed crates of powdered milk and vitamin supplements to eager survivors in the scattered camps from an armor-plated supply truck: Everyone suffered from PASD. Herkimer put it at seventy-five percent of the surviving population, with the other twenty-five percent under the sway of preexisting mental conditions that were, of course, exacerbated by the great calamity. In the new reckoning, a hundred percent of the world was mad. Seemed about right.

Buffalo shipped out "Living with PASD" pamphlets to the settlements in the packages containing work orders, dietary guidelines focusing on the realities of this age of scarcity (scurvy was a recurring character), and, of course, classified status reports on new reconstruction initiatives. The pamphlets were left on bunks and mess-hall seats; Buffalo knew exactly how many to print from the survivor rolls. Mark Spitz mulled the literature in the latrine. According to the specialists, symptoms included feelings of sadness or unhappiness; irritability or frustration, even over small matters; loss of interest or pleasure in normal activities; reduced sex drive; insomnia or excessive sleeping; changes in appetite leading to weight loss, or increased cravings for food and weight gain; reliving traumatic events through hallucinations or flashbacks; agitation or restlessness; being "jumpy" or easily startled; slowed thinking, speaking, or body movements; indecisiveness, distractibility, and decreased concentration; fatigue, tiredness, and loss of energy so that even small tasks seem to require a lot of effort; feelings of worthlessness or guilt; trouble thinking, concentrating, making decisions, and remembering things; frequent thoughts of death, dying, or suicide; crying spells for no apparent reason, as opposed to those triggered by the memories of the fallen world; unexplained physical problems, such as back pain, increased blood pressure and heart rate, nausea, diarrhea, and headaches. Nightmares, goes without saying.

A meticulous inventory with a wide embrace. Not so much criteria for diagnosis but an abstract of existence itself, Mark Spitz thought. Once American tongues tangled with the acronym, it got mashed up and spat out into an intriguing shape. To wit: the afternoon he returned to camp after a rainy day working the Corridor, in abominable Connecticut, and was about to check the day's survivor roll. He hadn't seen the name of anyone he knew for weeks. Mark Spitz was halfway to the rec center when he discovered one of the comm operators, Hank, crouching by the prostrate body of a teenage soldier whose fresh gear had obviously never been worn before. Probably the kid's first foray out of camp since he came in from the wild. The soldier sprang in and out of a fetal posture, collapsing and exploding, smearing his body through a clump of vomit.

"What happened," Mark Spitz asked, "he get bit?"

"No, it's his past," he heard the comm operator say. The recruit moaned some more.

"His past?"

"His P-A-S-D, man, his P-A-S-D. Give me a hand."

That afternoon in Human Resources, Mark Spitz was grateful for Kaitlyn's empathy in sparing him from ID duty, and it became evident that Gary relished the job. "Ronkonkoma?" he asked, holding one of the HR ladies' licenses. "Had a lump of that on our crotch once." Kaitlyn excluded this information from the report.

Inserting corpses into body bags, on the other hand, provoked no symptoms in Mark Spitz. He removed four body bags from his pack and unfolded them, a genie of new-vinyl smell untangling its limbs. "You got Aunt Ethel and Gums over there," Gary said.

Mark Spitz started with the skel in pink, to get the heaviest out of the way. He grabbed its ankles and dragged it onto the plastic, tucking its feet into the sleeve. Its pantyhose curled back over its toes like a banana peel.

He still had a soft spot for Miss Alcott, all these years later, for it had been in her English class that he realized he was utterly unremarkable. She gave Mark Spitz and his classmates a vocab test every Thursday—"Use this word from the assigned reading in a sentence"—and by December it was hard not to notice the pattern. He was a thorough, inveterate B. It was his road. He studied for hours and there it waited for him, circled in red ink, oddly welcoming, silently forgiving. Or he refused to open his books and gorged instead on a prime-time platter of sitcoms: he'd still get a B. It was a little play he performed each week and he hit his marks instinctively, stalking the boards of mediocrity. He was not unintelligent; in fact, his instructors agreed that he was often quite perceptive and canny in his contributions to discussion, a "true pleasure to have in the classroom." The adjectives in his report cards, drawn from a special teachers' collection of mild yet approving modifiers, described an individual of broader gifts than implied by the grades delivered at the end of each term. All the parts were there. Extra screws, even. There was just something wrong in the execution.

Over the years, Mark Spitz reconciled himself to his condition. It took the pressure off. A force from above held him down, and a counterforce from below bore him aloft. He hovered on unexceptionality.

He zipped up the corpse that resembled, under the blood and contorted features, his elementary-school teacher and then he remembered. He looked around and crawled to the copier and retrieved its wig. He unzipped the black bag and dropped it on its face.

He tossed Gary a body bag and the mechanic grabbed the feet of the faceless skel. Mark Spitz got started on the Marge. He looked into her black teeth. His arm still flared in the aftermath of its assault, even though the lattice of fibers in his fatigues had absorbed most of the pressure. He didn't want to see what his bicep looked like under there. He'd probably have to tape a chemical compress around it for a week.

The Marge's broken teeth tilted hideously from its gums. He thought of the crumbling pilings across the water. Last month they'd swept the big apartment complexes of Battery Park, that crop of edifices jabbed deep into landfill. The western face of the buildings bristled with rows of terraces overlooking Jersey City. The week they worked that development, he stepped out on the balconies for air and stared at the withered stunts of the old Jersey docks. Remnants of a dead, seafaring era of trade and commerce. *What a view*. Make it to the edges of the island and the Palisades, Brooklyn, the Statue of Liberty scrolled before you in their stillness. (Give me your poor, your hungry, your suppurating masses yearning to eat.) What percentage of the residents' lips had formed, at one point or another, the syllables of a sweet, awestruck "What a view"? How could it be any less than a hundred percent. It was a banality no one could elude. What percentage of the residents surged with pride as they darted between the kitchenette and the living room to replenish the hors d'oeuvres when their guests whispered "What a view"? One hundred percent. The citizens were programmed by the vista-less city to utter such things at the correct triggers, so diminished were they from crippled horizons.

After four flights, Mark Spitz had the complex's blueprints in his pocket, a super's knowledge of the identical layouts of the apartments in their distinct lines. Windowless office nook or nursery, bathroom on the right, second bedroom at the end of the hall with a coffin-size closet. He recognized the area rugs and sconces and accent tables, for the residents had all shopped at the same popular furniture emporiums the rest of the country shopped at. They had shambled through the identical outlet showrooms and tested the same sofas with their asses, clicked through the drop-down menus of the same online purveyors, broadband willing, zooming in on See in a Room and mentally arranging the merchandise according to the same floor plans. In the D-line apartment on the sixth floor he discovered the plaid ottoman he came across in the A-line apartment on the fourteenth floor, an identical distance from the flat-screen television. They had been a community.

The only thing that truly changed was the view of Jersey, easing in perspective as his unit moved down the stairs from penthouse god to grub eye. Omega disposed of the bodies from the big Battery Park buildings the same way they disposed of bodies anywhere else. The vantages affected price per square foot, not their jobs. The bodies were equally ungainly in the black polyurethane, whether recovered in rooms that overlooked cliffs, or air shafts, or more extravagant apartments across the street. On the other bank of the Hudson River, the old pilings stuck up abjectly, rotten teeth in a monstrous jaw. Revolting gray water sloshed around them like saliva. Teeth everywhere. You make it across the water, Mark Spitz thought, and you'd get eaten up.

He zipped up the Marge, hastening when he arrived at the bloody mophead of her scalp. Was this skel a native New Yorker, or had it been lured here by the high jinks of Margaret Halstead and her colorful roommates? One of those seekers powerless before the seduction of the impossible apartment that the gang inexplicably afforded on their shit-job salaries, unable to resist the scalpel-carved and well-abraded faces of the guest stars the characters smooched in one-shot appearances or across multi-episode arcs. Struck dumb by the dazzling stock footage of the city avenues at teeming evening. Did it work, the hairdo, the bleached teeth, the calculated injections, did it transform the country rube into the cosmopolitan? Mold their faces to the prevailing grimace? The city required people to make it go. When citizens flee or die, others must replace them. As it expanded its magnificence, out over landfill or up in its multifarious and towering honeycombs, it required bodies to fill the vacancies. When the sweepers finished their mission, who would be the new residents of the island, bellies up to the boat rail, gaping as expectantly as those other immigrants who had come to the harbor, that first fodder? Where had all the previous tenants gone, what number would have been spared if they had remained in their stifling hometowns? How many had been indoctrinated by that enervating glow?

Infected by reruns. He sucked his teeth. Just as easy to get chomped up in a hayfield as in a subway tunnel. To be honest Mark Spitz had been hypnotized by the show himself, nestled inside the eighteen-to-thirty-four age demographic whose underdeveloped cultural immune systems rendered them susceptible to the series' shenanigans. The acquisitive debit-card swipers and the easily swayed. The obedient. Endure a minor epiphany by show's end and forget it by next week. At least that part of the program was true to life, he thought.

Kaitlyn said, "Probably one or two more downstairs and then we're done with this block."

"Oy, we need a new street, something," Gary said. "We're sick of this block."

"You need more time, Mark Spitz?" Kaitlyn asked.

He shook his head. He was ready. He had needed a reminder; he had received it. There was no when-it-was-over, no after. Only the next five minutes. Like all city dwellers, he had to accustom his eyes to the new horizon.

Gary zipped up the last of the corpses and lit another cigarette. He asked Kaitlyn for help bringing them down.

She shrugged. "You bag 'em, you drag 'em."

. . .

For the first few weeks they tossed the bodies out the windows. It was efficient. The likelihood of harming passersby was infinitesimal. The unsuspecting, the caught unawares, the out for a smoke. They lugged the bodies to the sill and heaved them out. Confronted with the beggar's slit of a safety window, they shot out the glass. Disinclined to lift the window, they shot out the glass. They awaited the sound of glass smashing into a million fragments and the splash of bodies bursting against concrete in equal measure.

It saved time and energy. They belonged to a nation enamored of shortcuts and the impulse persisted. It beat dragging the bodies down twelve flights and then humping back upstairs to resume the sweep. The higher up, the messier, naturally. In due course Disposal complained to the Lieutenant, to whatever brass at Fort Wonton was foolish enough to listen. "What's that?" the officers asked. It was hard to hear that team through their hazmat helmets.

"Defenestration!" Disposal shouted, louder, accustomed to this indignity. Defenestration unduly aggravated their job. It was disrespectful. It was unhygienic. Frankly, it was unpatriotic. Everything inside was bullied to a lumpy slime, and the zippers oozed a trail of crimson slush on the street, in the carts, the post-pickup staging areas. And that was when the bags remained mostly intact.

Mark Spitz conceded that Disposal had a point. There had been an incident where he had been brooding on the sidewalk when a body bag burst a few feet away, splashing him with ichor and clots of grue. Gary apologized for neglecting to offer a heads-up, but it had slowed the progress of their friendship, those early weeks.

The broken windows put an end to the practice. Disposal could whine until doomsday, so to speak, about contamination risk, but Buffalo wanted the city habitable for the new tenants. Especially given the marines' rampage through Zone One, necessary though it was. There had been no time for finesse, only the brute exigencies of clearing out thousands upon thousands of the dead. Now, with the introduction of the sweeper teams, they could proceed in a matter befitting the American Phoenix. The new era of reconstruction was forward-looking, prudent, attentive to the small details that will dividend in the years to come. The order came down: No more assaults on the windows of the fair city. The sweepers reconciled themselves to the new regulations. They took the stairs.

Mark Spitz and Gary tackled the heaviest bodies first. Per custom, they lugged, pulled, and kicked them down the stairwell, panting their way through the cinder-block intestine. Any witnesses would have moved their share of corpses and could sympathize. After a few floors, the muffled thump of skel heads bouncing against the stairs was replaced by a moist, unnerving thud. The body bags were equipped with handles on either end, but the realities of plague-era manufacture—the reclaimed factories were reconfigured to produce items outside the scope of their original purpose, often in a shoddy fashion—meant that the tenuously attached straps usually gave way after a few maneuvers. When that happened, the sweepers grabbed the bottom of the bag and felt the corpse's mulch squish through the plastic.

Gary said, "We're going to call it the Lasso."

Mark Spitz didn't answer. He had no idea what the man was referring to, so he waited for him to provide context. There was time. They were halfway to the street. The emergency lights still worked and they didn't have to worry about renegades lurching in the darkness. The two sweepers were so noisy that any devil maundering in the stairwell would have already made itself known.

"Our skel-catcher. We're going to call it the Lasso."

"I thought you were going to go with the Grabber," Mark Spitz said.

"The Lasso sounds more sophisticated."

In his downtime, Gary worked on an instrument for neutralizing skels. He recruited Mark Spitz and Kaitlyn into the only extant focus group on the planet, spitballing for weeks. The latest iteration involved a long rod with a ratcheted collar at the business end. The collar, in turn, was attached to a mesh bag, made of the same tear- and tooth-resistant material as their fatigues. When you came across a skel, you manipulated the collar around its head, then jerked back. The collar cinched tight like handcuffs, detached from the rod, "And voilà: Skel in a Bag." The captured monsters couldn't bite through, or see. They were neutralized. You could do what you wanted with them.

The problem was that the only thing to do with a captured skel was to put it down.

Mark Spitz and Kaitlyn had pointed this out to Gary on numerous occasions, among their other criticisms of the invention. The skel-catcher, or You-Grab-It or Lasso, whatever name Gary settled on (there had been brief flirtation with the Gary), was useless in close quarters. It required a low density of hostiles—with two or more creatures in the area, too many variables complicated execution. It tied up both your hands so that you couldn't pull off a last-second head shot if need be. But those were concerns of implementation. The main problem, of course, was that no one wanted a captured skel. In the early days, the government required a stock of the recently infected and the thoroughly turned for experiments, to search for a cure, cook up a vaccine, or simply investigate the phenomenon "in the name of science." The vaccine work continued—what were they going to do, boot out the epidemiologist now that priorities had shifted to infrastructure?—and in their subterranean labs Buffalo certainly still rode hard on the centrifuges and electron microscopes, but the market for fresh skels did not exist, the odd hillbilly torture dungeon aside. No one used the word "cure" anymore. The plague so transformed the human body that no one still believed they could be restored. Sure, rumors persisted that a team of Swiss scientists were holed up in the Alps working on processes to reverse the effects, but most survivors had seen enough skels to know the verdict of the plague could not be overturned. No. The only thing to do with a lassoed skel was to put it down. As soon as possible.

Gary was undeterred. He had been making diagrams for a patent, despite the small matter of there being no patent office in the land to process it. "I'm going to be rich," he maintained, as he sulked over his unit's lack of enthusiasm. Spoken like a true pheenie, Mark Spitz thought. Despite other contrary vectors of his personality, Gary maintained his own reservoir of pheenie optimism, a hazy vision, after all this time, of his insertion into the dreamscape of American prosperity. There would be room enough in his fabulous mansion for chambers devoted to his dead brothers' memory, along with the standard lap pool and 5,000 Btu gas grill. The sketches of his invention reminded Mark Spitz of cave paintings, but this was only appropriate given the culture's precipitous regression.

"The Lasso," Mark Spitz said. "You're really onto something there."

Although the sign at the exit informed them that an alarm would sound, this was not the case. They tugged the heaps across the black-and-white tile of the lobby and lurched into the slurry that passed for rain these days.

They left the bags in the middle of the street for Disposal, Gary darting back into the building to avoid the downpour. Mark Spitz felt the rain on his face. This was not stuff you wanted on your skin, to see the residue from the rain when it dried. It reminded Mark Spitz of when he visited his cousins in Florida and he emerged from the ocean with brown globs of oil on his chest and legs, the stuff still drifting ashore so long after the big spill. As a frigid worm of water snuck under his collar, he saw that this block of Duane Street appeared unruined. It was any city block on a normal day of that expired calendar, five minutes before dawn, say, when most of the city was still sleeping it off. Duane had not been allocated, so the army mechanics hadn't cleared it, and the spectrum of vehicles popular at the time of the ruin were lined up at the curb, waiting for the return from the errand, the commute, the trip home. Nothing had been boarded up, there were no firefight traces or other signs of mayhem, and a finicky wind had kicked all the litter around the corner. From time to time Mark Spitz happened on these places in Zone One, where he strolled down a movie set, earning scale as an extra in a period piece about the dead world.

The swiftness of the evac, and the fact the island hadn't endured a major engagement—been firebombed like Oakland or nuked like St. Augustine or whatever the hell happened in Birmingham—meant that entire stretches of the city were pristine. Not everywhere, of course. Storefronts had been hastily fortified, and the defenses were still fixed in place or piled on the sidewalk in disassembly. There had been collisions: streetlamps and mailboxes tombstoned over the corpses of crashed cars, and delivery trucks and police vans had beached themselves on the sidewalk like sad behemoths. And they strolled down plenty of blocks where the marines had really gone to town on a throng of skels, as the broken windows and bullet holes testified. Nonetheless, it was remarkable how well the skin of the city had survived the catastrophe. The exploratory missions sent in their reports and the committees in Buffalo concurred: The city was an excellent candidate for early reboot.

New York City in death was very much like New York City in life. It was still hard to get a cab, for example. The main difference was that there were fewer people. It was easier to walk down the street. No grim herds of out-of-towners shuffled about, no amateur fascist up the street machinated to steal the next cab. There were no lines at the mammoth organic-food stores, once you reached checkout after stepping over the spilled rice and shattered jars of bloody tomato sauce and environmentally conscious package of whatnot thrown to the floor during the brief phase of looting. The hottest restaurants always had a prime table waiting, even if they hadn't updated the specials since the winnowing of the human race got under way. You could sit where you wanted to in the movie theaters, if you could suffer sitting in the dark, where monsters occasionally shifted their thighs.

This street looked normal. It was a façade. Beyond the wall, more streets like this awaited, and beyond the city, expanses of formaldehyded territory, old postcard specimens of America preserved in tidy eddies. Expertise had been employed to produce the illusion of life in the cadaver, a kindness. Then you made a sound, Mark Spitz thought, and you saw the movement of creatures.

A worm of gray water slithered down his back. The last time he saw his childhood home was on Last Night. It, too, had looked normal from the outside, in that new meaning of normal that signified resemblance to the time before the flood. Normal meant "the past." Normal was the unbroken idyll of life before. The present was a series of intervals differentiated from each other only by the degree of dread they contained. The future? The future was the clay in their hands.

On Last Night, the sprinkler had pivoted and dispensed in its prescribed arc on his lawn. The floor lamp next to the living-room television transmitted its reassuring cone through the powder-blue curtains, as it had for decades. He was not a loser of keys, and held twenty-year-old front-door keys in his hand. When he fled the house minutes later, he would not stop to lock the door behind himself.

He and his friend Kyle had spent a few nights in Atlantic City at one of the new boutique casinos, adrift among the dazzling surfaces. Inside the enclosure, they imagined themselves libertines at the trough, snout-deep and rooting. The banks of machines trilled and dinged and whooped in a regional dialect of money. At the hold 'em tables, they visualized the hand rankings from their poker bibles and nervously joked about the guys who were overly chummy with the dealers, the local sharks on their nocturnal feed. They tipped the waitresses with chips, deducting these from their night's tally in the spirit of thorough accounting, and slid their fingers around the dice in superstitious motions before launch in the craps arena. They were heroes to strangers for a time, ticker-taped during sporadic rushes. On barstools they ogled the bachelorettes in the club and discussed their chances, recalling near-conquests from previous visits. In the buffet lines they foraged from the heat lamps and steam trays, and impaled and then swirled wasabi around tiny ceramic saucers, tinting soy sauce. After thirty-six hours they realized, according to custom, that they hadn't yet left the premises, and submitted happily to the artificial habitat that is the modern casino. They did not want. It was all inside. Their brains fogged over as possibility and failure enthralled them in a perpetual and tantalizing loop.

The casino was emptier than it had been on their earlier missions. The fresh casinos burst from the gaping, rebar-studded lots where the past-prime establishments had stood, and perhaps that explained it, they thought, the law of competition and the lure of the latest bauble. Everyone was at the new place they hadn't heard of yet. Fewer people milled about the tables, there were subdued shrieks at the craps, roulette stands shrouded in plastic, although it should be noted that the slots maintained their sturdy population of glassy-eyed defectives, the protohumans with their sleepless claws. Their favorite blackjack dealer, Jackie, a weather-beaten broad who dispensed smiles beneath a slumping orange beehive, was out sick, and the creature in her place kept fucking up the deal, but they decided against complaining to the pit boss after consideration of his imposing, deflecting mien. To be sure, this trip's pod of bachelorettes was a trifle depleted, running through their pantomime of excess with weary affect and listlessly brandishing the rubber penises on the dance floor. It occurred to them more than once that this trip would not live up to their lore, and they mourned over sips of subsidized liquor. Maybe they had outgrown these enthusiasms. Maybe those times were dead and they were only now aware of their new circumstances.

They did not watch the news or receive news from the outside.

They were up past dawn, crashed, were granted absolution in its secular manifestation of late checkout. They inserted themselves into the Sunday northbound stream and devoured the under-carbonated colas and turkey wraps purchased at the turnpike conveniences. The wraps were sealed, according to the label, in a plastic that degraded into eco-friendly vapor in thirty days. The traffic was atrocious and shaming, of that pantheon of traffic encountered when one is late to a wedding or other monumental event of fleeting import. Surely an accident unraveled its miserable inevitabilities ahead and now all was fouled, decelerated, the vehicles syllables in an incantation of misfortune. Drivers and their passengers misbehaved, steering onto the shoulder and jetting past the stalled unlucky, even seeming to abandon their vehicles. Figures lurched through the median. Fire trucks and police cars galloped past in their standard hysteria. Kyle and Mark Spitz traded playlists, which were broadcast from their digital music devices over the car speakers. The traffic did not cease when they emerged from the tunnel, the Long Island Expressway a disgrace in either direction.

"Big game tonight or a concert," Kyle said.

"They need to chill," Mark Spitz said. The Monday vise clenched. Here was that end-of-weekend despair, the death of amusement and the winnowing of the reprieve. Everyone on the expressways and turnpikes felt it, he was sure, this evaporation of prospects. What impotent rebellion they enacted, feebly tapping the leather facsimile of their horns and spitting the top-shelf profanities. In retrospect, perhaps the intensity of that moment, the pressure he felt, was the immensity of the farewell, for this was the goodbye traffic, the last latenesses and their attendant excuses, the final inconveniences of an expiring world.

They finally arrived at Mark Spitz's corner. A small team of boys played basketball at the other end of the street. The game was breaking up, it had been too dark to play for a while now, and he tried to identify the players but they didn't seem to be part of the block's pool of well-bred teens. Were they playing basketball? There was a small round shape on the pavement and they bent into a huddle. He didn't recognize their faces, only that deflated curl of the shoulders that marked Sunday night's recurring epidemic: Back to work.

Mark Spitz said goodbye to his childhood friend for the last time and walked up the pavestone path, the fruit of a recently completed replacement of the brick walkway that had skinned his knees many times. Except for college and brief, doomed stints here and there—a botched adventure in California pursuing a girl whom he hadn't believed when she professed to prefer girls, a season on a couch in Brooklyn—he had lived in this house his entire life. Technically, he lived in the basement, his childhood room having long been converted into his mother's home office, but his father's subterranean renovation—an undertaking that had kept him afloat when so many of his peers had been capsized by midlife's squall—made plausible Mark Spitz's explanation that he had moved down to the "rec room." This was no mere basement, with its touch-screen climate controls and programmed lighting routines, but a space capsule he piloted to the planet of his life's next stage.

The house looked normal from the outside. The shades were pulled and the lights were out save for the aforementioned glow of the floor lamp by the media center in the living room, that dependable illumination that had greeted him for years. His mother had been feeling "not so red hot," in her mom parlance, and he surmised that they were half asleep in front of the upstairs digital video recorder as the final fifteen minutes of last week's episode droned before them: the verdict of the judges and the expulsion of the latest scapegoat; the obscure precedents cited by the maverick district attorney; the reenactors of real crimes in their shabby thespianship. His parents often retreated to their old honeymoon nest after dinner, ceding to their son the living room, with its high-definition enhancements and twin leather recliners equipped with beverage holsters. The rec room was a marvel in every respect save its television, a rare impulse purchase on the part of his father, who consulted the roundups on the internet with dedication, often contributing his two- and three-star verdicts to the rabble chorus. The set was an off-brand mistake lately afflicted with a black bloom of dead pixels. Its sorry conjurations gave the family an excuse to enjoy the big television spectacles together upstairs, the ones that periodically reunited the riven nation, albeit in staggered broadcasts in the cascade of time zones.

He scowled at the mail on the hall credenza, speculating anew over what misbegotten opt-in had birthed, among other bastards, his identification as a member of the opposite political party. (In the catastrophe, the demonic mailing lists were struck. One was free to choose a fresh affiliation from the rubbled platforms.) He decided to crow about his winnings. He moved up the stairs and was startled by the sound of his sneakers on the naked planks. The pavestone renovation had been part of a larger project that embraced, in its broad manifest, the retiling of the kitchen's hexagonal expanse and the removal of the stairway carpet. This was a foot-level campaign. They worked on the house constantly, his parents. The projects took time. Although they were relatively young (*young* got younger and younger as the gatekeepers of media contemplated their mortality earlier and earlier), their makeover schemes betrayed an attempt to outwit death: Who had ever died during the installation of a backyard water feature, one that might dribble joy from polyvinyl chloride tubing? In bed, they thumbed adhesive notes into the margins of catalog pages and exchanged them like hostages over the sheets. Every room, every reconsidered and gussied square foot was an encroachment into immortality's lot line. The blueprints, the specs, the back-of-the-envelope estimates. It would sustain them. The guest bathroom was next.

Exhausted by the foot-level transformations, his parents were between renovation projects. Perhaps if it had been otherwise, they would still be alive.

When he was six, he had walked in on his mother giving his father a blow job. A public-television program about the precariousness of life in the Serengeti, glimpsed in passing, had introduced him to dread, and it had been eating at him the previous few nights. Bad dreams. The hyenas and their keening. He needed to slip into his parents' king-size bed, as he had when he was very young, before he had been banished to his own big-boy bed in accordance with the latest child-rearing philosophies. It was forbidden, but he decided to visit his parents. He padded down the hall, past the green eye of the carbon-monoxide detector, that ever-vigilant protector against invisible evil, and the bathroom and the linen closet. He opened the door to the master bedroom and there she was, gobbling up his father. His father ceased his unsettling growls and shouted for his son to leave. The incident was never referred to again, and it became the first occupant of the corner in his brain's attic that he reserved for the great mortifications. The first occupant, but not the last.

It was, naturally, to that night his thoughts fled when on his return from Atlantic City he opened the door of his parents' bedroom and witnessed his mother's grisly ministrations to his father. She was hunched over him, gnawing away with ecstatic fervor on a flap of his intestine, which, in the crepuscular flicker of the television, adopted a phallic aspect. He thought immediately of when he was six, not only because of the similar tableau before him but because of that tendency of the human mind, in periods of duress, to seek refuge in more peaceful times, such as a childhood experience, as a barricade against horror.

That was the start of his Last Night story. Everybody had one.

Mark Spitz and Gary returned to the law office and dragged the other two bodies down, Kaitlyn whistling behind them as they descended. She proposed lunch, and they squatted in the lobby underneath the glass case listing the building's occupants, which were detailed by easily recombined white letters embedded in black felt. Like most lists of people, it was now a roll call of the dead, an inversely colored obituary page.

"Are they a sponsor?" Gary asked. "We're hungry." He held up a chocolate bar retrieved from the spill of candy, breath mints, and hand sanitizer. The gate of the lobby newsstand had been ripped open and looted, probably by the marines, or else a post-evac survivor who'd run out of crackers and dared a raid.

"Not yet," Kaitlyn said.

"But they might come aboard next week. Could happen. In which case it's okay."

Kaitlyn shook her head.

"The marines took what they wanted when they came through. How do you think they got all those NFL jerseys?"

"That was before the regs came down. You have chocolate chip cookies in your MRE."

Gary tossed the candy bar and declined his standard joke. Usually when someone mentioned meals ready to eat, their military rations, Gary pointed out that survivors were MREs to the skels, hardy-har, punctuating it with his gravelly chuckle. Perhaps Gary was exhausted; it was the end of the week. "Just gonna get eaten up by the residents," he said. "Pheenie bastards."

"Maybe they'll put you here," Mark Spitz said. He didn't believe it.

Buffalo had not yet divulged who was going to get resettled in Manhattan once the sweepers were finished, but Gary had long been skeptical that he would be among them. "You think we're going to end up here? We ain't special. They're going to put the rich people here. Politicians and pro athletes. Those chefs from those cooking shows."

"It's going to be a lottery," Kaitlyn sighed. She opened a meat tube and squeezed it into her mouth.

"Lottery, shit," Gary said. "They're going to put us on Staten Island."

"I thought you liked islands," Mark Spitz said. Gary was a firm believer in the Island Theory of plague survival.

"We like islands. Natural defenses. You know we like islands. But we wouldn't live on Staten Island if they were giving out vaccines and hand jobs right off the ferry."

"They screen for DNA, you'll be lucky they don't turn you out the gates." Trevor, one of the sweepers in Gamma Unit, maintained that he'd heard that Buffalo was working on a system of screening settlers according to their genetic desirability. Mark Spitz didn't believe it but rationalized that he had a decent chance of getting a nice spot somewhere. Surely many of the high-functioning members of society had been killed off, allowing mediocre specimens such as himself to move up a notch.

Kaitlyn tapped her headset distractedly, as if she'd been trying to make a weekend plan with one of her gal pals and her cell dropped the call. Did you lose me or did I lose you?

"Anything?" Mark Spitz asked.

She shook her head. They'd been out of contact with Fort Wonton for a week, ever since they departed for this grid. The comms went out with nettlesome frequency. It was hard to get a signal through on the best of days—the buildings bounced the waves between each other like kids playing keep-away—but the big culprit was mischievous bugs deep in the military communications software. The machines froze, chronically, and then they'd have to be rebooted and it took forever for the equipment to reinitialize. It was highly unlikely that the defense contractor awarded the bid would be prosecuted in the future, but this was the case even if the plague hadn't cleared the halls of justice of everyone save the odd robed straggler gripping a gavel in the empty chamber.

The comm failures were annoying, but fortunately the sweepers didn't need any orders apart from what grid was up next, and they got that every week when they returned to Wonton. "Let's get going," Kaitlyn said. "We'll check in when we go back on Sunday."

As they packed their gear they saw that the bodies were gone. Disposal had picked them up without the sweepers observing, with the eerie efficiency that was their trademark. Outside Wonton, the most you ever saw of Disposal was their cart disappearing around a corner a block or two blocks ahead, as they slumped in their bright white hazmat suits. The carriage and the horse had been players in the Central Park tourist-ride industry, the former enduring the elements as it waited for reassignment—obviously, sightseeing had taken a hit the last few years—and the latter presumably living off weeds in the Great Lawn until they established Fort Wonton. The horse had been choppered to the Zone after it was spotted during an early uptown reconnaissance mission. "It seems like the right thing to do," General Tavin said, and indeed the rescue operation's planning and execution had fostered a great deal of morale, even more than news of the beer distributor's sponsorship.

The chopper pilot who brought Mark Spitz from the Northeast Corridor sustained a tour-guide spiel the whole trip down, narrating the eastern seaboard's points of interest with an oddly perky flair. Mark Spitz suspected he was on drugs. When they reached Manhattan, he took them for a quick circuit over Central Park, "laid out by Frederick Law Olmsted in one of the greatest landscaping undertakings Jesus has ever seen." Mark Spitz had seen the park unscroll from the windows of the big skyscrapers crowding the perimeter, but never from this vantage. No picnickers idled on their blankets, no one goldbricked on the benches, and nary a Frisbee arced through the sky, but the park was at first-spring-day capacity. They didn't stop to appreciate the scenery, these dead visitors; they ranged on the grass and walkways without purpose or sense, moving first this way and then strolling in another direction until, distracted by nothing in particular, they readjusted their idiot course. It was Mark Spitz's first glimpse of Manhattan since the coming of the plague, and he thought to himself, My God, it's been taken over by tourists.

Diesel supply being what it was, the horse made sense, and the nag was game enough to lug the big metal cart attached to the carriage as Disposal made their circuit downtown, cleaning up after the sweeper units. Bring out your dead. The guys and gals in Disposal never removed their hazmat suits, in public at least, even when off the clock and prowling around Wonton with everyone else. Maybe they know something we don't, Mark Spitz thought, as he saw them take their rations and scurry back to whatever building they'd staked out. They had duct-taped a shower-curtain rod to the carriage's dashboard and tied a brass bell to it, which somehow ended up sounding more cheerful than macabre, sounding off in the distance.

Gary snatched the stack of replacement body bags left by Disposal—they kept track, meticulously, dropping off new ones when a unit was running low—and the three of them headed up the stairwell to finish the building.

It was always disquieting to see empty pavement where you'd dumped some terminated skels. It was as if they'd just walked away.

. . .

They stoppered the tunnels and blocked the bridges. They plugged the subways at the preordained stations, every one south of where the first wall would stand. The choppers lowered the swaying concrete segments one by one across the breadth of Canal Street as the dead gaped and clawed through the dust kicked up by the blades. More than a few of the unfortunates were pulverized. Perhaps this was the pilots' intent. The final section went down at the edge of the river. Now they had a zone.

The soldiers landed at the Battery Park staging area, near the Korean War memorial. They disembarked from the troop transports, this generation's marines, and initiated the first sweep. Buffalo's estimates vis-à-vis skel density south of Canal were stupendously botched. How could they have reckoned the numbers skulking in the great buildings. The dead poured into the street at the soldiers' noise. Which was part of the plan. The grunts used themselves as bait, their invectives, war cries, and tunes drawing schools of the dead into their machine-gun fire.

They rappelled from gunships into key intersections, eliminating a hundred shuddering skels before clipping back to the cables and floating out of the strike zone, camoed fairies of destruction. They strafed, loosed fusillades, and mastered the head shots, spinal separators, and cranial detonators that diverted the dead to the sidewalk against newspaper boxes, fire hydrants, antiterrorism planters, and inscrutable corporate-sponsored public art. The soldiers terminated targets on fire escapes, where they slumped like moths caught in wrought-iron cobwebs. Kill techniques cycled in their fads, in this week and out the next, as the soldiers refined and traded tips and accidental discoveries. Everyone had their own way of handling things. The red tears of tracers shrieked through the thoroughfares and stray bullets cratered the faces of banks, churches, condos, and franchises, every place of worship a city has to offer. Exquisite glass panes crashed down in their music, manufacturing geometric shapes that had never before existed in the history of the world, which in turn sharded into newer shapes and brilliant white dust. Shell casings danced and skipped on the asphalt like tossed cigarette butts. The gun smoke was sucked up into braids and curtains by the atmospheric patterns created by skyscrapers and avenue crevices, those mountain faces and valleys, and when it cleared the creatures gushed in renewed fortified lines.

The soldiers discussed work over dinner. While they sucked meat paste off the roof of their mouths, they pondered how every type of store and building cultivated its own rhythms and customs, kept likely suspects loitering by the checkout counters, the help desks, and You Are Here maps of subterranean midtown concourses. The health clubs in the basements of rental buildings catering to young singles commanded their regulars and habitués, and the faculty lounges of mammoth public high schools maintained their assortments ricocheting off the coffee-machine counter, as they had before the plague. The major fast-food purveyors became, over time, reliable for a certain kind of experience and the reasonably priced surf-and-turf chain offered its own fortifying menu as the dead city continued its business in mirthless parody.

One day they noticed the ebb. Impossible not to. The grotesque parades thinned. Slaughter slowed. The dead creaked forth in groups of a dozen, then five at a time, in pairs, and finally solo, taking their proper place atop the heaps of corpses as they were cut down. The soldiers steadied themselves atop the corpses in turn and drew a bead. They made hills. Putrefying mounds on the cobblestones of the crooked streets of the financial district. They rid the South Street Seaport of natives and tourists alike, and the breeze off the water carted away buckets of the stench. Snipers crosshaired on swaying silhouettes six, seven blocks crosstown, that sensible, age-old grid layout allowing passage for traffic that traveled at the speed of sound. As the numbers of the creatures thinned, the soldiers no longer offered themselves as lures. They hunted, ambled, leisurely, easygoing flaneurs drifting where the streets took them. The soldiers were the arrowhead of a global campaign and they understood it each time they overcame the resistance in the trigger, felt good about it. The soldiers took longer rest breaks, devising new branches of gallows humor, jokes that took root. They knew they were being fundamentally altered, in their very cells, inducted into a different class of trauma than the rest of the survivors. Semper fi. Then they went inside.

They dispensed with the superstructures one by one, the global headquarters brimming with junior VPs and heads of accounts, the great sinks of money and insurance, the public housing projects with their cinder-block labyrinths and denimed minotaurs, the middle-income megaplexes and prewar co-ops. They stormed the municipal buildings whose functions were engraved in great stone blocks over the entrance for easy identification. Initially surprised at how many skels they found ricocheting inside the government buildings, but it made sense once they thought about it. They landed on the roofs and rammed the stairwell doors, grateful for daylight whenever it penetrated. The most unexpected places pullulated with the things, for no reason they could fathom. Why this particular juice joint and not another, why this neighborhood greasy spoon, synagogue, bookstore, 99 cent store? Bas-reliefs of gryphons, sea serpents, and chimaeras coiled the length of the monumental old buildings, indicators of another era's idea of craftsmanship and of what monsters might look like. The pulverized faces of the dead increased the zone's percentage of faces that were less handsome than those of the cornice gargoyles. It had been a small number before the plague, despite the coteries of investment bankers.

The marines eliminated the outside stragglers, the ones standing on the sidelines as the dead made their implacable sallies. The street vendor at his rolling cart brandishing a small rod covered with caked, dry mustard. The skateboarder posing on the filigreed manhole cover at the bottom of his favorite declivity. The window-shopper bewitched before a boarded-up department-store window, taking in a long-removed display that nonetheless unfurled its exquisitely arranged baubles behind the plywood. Who knew what went on in what remained of their minds, what mirages they made of the world. The marines shot them in the head, harmless or no.

Some of the marines died. Some of them didn't hear the warnings until too late for all the gunfire. Some of them lost their bearings in the macabre spectacle, drifting off into reveries of overidealized chapters of their former lives, and were overcome. Some of them were bit, losing baseballs of meat from their arms and legs. Some of them disappeared under hordes, maybe a glove sticking out, waving, and it was unclear if the hand was under the direction of the fallen soldier or if it was being jostled by the feasting. Funeral rites were abbreviated. They incinerated the bodies of their comrades with the rest of the dead.

They nozzled diesel into the bulldozers and dump trucks. The air filled with buzzing flies the way it had once been filled with the hydraulic whine of buses, the keening of emergency vehicles, strange chants into cell phones, high heels on sidewalk, the vast phantasmagorical orchestra of a living city. They loaded the dead. The rains washed the blood after a time. The New York City sewer system in its bleak centuries had suffered worse.

The marines were redeployed, some upstate to hasten completion of the northern initiatives, others to hush-hush engagements out West. Not many details apart from that. The army arrived, then the corps of engineers with plans for the next phase. They cradled the tubes of blueprints and schematics of the metropolitan systems under their armpits, bestowed upon them by Buffalo after excavation from some undisclosed climate-controlled government storehouse.

Any structure under twenty stories was left to the sweepers. Hence Mark Spitz. When his unit finished number 135, they were done with Duane x Church, Mixed Residential/Business. Then it was on to the next.

"Shouldn't be too many hostiles," Kaitlyn said. They started back up the stairs of 135 Duane. The sweepers gobbled and assimilated the military lingo into their systems with gusto. Mingled with the fresh slang, the new vocabulary of the disaster was their last-ditch armor plate. They tucked it under their fatigues, over their hearts, the holy verses that might catch the bullet.

Other phrases in vogue were less invigorating and uplifting: extinction, doomsday, end of the world. They lacked zing. They did not stir the masses from their poly-this poly-that inflatable mattresses to pledge their lives to reconstruction. Early in the reboot, Buffalo agreed on the wisdom of rebranding survival. They maintained a freakish menagerie of specialists up there, superior brains yanked from the camps, and what did these folks do all day but try and think up better ways to hone the future, tossing ideograms up on whiteboards and conferring at their self-segregated tables in the sublevel cafeteria, lowering their voices when outsiders walked by balancing orange trays. Some of them were hard at work crafting the new language, and they came up with more than a few winners; the enemy they faced would not succumb to psychological warfare, but that didn't mean that the principles needed to remain unutilized.

It was a new day. Now, the people were no longer mere survivors, half-mad refugees, a pathetic, shit-flecked, traumatized herd, but the "American Phoenix." The more popular diminutive *pheenie* had taken off in the settlements, which also endured their round of cosmetics, as Camp 14 was rechristened New Vista, and Roanoke became Bubbling Brooks. Mark Spitz's first civilian camp was Happy Acres, and indeed everyone's mood did brighten a bit on seeing that name on the gate next to the barbed wire and electric fencing. Mark Spitz thought the merchandise helped out a lot, too, the hoodies and sun visors and such. The frigid hues and brittle lines of the logo conformed to a very popular design trend in the months preceding Last Night, and it was almost as if the culture was picking up where it left off.

Omega discovered 135 Duane's lone straggler on four. After the conference room, it was clear sailing, no skels, and since this was not a residential building, no pets, the odd bichon frise or hypoallergenic kitty decomping on the scuffed aquamarine corridor tile. The fourth floor had been hacked into a warren of one- and two-room offices, most without windows. Last-chance operations outracing collection agencies and bankruptcy judges, slumping into sadder and shoddier offices in their withering prospects. Half extinct before the coming of the plague, it was that last bad winter that wiped them off the Earth.

The straggler stood in the back room of an empty office. No telling what the former enterprise had been. Half-crushed cardboard boxes rested on the beige carpet next to crumpled sheets covered with the black lines and rows of the best-selling spreadsheet program. A beat-up telephone trailed its umbilicus, caught mid-crawl from the premises. The copy machine dominated the back room, buttons grubbed by fingerprints, paper tray sticking out like a fat green tongue. The straggler's right hand held up the cover and he bent slightly. Like all stragglers, he did not flinch at their approach. He peered into the glassed-off guts of the machine, as still as the dust, bent paper clips, overnight-mail packaging, and other assorted leavings in the room.

"Ned the Copy Boy enjoyed his job. Enjoyed it too much," Mark Spitz said.

"Come on, you can do better than that," Kaitlyn said.

He was a young man, dwindled in his clothes like all skels, but his red bow tie cinched his collar around his neck. He appeared to have been bitten in his armpit; a cone of dried blood terminated there, fanning out in the lumpy shape of a rocket ship's exhaust.

Gary thought and contributed, "More toner, stat!"

Kaitlyn rattled off in quick succession: "My God, it's full of stars." And, "If we can identify whose gluteus maximus this is, we'll have our culprit." Finally, "I can see my house from here."

Solve the Straggler broke up the day with its meager amusements and unearthed a vein of humor in Kaitlyn, a glimpse of the kind of wit she had shared with her friends, family, and members of her favored social-media networks. The game served another purpose in that it gave the sweepers mastery over a small corner of the disaster, the cruel enigma that had decimated their lives. How did the copy boy, or copy repairman, or toner fetishist end up here? Had he traveled miles, had he been here since Last Night? Had he worked in this office six incarnations ago, when it was an accountant's or dietitian's office? The most frightening proposition was that he had no connection to this place, that this fourth-floor office was simply where he broke down. If his presence here was random, then why not an entire world governed by randomness, with all that implied? Solve the Straggler, and you took a nibble out of the pure chaos the world had become.

It was certainly less bleak than Name That Bloodstain!, another pastime. What do you see?—that kid's cloud game gone wrong: Mount Rushmore, Texas, a space shuttle, a dream house, my mom's grave. Like all sweepers they joshed about the strange creatures before them, trying to muster the most clever hypothesis about how the Girl Scout ended up in that boxing ring, or why the guy in the bus-driver uniform was bent in the ice-cream store freezer scooping up dried cakes of mud. The answers to Solve the Straggler were logical, fanciful, or absurd ("Bananas!" Kaitlyn shouted once), according to the tenor of the day.

Skel mutilation was another popular amusement, although not on Kaitlyn's watch, not that Mark Spitz was so inclined. He assumed that Gary had indulged in abhorrent Connecticut, where it was a local custom. "Just having fun," the excuse went, on the rare occasions when one was asked for. A neutralized skel was a perfect stage for one's sadism, whether you were a dabbler, merely taking your time in terminating the thing before you, pruning a finger here or an ear there, or a master-level practitioner, restless all night trying to think up novel variations.

The stragglers posed for a picture and never moved again, trapped in a snapshot of their lives. In their paralysis, they invited a more perplexing variety of abuse. One might draw a Hitler mustache on one, or jab a sponsor cigarette between a straggler's lips. Administer a wedgie. They didn't flinch. They took it. And then they were deactivated—beheaded or got their brains blown out. Although the subject was not mentioned in the PASD seminars Herkimer held with the camp shrinks, it was generally assumed that this behavior was a healthy outlet. Occupational therapy.

Mark Spitz had noticed on numerous occasions that while the regular skels got referred to as *it*, the stragglers were awarded male and female pronouns, and he wondered what that meant. "What's his name?" he said.

"What do you mean, what's his name?" Gary said.

"It has to be something."

"Buffalo don't want the names."

"Still."

"His name is Ned the Copy Boy."

"What if we let him stay?" Mark Spitz didn't know why he said it. "He's not hurting anyone. Look at this room. We're standing in the most depressing room in the entire city."

His comrades looked at each other but did not comment. "Let's wrap this puppy up," Kaitlyn said, and popped him in the head.

If they had played Name That Bloodstain!, Mark Spitz would have said, North America. They would need a lot of new windows in the days to come, he thought. And plenty of bleach. These would be thriving industries, full of opportunities. Perhaps Gary should hang up his Lasso and get into the blood-scrubbing industry. Get in on the ground floor. Erase the stains.

The copy boy was the final straggler in the building. Kaitlyn recorded his details in the notebook. They dragged the body out into the twilight and punched out for the day as Disposal's bell jingled in the distance. Mark Spitz listened to it fade. It was the sound of the god of death from one of the forgotten religions, the one that got it right, upstaging the pretenders with their billions of duped faithful. Every god ever manufactured by the light of cave fires to explain the thunder or calling forth the fashionable supplications in far-flung temples was the wrong one. He had come around after all this time, preening as he toured the necropolis, his kingdom risen at last.

. . .

His unit had slept the last four nights in a former textile warehouse that had been converted into spectacular lofts, alcoves of glamour notched into the cliff face of the city. The apartment they chose belonged to the drummer of a minor rock outfit whose one big charter was a muscular anthem that tried to identify, verse by verse, the meaning of stamina. It was a stadium staple, a real rouser, the royalties evidently providing ample down-payment money. In the blown-up magazine covers on the walls, the owner was perpetually on the verge of being elbowed from the frame by the rest of the band, who were of a more rarefied attractiveness. Such was the drummer's lot. An orgy tub squatted in the center in the master bath, roomy and guardrailed.

Omega slept in the living room, taking turns on the white sectional. It was pleasant in the loft; one night they even made a fire. Kaitlyn discovered a tube of her favorite moisturizer in the medicine cabinet and Gary caught her taking a dab. He tsk-tsked and pulled out his No-No Cards, brandishing the one depicting a red slash across an open fridge door. The massive, oversize windows didn't have shades or blinds, but there were no neighbors gathering gossip in the beyond, no ambient street light to keep them awake, no light at all.

They spent their last night on this grid, however, on the eighteenth floor of number 135, at Mark Spitz's request. In general, they bivouacked on the lower floors, for obvious reasons. In normal circumstances, Kaitlyn and Gary would have vetoed this choice of camp, but they relented without protest. Mark Spitz had been unusually quiet ever since the attack, save for his strange intercession on behalf of the copy boy. If he sought something in this place, something he needed, they were willing to climb all those flights and help him out. This time. He'd used up his chits for a while.

They unrolled their sleeping bags in the conference room of a consulting firm, shoving the gargantuan desk up against the wall and laying their packs across it. They consumed their MREs and eased into their nocturnal rituals after activating a motion detector in the hallway: Gary smoked and skipped through sections of his foreign-language audiobook, Kaitlyn speed-read one of her biographies of dead celebrities, and Mark Spitz paced. After so long in the wild, it still took Mark Spitz a long time to power down his myriad subsystems. There are pills, Gary told him, but he didn't want to be dulled. He was wired at night, bucking on a vector of PASD, but it had kept him alive.

The sleeping bag was comfortable enough on the teal carpet squares, but he missed sleeping in the trees, entwined in the branches like a kite. In the woods bordering the dead subdivision, in a public park going native according to primeval inclination, levitating over koi in the acupuncturist's backyard garden. In those early days, he roved from empty house to empty house like the other isolates, making it up as he went along. He cased the abode in advance of night, selected his entry point, and then swept the ranch house or split-level or other locally popular construction room by room. He checked the basements, the closets, the dryer (you never know), made test noises to draw out any skels inside, but not loud enough to alert a pack cruising outside. He discovered plague-stricken unfortunates who had been locked away in attics like the photo albums of bad weddings, and came upon leaking wretches handcuffed to bedposts by fluffy erotic handcuffs. He put down any skel or skels who emerged from the den or romper room and he made a hasty retreat if it got too hot, taking the pile-covered stairs two at a time or vaulting out the window, the inevitable window, landing messily on the patio set. He knew when it was time to split. It clicked in his brain, the same way he'd known which desk to choose in a new classroom on the first day of a fresh school year, the one that would place him in a zone that reduced the chances of being called on, amid a high concentration of smart kids and inveterate hand-raisers but at a distinct and quirky angle to the teacher's vision that enabled Mark Spitz to pop in and out of his or her attention. The same way he knew exactly how late he could roll into work without it becoming "an issue," how often he could pull off this feat, and how busy he had to appear at different times of the day according to his boss's scofflaw-seeking trawls through the cubicles. He'd always known when to say "I love you" to keep the girlfriends cool and purring, how much to push a deadline without repercussion, how to smile at the representatives of the service industry so that he got a decent table or extra whip. In his mind, the business of existence was about minimizing consequences. The plague had raised the stakes, but he had been in training for this his whole life.

Gary said, "Day ha-may in poz. Day ha-may in poz."

He went into a tree cycle for months at a time, weather permitting (that quaint picnic language), because he hated bunking in an empty house knowing that its occupants were most likely some variety of dead. Perhaps this was the start of his aversion to ID detail, all those times he pushed a bureau up against the door of a bedroom and watched the crap on top tumble to the floor, boxes of gaudy jewelry, cologne in turquoise glass, the family pictures in the fragile plastic frames. It was worse when he came across a straggler, although he didn't know the word then. A woman in a bathrobe measured out coffee into the Swedish machine, frozen there. A teenager wielded a lacrosse stick in his funky bedroom, and in the next town over the pigtailed little princess arranged chewed-up unicorns on the cardboard top of an old board game that had never made it into her family's regular rotation, a fad game with too many or too few instructions. He bashed their heads in with a baseball bat of course; he'd quickly cottoned on to their harmlessness, but didn't know back then if they'd suddenly awaken at some inner cuckoo chime and start the chase. The plague didn't let you in on its rules; they weren't printed on the inside of the box. You had to learn them one by one. The majority of skels were rabid, and then there was this subset. It was early enough in the unpleasantness that they hadn't begun to waste away yet, earn the name skeleton. Which made it worse. In the half-light, before he could see their wounds, he was a harmless cat burglar who accidentally broke into the wrong house, the one next door to his target. The occupants were home. He wanted to apologize, and did on a few occasions. They didn't respond. They looked like regular people, until he saw the missing parts or the make-shift, suppurating bandages. Cemetery statuary, weeping angels and sooted cherubs, standing over their own graves. Stick to the trees, he told himself.

Gary said, "Kwan-to kwesta? Kwan-to kwesta? Kwan-to, kwan-to."

He learned to keep still, ease into a sleep shallow enough to still perceive and react to peril, practicing a quick jungle swing/running/landing combo in case one or more of them looked up and saw him, which they never did. They never came when you were vigilant; they came for you when you had one foot in the past, recollecting a dead notion of safety. Way he saw it, if you were going to get surrounded, you were going to get surrounded—if your luck went that way, it didn't matter if you were up an oak or in a colonial revival.

The first time he'd shared his tree affinity with another survivor, she said, "So what? Everybody sleeps in the trees from time to time." They'd all done the same things during the miseries. Manhattan was a template for other feral cities and Mark Spitz was a sort of template, too, he'd figured out. The stories were the same, whether Last Night enveloped them on Long Island or in Lancaster or Louisville. The close calls, the blind foraging, the accretion of loss. Half starved on the roof of the local real estate office, crouching so they wouldn't be seen from the street and have the ravenous dead clot around the only exit. Contorted in a stainless-steel restaurant cabinet and waiting for morning to break, when it was time to split for the next evanescent refuge. Listening, ever listening for footsteps. The insomniac's brutal scenario had become the encompassing reality across the planet. There were hours when every last person on Earth thought they were the last person on Earth, and it was precisely this thought of final, irrevocable isolation that united them all. Even if they didn't know it.

Kaitlyn said, "Can you not do that in here? Hello—secondhand smoke kills."

Mark Spitz wondered how Gary would handle changing these common Spanish phrases for use with his dependable "we." "Gary, you gonna catch a ride on that sub to get to your island?"

Gary removed his headset. "If we have to. We can get assigned no problem, all the stuff we've done out here for them."

"You probably have to be in the navy," Kaitlyn said.

"Half the navy's been eaten. We're not worried. We'll swab the decks, whatever." He replaced his headphones and loudly added, "Soon as we get to the island, we're done climbing stairs."

Gary wouldn't spill which island he had in mind: "You'll tell everybody and then it will be ruined." Mark Spitz caught him reaching for Spain guidebooks on two occasions, Gary about to furtively pluck them off bookcases in silent apartments before aborting the mission, so he had discounted the landmasses and archipelagoes of the lower hemisphere. The Mediterranean, then. It was hard to argue with the logic of the Island die-hards and their sun-drenched dreams of carefree living once every meter inside the beach line had been swept. The ocean was a beautiful wall, that most majestic barricade. Living would be easy. They'd make furniture out of coconuts, forget technology, have litters of untamed children who said adorable things like, "Daddy, what's 'on demand'?"

In practice, something always went wrong. The Carolinas, for example. Someone snuck back to the mainland for penicillin or scotch, or a boatful of aspirants rowed ashore bearing a stricken member of their party they refused to leave behind, sad orange life vests encircling their heaving chests. The new micro-societies inevitably imploded, on the island getaways, in reclaimed prisons, at the mountaintop ski lodge accessible only by sabotaged funicular, in the underground survivalist hideouts finally summoned to utility. The rules broke down. The leaders exposed mental deficits through a series of misguided edicts and whims. "To be totally fair to both parties, we should cut this baby in half," the chief declared, clad in insipid handmade regalia, and then it actually happened, the henchman cut the baby in half. Sex, the new codes of fucking left them confused. Miscreants pilfered a bean or two above their allotted five beans when no one was looking and the sentence at the trial left everyone more than a tad disillusioned. Bad luck came to call in the guise of a river of the dead or human raiders rumbling up the lone access road despite the strategically arranged camouflage brush. He'd seen this firsthand during the long months. People are people.

Now the big groups were in again: the elite antsy to drop their pawns, and the pawns hungry for purpose after so long without instructions. One day Mark Spitz looked around and found he no longer knew each person in camp, how they had arrived, who they'd lost—suddenly this settlement had become a community. Buffalo implemented food-distribution networks, specialized scavenger teams, work details keyed to antediluvian skill sets, and the survivors had something to hold in their hands besides the makeshift weapons they had nicknamed and pathetically conversed with in the small hours. The leaders toiled over the details of the paradigm-shifting enterprises like Zone One. So tentative bureaucracy rose from the amino-acid pools of madness, per its custom.

Mark Spitz had to admit that he preferred things now that Buffalo was in charge, replicating the old governmental structures. He liked the regular meals, for one thing: beef jerky and room-temperature high-fructose colas had devastated his insides.

Others resisted the transition back. Sometimes the soldiers had to convince a well-armed doomsday cult that it was safe to come out from behind the fortified hatch, or rough up some hippies to get them to come off the farm, hydroponic breakthrough or no hydroponic breakthrough, but it seemed to work, the return of the old laws. In reconstruction, you knew where you stood.

His arrival at Fort Wonton was a deep immersion into the reanimated system. After finishing his tour of Central Park, the pilot beat it south over the crest of midtown edifices. From above, Mark Spitz registered the flaws in the skyline, the gaps, the misbegotten architecture of some of the specimens, the cheerless monotony of the glass surfaces. They did not seem so magnificent from above; they were pathetic, not a brigade charging the sky in unchecked ambition but a runty gang stunted and stymied. A botched ascension. The other passenger was similarly unmoved, for different reasons. He didn't speak the entire trip or acknowledge Mark Spitz's presence. He wore a smart black suit, spy sunglasses, and rested the black cylinder that was chained to his wrist in his lap, petting it slowly from time to time. He barely looked out the window save for the periodic robotic glance, followed by a nod, as if comparing his mental track of their journey with the landmark evidence below.

When the chopper touched down on the bank the man with the cylinder was met by two men in similar dress, similarly mute. Mark Spitz was invisible to them and vice versa: he never again saw the agents of this hush-hush division during his tour of duty in Zone One. He presumed they operated out of an anonymous building they had requisitioned, or in a government complex that had bided the disaster, alive with the hum of its sublevel generators.

As for Mark Spitz, the pilot gave him a thumbs-up, took off, and stranded him in the middle of the bright reflective paint of the landing X. He felt as if his ride had forgotten to pick him up at the airport or train station, and he decided that he was more far gone than he thought for this comparison to occur to him. A walk to the edge of the roof and the sight of the beautiful wall cured him of disappointment. He'd been granted a glimpse on the approach, whirring over the desiccated skels writhing on the sidewalk in their mindless pantomime, then over that other territory beyond the wall, the human side, but it was different up close. The machine gunners strafed and perforated the intermittent skels from their catwalk nests, the beefy crane operators clawed up the sopping corpses and plunked them in cherry-red biohazard bins. The snipers lounged on scattered rooftops, taking potshots up Broadway and goofing off. This was real live human business even though only a thin concrete wall separated them from the plague and its tortured puppets. The world was divided between the wasteland he had roamed for so long and this place, loud and rude, cool and industrious, the front line of the new order. He put aside his petulance over his meager welcome. This was chicken soup.

The stairwell door opened on the controlled mania of a military operation in full swing. He'd served on the new bases before and taken orders in the mobile trailers of the ad hoc HQs, but on the island it was different. It felt like a city, as if order did not terminate at the electric fence but strode forth, extending up every avenue and inside each building. The city was back in teeming business behind every bleak window and street entrance. He'd soon take it for granted, when he returned to Wonton for check-in and turned a corner to suddenly find himself on living streets. In the hallway, he squeezed past soldiers, clerks, and officers. He had yet to parse the hierarchy. Comms squealed and buzzed behind closed doors. Pictographs and signs on the walls hectored about sanitation procedures and vandalism edicts in Buffalo's pet font. He stood in the middle of the stream, pack dangling in his hand, as he listened to conversation phase in and out. Noise, fabulous noise.

Three privates sniggered as Mark Spitz blinked in the current, a hick stupefied by the bright lights of the big city. He was dressed in an old SWAT uniform taken from a locker in a Bridgeport police station, back in accursed Connecticut. When off duty, the civilians working the Northeast Corridor wore old cop gear to distinguish them from the regular army, as if their general conduct and deportment did not suffice. He'd sewn up parts of it over the months, poorly. "Hey, you missed a spot," one of the soldiers jeered, lobbing the standard sweeper joke. As in, broom. He'd heard it before.

Fort Wonton's nerve center was an old bank. The owners had changed over the years in the inevitable consolidations, liquidations, and takeovers, but the building still stood, a tiny granite hut among the furious high-story construction in downtown over the last hundred years. The offices overlooked the main intersection of the wall, Broadway and Canal.

A soldier carrying a stack of folders whistled. "You Spitz?"

Fabio led Mark Spitz to the office. When he saw his new charge flinch at a sudden round of machine-gun fire, Fabio told him, "They usually come in three waves these days. Kinda regular, so we call it Breakfast, Lunch, and Dinner." The artillery increased for a short burst. "That there," he said, "is Lunch."

The Lieutenant's office had eastern and northern exposure, and perhaps at one time enjoyed a healthy wash of morning light, but the skyscrapers and the sun's reluctance to bless the zone surely extinguished that phenomenon. Maps of different segments of the Zone hung on the walls, covered in incomprehensible marks, tinted different hues, and the old, varnished desks made Mark Spitz think he'd wandered into a World War II campaign, on another island in the Pacific. The ceilings were twelve feet tall, and the large half-moon windows overlooked the wall. A ponytailed soldier prowled lazily across the scaffolding, looking at something or someone at the foot of the barricade, on the other side. She took a quick shot, shook her body like a wet dog, and stretched.

People carried themselves differently in the thrall of PASD. Per Herkimer, each was marked. Everyone he saw walked around with a psychological limp, with a collapsed shoulder here or a disobedient, half-shut eyelid there, and that current favorite, the all-over crumpling, as if the soul were imploding or the mind sucking the extremities into itself. Mark Spitz sported this last manifestation from time to time, in maudlin moods, only unwrenching when adrenaline straightened him out. Anyone with perfect posture was faking it, overcompensating for entrenched trauma. In the Lieutenant's case, the man's movements were marked by a distinct reluctance, the slightest gesture requiring a hesitation before it could be completed—it needed to be vetted, triple-checked before morose execution. The input could not be trusted, as if the logic of the lost world were struggling to reassert itself: Surely this is not happening.

He spotted Mark Spitz and his hand ratcheted up to a slow come-hither wave. "Sit, sit, sit," he said. His thumb was pressed to his temple and his index finger was embedded in the middle of his brow as he squinted at his desk.

"Have your file right here," the Lieutenant said. "On sponsored paper—they browbeat some recycling magnate into giving the okay. Writing on paper like in the Stone Age. Used to be everything was in the cloud, little puffy data floating here and there. Now we're back to paper. You hear people talking, they miss cable TV, basketball, they miss local organic greens cold-washed three times. I miss the cloud. It was all of me up there. The necessary docs and e-mails and key photographs. The proof." He coughed into his fist. "Now it's evaporated. Least we still have the old-fashioned clouds. What about you?"

"Me what, sir?"

"What do you miss?"

Mark Spitz sat up straight. "Traffic."

"And where do you fall on the question of cumulus versus cirrus?"

"The puffy ones."

"Cumulus! Has its plus sides, the Rorschach thing, but I'm a cirrus man born and bred. Can't beat a coherent layer of cirrus, self-organized, covering the sky. Sunset, bottle of Shiraz, and the usual double entendres? The way we used to do it. Nonetheless, I see where you're coming from, young man."

The Lieutenant glanced between the file and Mark Spitz to confirm the man before him. As the Lieutenant talked, his manic delivery gave counterpoint to the physical hesitancy. "Says here you did a good job mopping up I-95, adjusted to the transition from camp life to active duty. Except for an incident on a bridge? Some people, you know. But you made it out, that's the important thing, right? 'The mighty Phoenix shall spread its wings.' What do I call you?"

"Mark Spitz is fine," he said. It was the truth. "It's caught on."

"Wanted to make sure. People like to be called what they like to be called. Served under Corporal Kinder?"

"Yes, sir."

"Fucking idiot. Part of the brain trust working on phase one around here, forgot to cap the island."

Mark Spitz had heard tell of the so-called technical difficulties, but he wanted the Lieutenant's description of it. He was starting to like this character. He'd been forced to endure such a low variety of PASD in Happy Acres—a host of inappropriate staring, unabated drooling, and compulsive finger-sniffing—that the man's almost sophisticated strain was refreshing. Urbane and citified compared to that bumpkin sniveling.

"We have to quarantine the island," the Lieutenant said, "so we can clean it out. The subways, the bridges, tunnels. Secret exits most people don't know about. Civilians anyway, but we do, we have the maps. All kinds of holes in the island of Manhattan. It's startling. They do the big sweep of Zone One, guns blazing, turkey shoot, put the wall up, but then they notice something. Every day there are more and more skels up at the wall. The marines cut them down—you saw the .50-.50s on your way in. But still. Proper ordnance is not the point. Everybody's, What the fuck.

"They finally have this big confab, right down the hall in fact, General Carter's down from Buffalo and he wants to know what the problem is, where they're all coming from. Because there's too many to only come from uptown. Then one of the bright boys asks, 'Is it possible they're using the George Washington Bridge, maybe?' Like they're commuting from Jersey. Then it hits them. They didn't shut it down above Canal. All that shit is still wide open. Lincoln Tunnel, GWB, Triborough, all of it. Plum forgot. All these skels visiting the Big City like they did before all the shit went down. Piling into tour buses for a Broadway matinee."

"Wow."

"But by this time the Army Corps is redeployed on that crazy shit they're cooking up in Baltimore, and we're not going to get the manpower to block uptown for months. The marines tasked elsewhere, too. Crazy. Buffalo's attitude is, Let the sweepers do their thing and then we'll fix that little glitch when we start on Zone Two. In the old days, we'd have a court-martial, but good old Tattinger, the guy in charge of this clusterfuck, got his face eaten off a week later, so there's that I guess." He shook his head. Laboriously, as if commanding the muscles one by one. "You don't have to call me 'sir,' by the way. You're a civilian. We work for you, although some of them have forgotten that around here."

The sudden menace of gunfire interrupted. He talked over it. "You have a lot of experience with stragglers?" he asked. "That wasn't your bailiwick out on the Corridor."

"Same as anyone else. You can't help it, being out there. Pop 'em and drop 'em." That easy vernacular.

"Where was your first?"

The question surprised him. No one asked questions like that. Mark Spitz had been navigating repulsive Connecticut. Behind a half-built housing development there was a field that had been chewed up by dozers to make room for another line of houses. At the far side of the field a highway ran north–south, and that was his day's mission, make it a few paces up his map. He saw the man standing in the middle of the dirt. At first he thought it was a scarecrow, it was so still, even though it eschewed stereotypical scarecrow stance and this was no farm. The figure's right arm stretched to grasp the sky. Mark Spitz waited for him to move. He scanned the territory, then tried to get the man's attention in that moronic stage whisper he used so much in those early days. If it was a skel, he'd kill it; he didn't see any others around. That was the rule: Don't leave them around to infect other people if you can get away with it.

He crept toward him. Mark Spitz was in a baseball-bat phase and he got his slugger grip ready. The figure was an older man, dwindling inside his red polo shirt and khaki pants. A string trailed from his hand, leading to a roughed-up box kite that had been dragged a great, difficult distance from the look of it. Was the man in shock? Mark Spitz didn't know if the guy had shrunk from malnutrition or the plague. He didn't want to know, actually. He gave the thing's shoulder a pro forma shake. He'd abandoned his share of crippled survivors. Couldn't save everyone.

The man's mind had been eliminated. He didn't stir when Mark Spitz snapped his fingers in his ears, blink at the stimuli. The man's gaze, if such a barren thing could be called that, was leveled at a void above the horizon. Any activity or process in him was directed at pouring some undetectable message into that spot in the sky. Mark Spitz shook his shoulder, prepared to jump away if necessary. What did he see there?

He abandoned the man in the field. Then it was like in the

old days when he came across some energetic new fad, a nouveau jacket or complicated haircut: He started seeing them everywhere, sitting patiently at a bus stop or holding a leaf up to the sun or standing in the field they'd played in as a child, before they grew up, before the dozers. When he mentioned these creatures to a band he hooked up with for a brief time, they gave him the term: stragglers. "They're all messed up."

Mark Spitz related a version of this to the Lieutenant, who stroked his chin skeptically. "Buffalo's still trying to explain what makes one person become your regular pain-in-the-ass skel," the Lieutenant said, "and what makes another into a straggler. That one percent. Buffalo's not really known for explaining shit. How they can walk around for so long just feeding off their own bodies. Why they don't bleed out. Buffalo will tell you that the plague converts the human body into the perfect vehicle for spreading copies of itself. Thanks for the news flash. But what's up with this aberrant one percent?"

Mark Spitz said, "I don't know." He could have added his own questions. How come, rain or shine, the stragglers stand at their posts? Hottest day of the year, monsoon, they're standing there foul and oblivious. Caught in a web.

"They're mistakes," the Lieutenant said. "They don't do what they're supposed to. You know that super-secret bunker in England? Those guys are the real deal, three more Nobel Prize winners on tap than Buffalo. They've been studying this thing, squinting at the microbe, cutting it up, and all the British guys can come up with is that the stragglers are mistakes. Nobody knows anything."

Mark Spitz turned to the movement at the border of his vision. Outside the window, ash had begun to fall in drowsy flakes.

The Lieutenant said, "You figure it out, you get back to me. Personally, I like them. Not supposed to say it out loud, but I think they've got it right and we're the ninety-nine percent that have it all wrong." He waited for Mark Spitz to turn away from the window. He tapped his desk, lightened the register of his voice, and the new sweeper rejoined him. "Who knows? Maybe it'll work. The symbolism. If you can bring back New York City, you can bring back the world. Clear out Zone One, then the next, up to Fourteenth Street, Thirty-fourth, Times Square on up. Those sweet crosstown bus routes. I used to take the bus all the time when I lived here, to see the Famous New York Characters in all their glory. Spitting, scratching, talking in voices. Them, not me." He batted at a fat fly. "We'll take it back, barricade by barricade. Tell me, Mark Spitz, are you known for your optimistic disposition?"

"Sure."

"I can tell." The Lieutenant smiled. "That wall out there has to work. The barricade is the only metaphor left in this mess. The last one standing. Keep chaos out, order in. Chaos knocks on the door and bangs on the wood and gets a claw in. Will the boards hold until morning? You know what I'm talking about if you made it this far. There are small barricades—across the apartment door, then a whole house nailed up—and then we have the bigger barricades. The camp. The settlement. The city. We work our way to bigger walls." Across the room, Fabio tried to catch his attention, but the Lieutenant dismissed the man with a flick. From his assistant's expression, he was accustomed to his boss's rhetorical flights. "One naturally thinks of the siege, but we overlook that because the word takes away our agency. Sure, I can play that game. We are safe inside from what is outside. We had our modern conveniences, the machines at the end of the power strip that kept away the primitive. I had my beloved cloud, you had yours.

"I notice you are not staring vacantly at your palms. Good. Sometimes they ship these mopes in here, they've had their souls scooped out. They wash out pretty quick. The hard way. Now I screen everybody who comes in. See what kind of business they got behind the eyes. You passed the quiz. You're still alive. Congratulations. Even got all your fingers. Which is a big plus in this line of work."

The Lieutenant held up a hand to his assistant, acquiescing. "We're almost done and then you can go. I know the first thing people want to do when they get to Zone One is walk around. See the sights." Outside, the lunchtime fusillade erupted anew. He rolled his eyes. "You get used to it. Spend some time here and you get used to it. What made you volunteer? You don't like farming? I come from a family of farmers."

Mark Spitz didn't know in that moment. It would take some time in the Zone for him to discover the reason. He said, "Just trying to do my part."

"Good answer! That can-do pheenie attitude. Personally, I say wake me when you bring back cilantro. Got any family?"

He thought of Uncle Lloyd, but what was there to say. "I don't know."

"Mostly joking with that one. I've been thinking about how in the old days, we had these special-ops dudes who did all the batshit stuff. Parachute into hostile territory, baroque wetwork, tiptoeing into the tent to garrote the warlord—pretend I didn't say that—and these batshit killing machines were always single guys, single men and women, no families. What do they have to lose, right? But who has a family anymore? Everybody's dead. All those vacation pictures floating in the cloud. Zip. Been thinking about that. Now we're all batshit killing machines, could be a motherfucking granny wielding knitting needles. I digress."

The Lieutenant hesitated, then nodded wearily. "What we have here in Zone One is not a suicide mission. Just a bunch of stragglers. Welcome to the team."

The Lieutenant stared at him and Mark Spitz wondered if he was dismissed. Then the man clicked on once more. "You bunk where you want in the grid. Take your pick. Try not to break anything. They're really big on that now. Sundays you come back here for check-in. Besides that, pop 'em, bag 'em, drag 'em. Any questions?"

"Seems pretty straightforward," Mark Spitz said. "This has been very informative." Fabio handed him some paperwork. He was pulling the door shut behind him when he heard, "Think it might rain today. That's what the old clouds say."

It did rain. It had been raining pretty much constantly since that day. At the window of the conference room, Mark Spitz looked out into a solemn nigrescence that was interrupted only by a white dome of light leeching out of Fort Wonton. The light climbed up a few stories on the Canal buildings like mold. He visualized the hard-core military lamps bleaching the concrete wall to sun-beaten bone white while the night-shift gunners sat in their nests or patrolled the catwalk, listening to the dead songs on their digital music devices. The cranes motionless, maybe being hosed off with sterilizing compound by Disposal. Tomorrow at Breakfast the machines would whine over the wall and clutch the corpses in their firm metal grip and drop them on our side.

Kaitlyn and Gary slept. He resisted the urge to tug Kaitlyn's paperback out of her hand—with her reflexes, she'd probably stab him in the eye. Still awake in a shallow layer of her mind. Mark Spitz had pretended to be asleep when his father used to check on him when he was a kid, but he was always awake before the door even opened. His brain processed the distinctive think-I'll-peek-in-on-my-offspring gait out in the hall and a clerk in his awareness woke him in time for the turn of the doorknob, the creak at ten degrees, the second creak at fifty-five degrees, and the sliver of hall light prying under his eyelids. He fell asleep knowing someone watched over him.

Gary and Kaitlyn would sleep until their personal danger detectors went off or morning arrived. They were exemplary sleepers, not that kind of pheenie who was up all night rewinding their private pageant of horrors. So much more efficient to be obsessed with such things when awake, to save it for when it might be converted into fuel.

Who was his family now? A specter of an uncle floating half a mile uptown in a blue building. He had these two mutts. Mark Spitz lost his parents on Last Night, and Gary's brothers perished in that initial wave as well, when the triplets joined the posse handling the Incident at the Local High School. This when the villagers still believed they could set up a quarantine, and it would work. That tooth-fairy period.

The PTA meeting went worse than usual, even by the deplorable standards of Milton High School. The engaged, the outraged, and the merely trying to fill the blank space that was their lives had convened to argue over that spring's big scandal, when one of the lesbian seniors announced her intention to bring her girlfriend to the prom. It had hit the national media as a fully operational event, with a berth on cable network chyron, pro-and-con expert panels, and mortifying nightly-news graphics. Lawsuits had been filed, the late-night wits bon-motted, and the Milton community wanted to see how to prevent such a thing in the future.

At any rate, the assistant principal had been infected the previous afternoon while breaking up a fight between two elderly ladies in the parking lot of a discount-sneaker chain and had been lurking around the bio labs all day. Attracted by the noise, he interrupted the proceedings with brio. When the police arrived they locked the doors of the premises per the measures suggested by the web videos that had been uploaded by the government about the emerging epidemic, segregating the bitten from the unbitten, employing the gymnasium and assembly, respectively, and waiting for further instructions from the authorities. Who by this time were not even listening to the voice-mail messages from the less consequential municipalities, let alone dispatching a scramble team. It wouldn't have mattered anyway. It was too late. It had always been too late.

Gary and his brothers were giddy over their deputization, only slightly deflated when told there weren't enough badges to go around. They'd butted heads with Sheriff Dooley and his officers plenty of times, sure, but in these new circumstances it was easy to see that they were good men to have by your side, shitkickers. They didn't take any mess, a trait that had hampered their upward mobility in former days but now provided opportunity. The brothers were even issued guns; Gary held on to his for almost a year in the following madness, before he accidentally dropped it while hightailing it out of a disused coal mine in South Carolina, no time to stop.

The guards hadn't heard anything from inside the school for twelve hours when the sheriff decided to go in. They peered past the wire-reinforced glass set in the thick institutional doors and into the halls they'd bullied through and grab-assed in during their teenage glory days. Saw nothing but shadows. Was this even the same place they remembered? In mistaking this place for something they knew, they undid themselves. For they were now in an entirely different country. It should be noted that as a general rule, the early rookie posses were not as successful as the later posses. Steep learning curve.

As for Kaitlyn, she never saw her parents again after she departed on her trip to see her best gal pal Amy in Lancaster, Pennsylvania. Another member of their college-rooming group drove over from Philly and it turned out they hadn't changed all that much since graduation. The same dull boys skulked around, indulged or ignored, and the trio didn't have to force the in-jokes at all. They'd lost sleep fearing it would be otherwise. At the end of the weekend, however, the Sunset Dayliner did not return her to home and hearth. The train didn't budge at all after the conductor got a report about the incident in the dining car and pulled the brakes outside Crawfordsville to wait for the National Guard. She was stuck. Untold misfortunes later, she was in New York City.

Mark Spitz turned off the lamp. Outside, one of the potbelly transport planes cut the sky, red lights trailing. Grunts and experts rocked on the bucket seats, en route to where? Buffalo, or a makeshift landing field outside one of the camps? Bearing their disparate ammunition.

In the days following his arrival in the Zone, he'd mulled over the Lieutenant's theory of the barricades. Yes, they were the only vessel strong enough to contain our faith. But then there are the personal barricades, Mark Spitz thought. Since the first person met the second person. The ones that keep other people out and our madness in so we can continue to live. That's the way we've always done it. It's what this country was built on. The plague merely made it more literal, spelled it out in case you didn't get it before. How were we to get through the day without our barricades? But look at him now, he thought. They were his family, Kaitlyn and Gary, and he was theirs. He owned nothing else besides them, and the features of his dead that he superimposed on the faces of the skels, those shoddy rubber masks he pulled out of his pockets. He knew it was pathetic to carry them with him, a lethal sentimentality, but it warded off the forbidden thought. The faces of his dead were part of his barricade, stuck on pikes atop the length of the concrete.

He volunteered for Zone One while the rest of the wreckers on the Corridor remained because he was from around these parts. The lights of the broken city were few these days. A dim constellation hovered around the wall, smaller halos in the windows of the buildings that personnel staked out in far-flung Wonton, and in silent buildings across the downtown where drones like Mark Spitz cupped their palms around their little flames. North of the wall was darkness and the dead that scraped through that darkness.

The city could be restored. When they were finished it could be something of what it had been. They would force a resemblance upon it, these new citizens come to fire up the metropolis.

Their new lights pricking the blackness here and there in increments until it was the old skyline again, ingenious and defiant. The new lights seeping through the black veil like beads of blood pushing through gauze until it was suffused.

Yes, he'd always wanted to live in New York.

SATURDAY

"The age demanded an image
of its accelerated grimace."

Initially the dreams, when safe nights permitted them, favored a classic anxiety paradigm. He was enmeshed in the institutional structures of his previous existence—in school, one of his blank jobs—and the other students and the teachers, fellow employees, and bosses were dead. Dead in a precipitous state of decay, winnowed by the plague: bones visibly gliding under taut skin at every movement, blackened gums bared when they told a joke or introduced a complicating element to the setup (the exam is today, the supervisor is on the warpath), their wounds mushy and livid. They leaked, leaked constantly from sores, eyes, ears, bites. In the dreams he was not bothered by their appearance, nor were they. They informed him that they'd all studied for the test save for him, the big assignment was due after lunch and not next week, the performance review was already under way, abetted by secret cameras. Not that he'd ever had a performance review in his life—it was a neurotic curveball his subconscious came up with to freak him out, employing the exotic cant of bona fide grown-ups. They were not the rabid dead or stragglers. They acted pretty much the same as they had before, his best friend, his insidious science teacher, his distracted boss. Except for the plague thing, these were the dreams he'd been having for years.

The dreams changed once he made it to his first big settlement. He was no longer late for the final exam of a class he didn't know he'd enrolled in, or about to deliver the big presentation to higher-ups when he suddenly realized he left the only copy in the backseat of the taxi. His dreams unfurled in the theater of the mundane. There was no pulse-quickening escalation of events, no stakes to mention. He took the train to work. He waited for his pepperoni slice's extraction from the pizza joint's hectic oven. He jawed with his girlfriend. And all the supporting characters were dead. The dead said, "Let's stay in and get a movie," "You want fries with that?," "Do you know what time it is?," while flies skittered on their faces searching for a soft flap to bury eggs in, shreds of human meat wedged in their front teeth like fabled spinach, and their arms terminated at the elbow to showcase a white peach of bone fringed with dangling muscle and dripping tendons. He said, "Sure, let's stay in and snuggle, it's been a long day," "I'll take the side salad instead, thank you," "It's ten of five. Gets dark early this time of year."

He downward-dogged in a drop-in yoga class as the skel next to him broke in half while essaying the pose. No one remarked upon this sight, not him, not the dead teacher, not the enthusiastic and limber dead around him, and not the bisected skel on the floral-patterned hemp mat, who flopped grotesquely through the rest of the hour like a real trooper. He got into his street clothes in the locker room as the yuppie skel beside him dragged an expensive watch over his wrist, grating the fresh scabs there. On impulse he purchased a deluxe combo juice at the café on the way out and decided not to say anything when the pimply skel dropped a banana slice into the blender. He hated banana. He drank it anyway, blowing into the striped straw to dislodge a plug of pulp, and stepped out to the sidewalk into the rush-hour stream of the dead on their way home, the paralegals, mohels, resigned temps, bike messengers, and slump-shouldered massage therapists, the panoply of citizens in the throes of their slow decay. The plague was a meticulous craftsman, dabbing effects with deliberation. They were falling apart but it would take a long time until the piece was finished. Only then could it sign its name. Until then, they walked.

He took the subway to the commuter rail, curling his fingers around the pole still warm from the skel who had grasped it moments before. In the advertisements lodged just above eye level, airbrushed heads of the dead hawked trade schools and remedies. Some of the dead entered the train politely and others were quite rude as they shouldered into the car when he tried to gain the platform. Everybody trying to eke it home. On the commuter platform he made sure his monthly pass was secured in the nook in his wallet and he pictured the night ahead. Order in from his go-to takeout spot, pop open one of the beers, and watch the reality show he'd DVR'd three days before. He woke up as the train left the tunnel and they were out of the underground.

The only unsettling thing about the dream was that he'd never taken a yoga class in his life.

This series eluded the category of nightmare. He awoke refreshed, or at least aloft in a routine state of morning dread in equilibrium for months. The new vintage of dreamscape left him feeling curiously indifferent. The dead small-talked, recited speculation over tomorrow's cold front, numbly caromed from task to task as they had before, but they were sick. He recalled a theory of dreams from the old days that declared them wish-fulfillment, and another declaring that you are every person in your dreams, and each theory seemed equally plausible and moot and in the end he didn't spend too much time analyzing. He was a busy man these days.

To the next grid, and Godspeed. His unit squeezed MRE bacon-and-eggs paste onto their tongues—amber with brownish-red swirls—and packed up their gear. Kaitlyn deposited her celeb bio on the windowsill, as if gifting it to the next guest at the sun-splashed resort. They almost made it to the stairwell when she remembered the motion detector. She went back for it. That happened a lot these days. It was nice to know it was there even though it hadn't sirened once since the start of their tour.

Their new assignment was Fulton x Gold, Mixed Residential/ Business, a few blocks east. It started as a no-bother drizzle but Mark Spitz pulled on his poncho on account of the ash, and the others followed suit when the rain intensified.

They progressed without speaking, still waking up on their march. Kaitlyn whistled "Stop! Can You Hear the Eagle Roar? (Theme from *Reconstruction*)," that irrepressible pheenie anthem, as they stomped through the gray puddles. "What if we get there," Gary said finally, "and they've all keeled over? They finally caught what those kill-field skels got and all we have to do is bag them from now on?" He made this offering whenever they switched grids.

"That would be nice," Mark Spitz said. The discovery of the kill fields that spring hastened the start of many a reconstruction operation. Word first arrived with the new survivors stumbling through the camp gates with their extravagant tales of meadows and mall parking lots brimming with the fallen dead. It wasn't as if someone had neutralized them and departed without sterilizing the area—their heads were intact, they said. The dead looked as if they'd dropped in place.

Reentry into the anterooms of civilization was always difficult, and the longer the survivors spent out there, the harder it was to come back. But even after a hot shower, sleeping like stones for twelve hours straight, and tasting the corn (everyone was quite proud of the corn harvest, and rightfully so), the refugees continued with their wild stories. Then recon units came back with confirmation, video, up and down the coast. In wide-open places, the dead were falling en masse. A high-school football field in faraway Raleigh bumpy with bodies, a public park in Trenton where black flies zipped at the banquet. Buffalo sent down word of their think-tank scuttlebutt: The plague had finally, inevitably, exhausted what the human body could endure. There was a limit to the depredations, and that meant a limit to the devastation.

The reports of the scattered kill fields emerged at the same time, suggesting (according to some) a time frame for the course of infection. It was the season of encouraging dispatches. The establishment of steady communications with nations abroad, the intel traveling back and forth over the seas. Throw in the continued consolidation of the uninfected groups and clans, and the simple fact that skel attacks and sightings had diminished by all empirical measure, and one had reason to dust off the old optimism. You had only to look at the faint movement in the ashes: surely this is the American Phoenix Rising. At least that's what the T-shirts said, lifted from the biodegradable cardboard boxes fresh from Buffalo. Toddler sizes available.

Mark Spitz observed the reduced skel numbers firsthand. There were simply fewer of them around, the chancred losers, a blessing during his time on the Corridor in accursed Connecticut and beyond. But kill fields aside—and there were no solid numbers regarding these sundry fallen, given the general appetite for a quick bonfire—no one could account for where the skels had gone. One school maintained that exposure had cut a lot of them down, the winter in its savagery. Speculation was above his pay grade, never mind that he was paid in socks and sunscreen.

Kaitlyn said, "Haven't heard of that happening in urban areas yet." She registered Gary's deflated expression and, checking her usual impulses, added, "But maybe."

Mark Spitz slapped his arm across Kaitlyn's chest to stop her, a gesture he'd lifted from his parents, who had lifted it from their parents, who had remembered a time before seat belts: There was movement across the street.

The wasteland protocols booted up, obsolete or no. His brain compared the warehoused scenarios and previous engagements to the scene on Fulton Street, running demeanor, gear, posture, and facial expressions through the database. Dead or bandit, straggler or survivor, it was often hard to tell. Did they speak, that was the first test. Did they still have language. You took it from there. Before the rise of the camps, out in the land, you had to watch out for other people. The dead were predictable. People were not. Most were like Mark Spitz, isolated and squeaking by in the great out there, power bar by stale power bar. Once you ensured that you were both sentient, you gingerly approached to parley. Where are you coming from, onto what mirage have you fastened your hopes, have you seen any other people according to the old definitions, where shouldn't we travel. The essential information.

If you chose to hook up for a time, eventually you traded Last Night stories. In their bleak adventure, the survivors tried to crawl to the mythical settlements and forts they'd conjured in their minds, where the plague was part of a news segment recounting some other town's tragedy, filler before the weather report, where there was electricity and local produce right out of the bag and kids played and there were little jumping rabbits. Haven, finally. Each retelling of one's Last Night story was a step toward another fantastic refuge, that of truth. Mark Spitz had refined his Last Night story into three versions. The Silhouette was for survivors he wasn't going to travel with for long. He had quickly soured on this stranger standing before him by the cellar door of the farmhouse, or by the metal detector of the department of motor vehicles, out of skel sightline, and he concocted the thin broth of the Silhouette from this despair over the death of connection. At their core, Last Night stories were all the same: They came, we died, I started running. The Silhouette sufficed. No need to hand over his heart, the good stuff. The two parties had departed before they even started talking.

He offered the Anecdote, robust and carrying more on its ribs, to those he might hole up with for a night, in a long-cleaned-out family-owned Greek restaurant, a dilapidated trailer with weeds growing out of the carpet, or atop a toll plaza, baking up there but grateful for the 360-degree view. He also trotted out the Anecdote version for hookups with larger bands, when the Silhouette might appear rude, but the Obituary was too intimate to share with the half-formed huddled faces around the flashlights. The Anecdote included a gloss on Atlantic City, the trip home (spectacularly foreboding in retrospect, the ghosts playing basketball), and concluded with the phrase "I found my parents, and then I started running." It was the smallest portion, he learned, that was acceptable to strangers to allow them to fall asleep without thinking he'd bludgeon them in their sleeping bags. The versions they gave in return were never enough to let him sleep, no matter the surfeit of telling details and sincerity.

The Obituary, although refined over the months and not without a rehearsed air, was nonetheless heartfelt, glancing off his true self more than once, replete with digressions about his lifelong friendship with Kyle, nostalgia for the old A.C. trips, the unsettling and "off" atmosphere of that last casino weekend, and a thorough description of the tableau at his house and its aftermath. Although the adjectives tended to be neutral in later retellings, the Obituary was the sacred in its current guise. The listener usually responded in kind, unless revisiting that longest of nights dispatched them into a fugue, which happened occasionally. They'd spent some time together. This might be the final human being they'd see before they died. Both speaker and listener, sharer and receiver, wanted to be remembered. The Obit got it all down for some calm, distant day when you were long disappeared and a stranger took the time to say your name.

Albatrosses materialized around the bend, of course, and two minutes of their company sufficed. They were too far gone. Sick, not with the plague but with the workhorse afflictions newly complicated in the wasteland, pneumonia and rheumatoid arthritis and the like. The things requiring generic meds that needed decoding in the stripped pharmacies. Or they were quite clearly mad. How'd this brain-wiped half-skel make it this far? God had watched over children and drunks, and now he watched over no one, but these unfortunates made it through somehow. They had no supplies, not a single weapon, owned nothing but their clothes and wounds. Perhaps they might snap out of it, that cough might disappear with a packet of rehydrated chicken soup, but he made a swift retreat, faster than if pursued by a hundred skels. Safer to assume they'd get him killed. A parent-child combo might pop up at the crest of the old country road, wan and wary, and Mark Spitz shrank from these, no matter how well outfitted they were. Parenthood made grown-ups unpredictable. They hesitated at the key moment out of consideration for their kid's abilities or safety, they were paranoid he wanted to rape or eat their offspring, they slowed him down with their baby steps or kept him distracted as he pondered their erraticism. They were worse than the bandits, who only wanted your stuff and sometimes managed to take it, on the spot, or at gunpoint later when the opportunity presented itself, when you were sleeping or taking a piss. The parents were dangerous because they didn't want your precious supplies. They possessed the valuables, and it hobbled their reasoning.

He hooked up with strangers for a while, exchanged a grimy jar of cranberry sauce or a juice box per the new greeting ritual, and swapped information on the big matters of the day, like dead concentrations, and small things like the state of the world. A few months into the collapse, only the fools asked about the government, the army, the designated rescue stations, all the unattainable islands, and the fools were dwindling every day. He hung with them until they decided on divergent destinations, got into an argument over skel behavior theories or how to spot lurking botulism in a dented can. People were invested in the oddest things these days. He hung with them until they were attacked and they died and he didn't. Sometimes he ditched them because they talked too fucking much.

He stopped hooking up with other people once he realized the first thing he did was calculate whether or not he could outrun them.

After Mim, Mark Spitz dispensed with good-luck speeches and see-you-down-the-roads. He crept at first light. He heard his temporary companions wake at the small scrabbling of his leave-taking but they didn't budge from their dingy sleeping bags once they realized he wasn't stealing their stuff, the batteries and pocket drives full of family photos. They didn't care for the good-byes, either.

That afternoon on Fulton, Mark Spitz shut down his welcome routines after they identified the three figures across the street. They were people. They wore ponchos, and what else but a being cursed with the burden of free will would wear a poncho. The dead did not wear ponchos. Gary shouted greetings, followed by endearing epithets. The gang rejoined with enthusiasm, crooning the chorus from a bit of schmaltz about islands in the stream.

It was Bravo Unit: Angela, No Mas, and Carl. Given the enigmatic pattern of the Lieutenant's grid assignments, it was rare that units stumbled on one another in the Zone. The ten sweeper units crisscrossed downtown like locals checking off a to-do list: to the overnight-delivery place to rush the application, jetting to the dry cleaner, to the specialty cheese store for that esoteric hunk after stupidly asking their host if they could bring anything. When they bumped into one another it was a pleasant diversion.

As usual, Gary had history with those they encountered. He served with all three while cleaning out maddening Connecticut before assignment to the Zone. Connecticut with its pustulant hordes sans limit and notorious talent for coining new faces of bad luck, degenerate Connecticut with its starless nights and famished mornings, Bad News Connecticut birthed ragged crews that stuck together. In comparison, Mark Spitz and the few sweepers from elsewhere were green recruits perpetually repeating their first day of duty. He had a particular dislike for No Mas, who bragged around Wonton about his scrapbook of straggler humiliation. "Who'd you see this week?" a sweeper might goad during Sunday-night R & R, whereupon No Mas dutifully chronicled his latest shenanigans. He carried a big red marker in his utility vest and liked to draw clumsy clown grins on the slack faces of the stragglers, christening each with a name appropriate to that profession. Then he pressed the muzzle of his assault rifle to the temple of Mr. Chuckles or Her Most Exalted Highness the Lady Griselda, smiled for the birdie, and had Angela take a picture before he splattered their craniums. Sunday nights at HQ No Mas shared a cot with a young clerk who printed out his souvenirs on glossy paper. "If you find Captain Giggles, give me a call—I hate that guy," one of his audience offered in return, extending an I Heart New York mug full of whiskey. Just having a little fun.

Angela and Carl were more discreet about their transgressions, at least in mixed company, but Mark Spitz had heard them reminisce about their time together in a bandit crew, ripping off weaker survivors for aspirin and thermal underwear and who knows what other bad acts. He effortlessly pictured their carefree promotion up the American Phoenix to stations of venal authority. Investigating individuals who had been narced on for illicit salvage—"I don't know how all those shoes got in my closet, officer, but aren't they divine?"—and then bartering the confiscated goods on the black market. Or working as a New York City landlord, say, assigning apartments to the newcomers according to appetite and mealy whim, accepting the odd bribe or sexual favor for a better building, better block, southern exposure. Two bathrooms, park views, and basement storage would resume their currency in the new order, and insalubrious bureaucracy create its avatars. They came from Connecticut, repugnant Connecticut.

The rain redoubled. The two units huddled under the purple-and-orange awning of a popular doughnut-and-coffee concern and debriefed each other on the week. Bravo related how they lost half a day and filled two packs of body bags clearing out a den of decomposing suicides from the pews of a Ukrainian church. The usual: Gather 'round and grab a cup everybody, it'll be quick. Halfway through, Bravo stopped trying to pry the crucifixes out of their hands and simply zipped them up with the corpses.

It had been a slow couple of grids for Omega, apart from Mark Spitz's takedown, and Kaitlyn, in her circumspection, did not mention that episode. She wound up telling them about the secret Chinese nightclub. Omega decided it had been a gangster hangout, up two flights of rickety stairs above a store that sold shriveled herbs that looked like the fingers of the dead. The back room was filled with electronic gambling machines, pistols with taped-up grips, and jail-bait pinups. A high-tech safe crouched in a wall cavity, full of who knew what, opium and sundry incriminations. It was a mobster den out of some movie, she told them. She forgot they'd actually found the place two weeks ago and had already told the story. No one stopped her. It was raining. They were taking a coffee break.

Mark Spitz rubbed his eyes. He would have told Bravo about the sad straggler in the repair shop, but he had a hard time articulating why it fascinated him. They'd found the tinkerer huddled at his majestically cluttered worktable, poised over the guts of a VCR. Around his hands the metal housings of machines abutted, a thin metal skyline. The old man was surrounded by obsolete technology, the ungainly array of devices that had been a previous generation's top of the line for listening to music or crisping toast. What brand of idiot loved these broken machines enough to search the internet for this joint, take time out of their lives to bring them here for removal of the dust bunnies perched on the motherboards? The kind of idiot that knows that idiots exist who sign a lease for this kind of thing. They nourished each other's delusions. The piles of pieces reminded Mark Spitz of when they'd swept through the prosthetics distributor's and they were surrounded by pink half arms and feet, dangling from the ceiling, climbing out of boxes. These incomplete people. All the dead parts.

No Mas and Gary lit cigarettes, prompting Kaitlyn to glower and commence to cough theatrically. Angela thanked Christ it was Saturday and they'd head back to Wonton for a night of R & R tomorrow. She asked if they'd seen anyone else around.

Kaitlyn shook her head. "Pretty dead."

"Ran into Teddy and them on West Broadway," Carl said. He grinned. "Saw the smoke first. They were having a cookout."

Gary chuckled. Kaitlyn requested coordinates.

"Can't remember," Carl said. He reeked of urine. "They dragged out a portable grill and set it up under the big glass canopy of some fancy condo. Red tablecloth on the sidewalk and everything."

"What were they cooking?" Kaitlyn asked, no doubt envisioning burgers molded from contraband processed meat. Stolen grill, pilfered tablecloth. Two infractions right there.

They grew cagey. Connecticut style. "Maybe it was MREs, you have to ask them."

"All I know is that it smelled good," No Mas said.

"Could get written up for that," Kaitlyn muttered. Gary shrugged. Angela changed the subject by asking where they were headed.

Gary stepped out, checked the street sign. "Here."

"You're incorrect," Carl said. His face tightened. "This is our spot."

Their grid assignments were identical. Fulton x Gold. They moved into the intersection to double-check they weren't bickering over adjacent blocks, and all of them couldn't help but notice that the east side of Gold had received the benediction of three- and four-story town houses, and that a huge open-air parking lot dominated the north side of Fulton. A bonanza. A four-day job max, but in the right hands it could be stretched out over a leisurely six or seven with Wonton being none the wiser. This would be a quarrel.

"We got here first," No Mas said.

"First's got nothing to do with it," Mark Spitz said. The parking lot was mostly empty. Not even the stray corpse slumped over a steering wheel to bag up. They didn't have orders to check the trunks.

"It's ours."

"Not like the Lieutenant to make a mistake," Kaitlyn said. "Call him on your comm. Ours is on the fritz."

"Comm?" No Mas said. "Haven't got shit on that all week."

"They got these pheenie grandmas making this crap, what do you expect," Carl said.

Gary loosed a series of expletives. "Ee-ho de puta. Fabio. Remember that time he gave Marcy a grid and it turned out it was on the other side of the wall? Up on Spring Street. That dude is off his meds." Gary looked at No Mas and Mark Spitz caught the other man swiftly glance down to examine the sidewalk.

Fabio had distributed their grid assignments the previous Sunday. The Lieutenant had been summoned to Buffalo and now his second was in charge. With the big man out of town, Fabio informed them there was no need for them to come up. He instructed them to skip their usual R & R and stay out in the Zone, Disposal would drop some rations on their rounds. He sent the grids out over the comm and wished them luck. "We better get that R & R back," Gary informed his unit, "or people will be sorry."

"Lieutenant's gonna have his ass when we tell him how he fucked up," Angela said.

They returned to the awning, waiting for the rain to let up, like in the old days, average citizens save for the assault rifles. And the rest of the gear. A fat drop landed on the back of Mark Spitz's hand; he wasn't wearing his gloves. Gray particulate described its outline on his skin. The rain captured ash on the way down, and looking out into the street he imagined the drops as long, gray, plummeting streaks. Giants wrung dirty dishrags over his head. "Look at this," he said to Gary. He pointed at his skin.

Gary frowned. "We don't see anything."

When Mark Spitz was a child, his father had shared his favorite nuclear-war movies with him. Father-son bonding on overcast afternoons. Fresh-faced rising stars who never made it big and crag-faced character actors marched through the acid-rain narratives and ash-smeared landscapes, soldiering on, slapping hysterical comrades across the face—get a grip on yourself, we're going to make it—dropping one by one as they chased the rumors of sanctuary. He asked, "What does 'apocalypse' mean, Daddy?" and his father pressed pause and told him, "It means that in the future, things will be even worse than they are now."

In college Mark Spitz coasted in his customary way through a history requirement about the cold war. They'd pegged their doomsday to split atoms. They were blind to the plague's blueprint of destruction, but they'd seen the ash. The pervasive, inexorable gray was a local atmospheric anomaly, and not what Buffalo had been thinking of when they devised their American Phoenix, but it suited. Up out of the ash, reborn.

Carl paused. The others turned. One of the dead came down the avenue. It was a strange sight after all this time, out there in the open. On their streets. Mark Spitz had only seen one other free-range skel since his arrival. This one had escaped the marines' sweep somehow, finally freeing itself from some crummy cell, the room in the bowling alley where they stored the past-prime shoes or the basement of the souvlaki joint. The skel had spotted them, awakened at their bickering, and it veered from the middle of the asphalt, crept between two foreign-made compacts, and slowly gained the sidewalk. It walked in the rain in the way no one walked in the rain, in a downpour like this, without shiver or frown, the water popping off its head and shoulders into a spray like a swarm of gnats. It approached them, implacable and sure, at the familiar grim pace.

The skel wore a morose and deeply stained pinstripe suit, with a solid crimson tie and dark brown tasseled loafers. A casualty, Mark Spitz thought. It was no longer a skel, but a version of something that predated the anguishes. Now it was one of those laid-off or ruined businessmen who pretend to go to the office for the family's sake, spending all day on a park bench with missing slats to feed the pigeons bagel bits, his briefcase full of empty potato-chip bags and flyers for massage parlors. The city had long carried its own plague. Its infection had converted this creature into a member of its bygone loser cadre, into another one of the broke and the deluded, the mis-fitting, the inveterate unlucky. They tottered out of single-room occupancies or peeled themselves off the depleted relative's pullout couch and stumbled into the sunlight for miserable adventures. He had seen them slowly make their way up the sidewalks in their woe, nurse an over-creamed cup of coffee at the corner greasy spoon in between health department crackdowns. This creature before them was the man on the bus no one sat next to, the haggard mystic screeching verdicts on the crowded subway car, the thing the new arrivals swore they'd never become but of course some of them did. It was a matter of percentages.

Carl took the shot and they resumed their negotiations.

"This isn't going to un-fuck itself," Kaitlyn said. "Mark Spitz, go up and see what the situation is."

"Why does he get to go?" Carl said. Mark Spitz had never seen a hard case pout before.

"Because he knows how to walk in a straight line."

Angela, Bravo's leader, did not protest. She looked resigned to losing the grid, steeling herself for the next inconvenience, whatever it may be.

Kaitlyn unslung her assault rifle and dropped her pack. She sat cross-legged on the concrete. "Now who's gonna go over there and zip up that skel?"

. . .

He met Mim in a toy store. The convenience marts, box outlets, pharmacies, and other likely suspects had been thoroughly excavated so Mark Spitz started hitting toy stores. The plague had reacquainted him with primal disappointments and in younger days he had been tormented by the fine print BATTERIES NOT INCLUDED often enough for it to leave a permanent dent. He thought this tactic ingenious—indeed, more than a few toy stores still had batteries behind the counter, even in loathsome Connecticut, where he encountered Mim during a noon raid. A handful of skels drifted down Main Street out front, the compasses in their veins quivering at no true north save the next square in front of them. He went around back to employee parking and spent a hairy ten minutes fretting the back door with a crowbar, scratching away, until he heard the muffled "Who is it?"

He said, "I'm alive," and she let him in.

Her name was Miriam Cohen Levy and she was the last person to give him a full name for a long time. She'd been hitting toy stores since the start. "I have three kids," she told him later.

They chatted in the robot aisle. Her gear sat at their feet in perky, neatly organized nylon packs. Her weapon of choice was a red-bladed fire ax, snatched from the wall of an elementary school or municipal building, and it was sparkling clean, even in the weak light trickling past the window display. "Germs," she said. "But I prefer running whenever possible. The cardio."

Mark Spitz noted that there were only two points of entry to the building. He pointed to the spiral staircase. "More toys upstairs. You can drop your pack there," she said, like a good host. "You heading to Buffalo?"

"What's there?"

"That's where the government is now. They got a big compound organized."

He hadn't heard that one, but it was in accord with his theory that every rumored sanctuary was located in a place he'd never had the slightest intention of visiting. "Last I heard people were going to Cleveland."

"That was awhile ago."

"Buffalo is the new Cleveland."

That's what people were saying, she told him. Mim had hooked up with some Buffalo-bound pilgrims for a week, but then she got some kind of stomach thing and had to lie on her side all day, the only thing that helped. They apologized, but they had to leave her behind, nothing personal. She didn't take offense. "Them's the rules," she told Mark Spitz, shoulders popping up in a brief shrug.

Mim had been mobile since her last camp imploded. She'd spent the summer and most of the autumn at a mansion in Darien: two and a half meals a day, stone walls, and a generator. The owners were dead, but the gardener's son, Taylor, had keys and set up camp at the start of the abominations. He'd played Space War on the grounds as a kid, knew the clandestine tunnels dug during the reign of prohibition and maintained during the heyday of infidelity. Plenty of spare exits if others got skel-heavy. Taylor recruited fellow survivors on gas runs, or he caught them clambering over the walls, backpacks full of cans and accessories. If he saw something in you he liked, you were invited to stay. He dressed like biker-club muscle but was a very sweet soul; it was a costume, and when he ran off people, they obeyed.

"It wasn't crazy-culty," Mim said, sucking powder from a protein packet, licking the excess from her fingertip. "He didn't try anything nuts, like you have to kill the oldest every Thursday at midnight—he just wanted people he could get along with. Potheads, mostly." Willoughby Manor was thirty people at its biggest population, and well run. Organized forage runs, an activity board. "No bullies, no rapes. Low profile kept the dead from hanging around outside." Lights out after dark was the rule, whereupon they gathered in the wine cellar for mellow evening tastings. Down in the branching tunnels there were ample amusements to pass the time. They played poker among the Brunellos, charades before the Argentine vintages, watched the cherished sitcoms in the final, unfinished room that was actually underneath the pool, imagine that. They'd plucked Mim from Darien's main drag after she miscalculated the margin of safety while trying to outrun a skel swarm she'd accidentally wandered into. "Don't you hate it when that happens?" she asked. "Minding your own business, on a lip balm mission, and then boom." The Willoughbys scooped her up in an SUV and she enlisted.

"Sounds like a nice setup."

"It was great. I really thought I'd wait it out there." She changed her tone. She was not the first to misread his face. "I still believe that—that we're going to beat this thing. However long it takes. And then we're all going to go home."

He mashed his teeth together so as to maintain his mask.

Their idyll was terminated by one of the number, Abel, who had developed some theories about the plague and its agenda. He was one of those apocalypse-as-moral-hygiene people, with a college-sophomore socialist slant. The dead came to scrub the Earth of capitalism and the vast bourgeois superstructure, with its doilies, helicopter parenting, and streaming video, return us to nature and wholesome communal living. No one paid much attention, Mim said; Abel was a good worker and one encountered crazier folk out on the wastes.

Mark Spitz had met plenty of the divine-retribution folks over the months. This was their moment; they were umbrella salesmen standing outside a subway entrance in a downpour. The human race deserved the plague, we brought it on ourselves for poisoning the planet, for the Death of God, the calculated brutalities of the global economic system, for driving primordial species to extinction: the entire collapse of values as evidenced by everything from nuclear fission to reality television to alternate side of the street parking. Mark Spitz could only endure these harangues for a minute or two before he split. It was boring. The plague was the plague. You were wearing galoshes, or you weren't.

"Then one night," Mim said, "it was over." Most of the campers were down in the cellar—it was game night—when Abel came downstairs and said that he could no longer sit back and watch while the household ignored the verdict of the plague. What right do we have to laugh and carol and play Texas hold 'em while the rest of the world suffered its just punishment? "Which is why," he told them, "I have opened the gates."

They ran upstairs. Abel did more than open the gates. The dead engulfed the grounds, spilling into the great room from the veranda "like wedding guests looking for cocktails after the ceremony." Abel must have lured them up the hill with promises of a buffet. The place was lost. "The usual helter-skelter," Mim told him. She was separated from everybody else but managed to scramble to some backup gear she'd stashed by the far wall of the grounds for this very occasion. "Settle in all you want to," Mim said. "Sign up for work duty and water the tomato plants. But you gotta stash a backup pack, 'cause it always comes tumbling down."

He liked her immensely, despite her belief in Buffalo. They were vapor: the big settlement beyond the next rise, the military base two days' walk, the utopian commune on the other side of the river. The place never existed or was long overrun by the time of your arrival, a stink of corpses and smoldering fires. Or it was lunatics and the crazy new society they'd cooked up, with a fascist constitution, or nutty rules like all the womenfolk had to sleep with the men to repopulate the race, or some other creepy secret you only discovered after you'd been there a few days, and when you had to split you found they'd hidden your weapons and stolen your bouillon cubes. Mark Spitz was off groups for now, but if the right outfit came along he'd start using Mim's solution. Stash a spare.

Mark Spitz was prepared to take whatever batteries Mim didn't want, but she insisted that they split them evenly. "I can't carry all this, that's ridiculous. Help yourself." He had filled his pack when he heard Mim curse.

She was at the window. "Bad weather," she said. He thought the snow had started; he'd smelled the impending snow since morning. Then he replaced her at the glass and saw Main Street. He dropped down. Was the back door locked? Yes. He and Mim crawled behind the aisles of toddler fare, the fake babies, squealing teddys, and assortment of cheap plastic shapes. It was the biggest dead stream he'd seen in months, a macabre parade walking from sidewalk to sidewalk in the wake of an invisible, infernal piper. Homecoming Day, Founder's Birthday, the End of the War. Did small towns still celebrate soldiers who made it back from the front? Salute that miracle of making it through the ordeal? The festivities honoring the defeat of the plague, the armistice with chaos, wouldn't match the spectacle outside. There wouldn't be enough people left to hold a banner. He shook his head. Fucking Connecticut.

The necrotic multitudes marched past the toy-store windows. This sick procession. Mark Spitz and his new companion repaired to the stockroom. Maybe the weather marshaled the dead into that big group, repurposed synapses in their spongy and riddled brains compelling them from the wind, the blizzard washing over the seaboard. Some unfortunate souls would discover where the dead army waited out bad weather. Not him. Mark Spitz and Mim remained in the back. When the dead finally disappeared, the big furry flakes stuck to the road and sidewalk. In the lost days when the pipes poured and electrons filled the multifarious cables, the ambient heat of the ground prevented such quick accumulations. Now the snow piled swiftly on the deadened earth.

They held off on Last Night. He knew he was going to give her the Obituary when she opened the back door and emerged from the gloom. Skull faces had replaced human faces in his mind's population, tight over the bone, staring without mercy, incisors out front. The stubborn ordinariness of her soft eyes and round, vigorous features were a souvenir. The yellow bandanna tight around her scalp tokened weekend chores, plucking acorns and twigs from the sputtering gutter, scraping last summer's black residue from the grill. The ancient rites. She was like him, one of the unlikely ones, pushing through. Normal.

Instead of Last Night stories, they indulged in Where Ya From, which tended to produce more positive hits than it had before the plague, or so it seemed to Mark Spitz. As if all the survivors shared a clandestine link, established here and there across the course of their lives for the arrival of this event. Or perhaps he was merely easily awed by coincidence now, in the disconnectedness of his days. "Oh, you're from Wilkes-Barre? Do you know Gabe Edelman?" "Really? That's funny, we met at a sales conference in Akron once." His life overlapped with the dentist duo, the bubbly truck driver, the insurance adjuster, and the rest of the sad-eyed lot, and it didn't matter that it was all meaningless. "She must have gone to rehab since then because she wasn't like that at all." It was a séance to penetrate the veil of the great beyond. The disembodied knocking of spirits brightened their respective corners of darkness for a time. "I was there once, ate at a coffee shop that had the best apple pie. Do you know it? That's it." "My cousin went there. But he's much older, you wouldn't have crossed paths with him." The associations hastened morning, when they went in different directions. Sometimes not until then. Sometimes the dead found them in the night.

He stayed with her, half in love with her before twilight. They didn't intersect, although over time they discovered they were both fond of the same television shows. But everybody loved the same shows back then and popular culture was not the same thing as people and places. He couldn't help but think that the juggernaut sitcoms and police procedurals were still in syndication somewhere on the planet, the laugh tracks and pre-commercial-break crescendos ringing out and lumbering forth in the evergloom. The shows had been so inescapable that they were past requiring electricity. At the very least, in a survivalist's underground rec room or a government facility (Buffalo had yet to reveal itself), seasons one through seven of the hospital drama groundbreaking in its realism and the extras-filled box set of the critic-proof workplace comedy unfurled on the screens as the watchers debated breaking out the good stuff, the cheese puffs they'd been saving for a special occasion. They tugged open the cellophane: special occasions were over. The commercials were the new commercials, he imagined darkly, for lightweight kerosene canisters (When You Need to Burn the Dead in a Hurry!) and anticiprant (Four Out of Five Uninfected Doctors Agree: Still the Only Antibiotic That Matters!). One did not fast-forward through these ads. These were essential consumer items.

He and Mim had no one in common, apart from the calamity. They were both its fleas. "I'm just a mom," she said, botching the tense. That first night they broke open a carton of birthday candles, which provided no heat but the concept of fire warmed them. Mark Spitz blocked the draft from the back door with a row of stuffed armadillos and others in the armadillo's troupe. She went first.

She was from Paterson, her husband's hometown. They moved there once they found out about the baby. Her parents were useless, trapped in a narcissistic loop, but Harry's mother was reliable and had a lot of time on her hands since her retirement. Mim came to love the town. She met some expectant moms online via the local parenting resource and in those disquieting postpartum days they assembled into a crew. They had plenty of babies over the next ten years, and she tapped a bona fide community into her auto-synced contact lists, especially after school started and she befriended the moms (and odd dad) she recognized from the two local playgrounds. "Didn't you use to go to that tot lot next to Café Loulou?" "We met during that heat wave—you were kind enough to give my girl, Eve, two water balloons."

Harry worked in sales at a company that compiled factoids for oldies stations: This plucky tune ruled the charts for an unprecedented twelve weeks in the summer of 1964. This irrepressible hit maker was born this day in 1946. Local DJs used them as a leavening agent in their patter and it was a sturdy business in an age of corporatized nostalgia, when each successive generation herded key favorites together to save them from nipping upstarts. Harry traveled a lot, but a religious webchat schedule erased the miles, especially in those early days when it was just the two of them. It was almost as if he were sitting on the couch when they grimaced and laughed into their minuscule lenses, as if Harry were on his laptop right next to her. When her ob-gyn told them their third child was on the way, they moved to their fourth and final Paterson address. New construction. Harry loved those old houses on the street he grew up on, but Mim never saw the appeal.

Gladys's youngest son, Oliver, was turning five. Miriam's son Asher had celebrated his birthday the week before. It was one of those enchanted, hyperactive months when the weekends were saturated with birthday parties and the moms (and odd dad) worked hard to coordinate their schedules—you can take Saturday and we'll take Sunday and next year we'll switch—reserve the vetted play spaces, discover new, uncharted play spaces, and ponder overlong what to cram down the gullets of the diaphanous goodie bags, the gooey, the plastic, the cavity-inducing. It was a kindhearted competition as far as these things go. Perhaps exhausted by the game, Gladys went old school by holding Oliver's party at home. Gladys downloaded the latest pastimes and tips from a parenting site she didn't think anyone else had heard of yet. The pool would finally be finished by then and, weather willing, it would be a splendid inaugural bash.

The pool wasn't finished. Gladys told Mim that Lamont had run out of patience and wanted to fire the contractor, but everyone else was booked up, they'd checked. The back of the house was a jagged hell and they'd have to stay indoors on account of liability. And to top it all off, Gladys told her, Lamont was sick upstairs with the flu. One aspect of the afternoon remained unblemished, however. It was a drop-off party, that two-hour oasis in the harried parent's calendar, egress to a world of manis and pedis, a pilfered nap, a glass or two of decent rosé. Mim left her kids there. They had buddies their own age, known each other since they were born. Asher, Jackson, and little Eve didn't even spare a goodbye, trotting into the playroom where the other kids toiled in their commotion. "Good luck," Mim said, as Gladys shut the door to keep the AC in.

When she returned an hour and a half later—she had resolved to straighten up her office but had scratched at her crossword instead—she saw the ambulance outside but immediately calmed herself: Gladys would have called her if it had been one of her kids. Then the squad cars ran her off the road as they sped past, almost driving onto her friend's front lawn and into her beloved hydrangeas and Mim thought, Maybe Gladys didn't have time to call and something has happened to her babies. She was correct: Gladys didn't have time to call.

Twelve hours later, Mim was on the run like everyone else. Cast out into the dreary steppes. Mark Spitz didn't ask about Harry. You never asked about the characters that disappeared from a Last Night story. You knew the answer. The plague had a knack for narrative closure.

Mark Spitz thought of Mim and the toy store as he walked up to Wonton because of the encounter with Bravo Unit. Other people in their surprises, the different social outcomes in the new world. He rarely hung out this far downtown before the plague, had never run into people he knew on these streets, so it was odd seeing Angela and the other two on their rounds. Mark Spitz was surprised at how calm he had been as the businessman skel approached, how far removed he was from out there. He was one of six heavily armed soldiers. This was not Last Night in its cruel ministrations. This was the new kingdom of Zone One. His turf after all this time.

The city—the pre-catastrophe city with its untold snares and machinations—intimidated him. He'd never lived on the island. He spent a sweltering August crashing with a college buddy in Bushwick, stranded on the L train, sure, but even when he could have scraped up enough dough for some miserable boot-camp apartment he had resisted moving to the city. He commuted to his job in Chelsea from his childhood home to save some money, he told himself. He wasn't the only one putting off the big move; a lot of the people he grew up with shuffled back to Long Island after college, knowing it was safe there or realizing this after getting slapped around and bruised out in the world. If they had ever left at all.

Looking back, it was silly. He wanted to find his bearings after his stint in California, have some sort of kick-ass job or unspecified achievement under his belt before he moved to Manhattan. To think that there had been a time when such a thing meant something: the signifiers of one's position in the world. Today a rusty machete and bag of almonds made you a person of substance. He had waited on a sweet internship from one of the globe-strangling midtown firms or . . . he couldn't think of it, what else would have made him comfortable walking down the New York streets in that hectic boil. He had been scared of the city. He knew how to dog-paddle and that was it. Now no one hogged the sidewalk so he couldn't pass, beat him to that vacant subway seat, jousted with him. He only encountered slow desperadoes and fellow sheriffs, meting out justice in the territory.

A feather of plastic stuck to his boot and flopped against the pavement. He tore it off. He was accustomed to the silence now, understood it as a part of himself, weightless gear he stowed in his pack next to the gauze and anticiprant. He walked in the middle of the street, between the ankles of the steel juggernauts. Past the barren windows. His beat was different than the marines'. The dead had poured out of the buildings when they heard the soldiers' dinner bell of war whoops and gunfire, and were cut down. His own tour of the tenements and high-end edifices was calmer: he had time to interpret the rooms of asylum. Emptiness was an index. It recorded the incomprehensible chronicle of the metropolis, the demographic realities, how money worked, the cobbled-together lifestyles and roosting habits. The population remained at a miraculous density, it seemed to him, for the empty rooms brimmed with evidence, in the stragglers they did or did not contain, in the busted barricades, in the expired relatives on the futon beds, arms crossed over their chests in ad hoc rites. The rooms stored anthropological clues re: kinship rituals and taboos. How they treated their dead.

The rich tended to escape. Entire white-glove buildings were devoid, as Omega discovered after they worried the seams of and then shattered the glass doors to the lobby (no choice, despite the No-No Cards). The rich fled during the convulsions of the great evacuation, dragging their distilled possessions in wheeled luggage of European manufacture, leaving their thousand-dollar floor lamps to attract dust to their silver surfaces and recount luxury to later visitors, bowing like weeping willows over imported pile rugs. A larger percentage of the poor tended to stay, shoving layaway bureaus and media consoles up against the doors. There were those who decided to stay, willfully uncomprehending or stupid or incapacitated by the scope of the disaster, and those who could not leave for a hundred other reasons—because they were waiting for their girlfriend or mother or soul mate to make it home first, because their mobility was compromised or a relative was debilitated, crutched, too young. Because it was too impossible, the enormity of the thought: This is the end. He knew them all from their absences.

He stood in the abandoned nests, kicking empty cans that had held the mainstay vegetables, backbone of a good American diet. Where terrified family units had quivered while waiting for the next-door neighbors to stop screaming for entry: Save us, let us in. When the screaming ceased, the residents waited for them to stop passing by the eyehole in the front door, deadly shadows in that tiny aperture. The plague-blind residents of apartments 7J and 9F, who had studiously ignored each other during the occasional elevator internment, had elected themselves to the condo board without dissenting votes and now patrolled the halls in search of bylaw infractions and flesh, pausing by the door as if they heard the breathing of those inside despite all those huddled critters did to silence themselves. In the living room on the fifth floor of the walk-up, the entombed lovers made a bed of expensive, hand-sewn blankets that was ringed by puddles of wax from the candles they'd used for dinner parties and romantic evenings at home, and murmured the newly minted endearments: "No, you take the last one, I ate yesterday" and "If I didn't have you with me right now I would have killed myself long ago." All of these waited for their moment of escape, those early days. All of these and the loners—the hipsters, the homesick transfer students and homebound retired teachers, the elderly who thought themselves long past being surprised by the invidious schemes of the world, the new arrivals with bad timing and zero friends and lacking anything resembling that false assemblage described as a "support system," and the biding cranks finally gifted with a perverted version of their long-awaited dream of liberation from humanity. They spent weeks or months holed up in their pads, devouring everything in the cheap cabinetry, every last morsel save for the upholstery, and even this occasionally bore marks of teeth, before finally making a break for it at whatever time of day they'd decided was safest, in the direction dictated by their mulled theories, toward the bridges, the river to search for a seaworthy vessel, the roof to wave down angels for a lift. Out, out.

They had lived in the city in the days of the plague. They finished off the food and hope of rescue and packed a small bag. In time they left their apartments or else snuffed themselves according to the recipes offered by the manual of pop culture. He'd never met anyone in the camps or the great out there who had made it out of the city after the first couple of days. They left the doors unlocked.

He became a connoisseur of the found poetry in the abandoned barricade. The minuscule, hardscrabble wedge of space between the piled-up furniture and the apartment door the departing had squeezed through. The wide, inviting arch of an old church that had been dwarfed by high-rises, the only open doorway on the block, the debris on the steps kicked away in the escape and the cleared path creating a kind of carpet for the bride and groom en route to the honeymoon limo. And out in the country, the one blank window among the other boarded-up windows on the first floor of the farmhouse, with its welcome mat of shattered glass. Those inside had made a break for it, and there the story ended. Did they make it? It was less depressing than the spectacle of the overcome barricade, the fortifications that failed, with their rotting, weather-lashed corpses and the expressionist eruptions of crimson across the surfaces.

When he used to watch disaster flicks and horror movies he convinced himself he'd survive the particular death scenario: happen to be away from his home zip code when the megatons fell, upwind of the fallout, covering the bunker's air vents with electrical tape. He was spread-eagled atop the butte and catching his breath when the tsunami swirled ashore, and in the lottery for a berth on the spacecraft, away from an Earth disintegrating under cosmic rays, his number was the last one picked and it happened to be his birthday. Always the logical means of evasion, he'd make it through as he always did. He was the only cast member to heed the words of the bedraggled prophet in Act I, and the plucky dude who slid the lucky heirloom knife from his sock and sawed at the bonds while in the next room the cannibal family bickered over when to carve him for dinner. He was the one left to explain it all to the skeptical world after the end credits, jibbering in blood-drenched dungarees before the useless local authorities, news media vans, and government agencies who spent half the movie arriving on the scene. I know it sounds crazy, but they came from the radioactive anthill, the sorority girls were dead when I got there, the prehistoric sea creature is your perp, dredge the lake and you'll find the bodies in its digestive tract, check it out. By his sights, the real movie started after the first one ended, in the impossible return to things before.

. . .

This is the story Mark Spitz told that final Sunday. The bite had stopped geysering blood. It was just the two of them, as Kaitlyn worried over the comm in the front room. Gary asked, "Why do they call you Mark Spitz?"

"I'd been at Happy Acres a few months, signed up for a bunch of work details, and I wanted to get out more. I missed it out there. I was malfunctioning—weird dreams, feeling gummed up—ever since I got picked up by the army."

When the convoy departed Camp Screaming Eagle, Happy Acres was still known as PA-12; on his arrival two days later, the signage proclaiming the new name was fresh and white and fragrant, the stencils curled in piles by the trash bins. Buffalo repositioned the settlements in the market—CT-6 into Gideon's Triumph, VA-2 into Bubbling Brooks—and perhaps Mark Spitz was being repositioned as well, from scarred and hollow-eyed wanderer into contributing actor of the American Phoenix. He worked in Inventory, tracking how many gallons of peanut oil and cans of asparagus tips were coming in and going out, tending to glitches in the supply train between local camps. Was Happy Acres receiving its fair share of recovered antiseptic or not, a proper allocation of that newly discovered cache of floss, and more important, was Morning Glory hoarding toilet paper with malicious intent, or were they merely embroiled in a camp-wide, gastrointestinal misadventure? He recorded everything on sponsored recycled paper, in longhand like in the dark ages before computers. It passed the time.

When word came down about the Northeast Corridor op, Mark Spitz was famished for change. He poked his ballot into the box and when they stapled the list of names on the rec center wall, right next to that day's survivor roll, he cheered for the first time since that final Atlantic City excursion, when Kyle lumbered into a hot streak and the craps table went bonkers for a time. As far as the new employment went, clearing the corridor didn't sound too terrible, capacious enough for both the orderly virtues of settlement life and the freebooting thrills of the wasteland shuck 'n' jive.

In the cinema of end-times, the roads feeding the evacuated city are often clear, and the routes out of town clotted with paralyzed vehicles. Whether government supercomputers have calculated beyond all doubt that the meteor will decimate downtown or the genetically engineered killer cockroaches are taking over the city, the inbound lanes are unimpeded. It makes for a stark visual image, the crazy hero returning to the doomed metropolis to save his kid or gal or to hunt down the encrypted computer file that might—just might!—reverse disaster, driving a hundred miles an hour into the hexed zip codes when all the other citizens are vamoosing, wide-eyed in terror, mouths decorated with flecks of white foam.

In Mark Spitz's particular apocalypse, the human beings were messy and did not obey rules, and every lane in and out, every artery and vein, was filled with outbound traffic. A disemboweled city, spilling its entrails, will tend to the disorderly side. If you want to fight against the stream of common sense, noble protagonist, you are going to have some trouble. For a time, the frenzied evacuees hack out precious distance between themselves and the blight. The cars and vans jerk forward, stop, stutter, a line makes a break for the shoulder and then there's a new lane, premium guzzlers with four-wheel drive ditch the roads altogether and tromp over the semi-landscaped greenery at the edge of the highway, mowing down the sign informing you THIS MILE OF ROUTE 23 MAINTAINED BY THE MORTVILLE SENIORS CHOIR. The drivers and passengers don't want to die. They have witnessed the grisly denouements of others, are panicked and shamed by how quickly they have jettisoned the props of civilization. A certain percentage will make it through, will escape to one of the rescue stations they've been hearing about on the radio, we have to, and hey, is it just me or have the announcers stopped mentioning Benjamin Franklin Elementary, do you think it's still operational?

The vehicles stop. Some obstruction they can't see at the head of the line. Distressing. People shout rumors down the turnpike. Aunt Ethel stirs in the backseat, her new brain issuing commands, her macramé shawl drops from her bosom and she takes a hunk of meat out of Jeffrey Fitzsimmons's neck, and nephew Jeffrey steers the two-year-old sport-utility vehicle into the Petersons' Japanese compact, which is so crammed with heirlooms and bottled water and camping gear that Sam Peterson can barely see out the windows, not that he woulda had time to get out of the way even if he'd seen the Fitzsimmonses coming. Bang, crash, ploof of airbag expanding, squish of metal impaling flesh in arrangements unforeseeable by crash-test professionals. The eight-car pile brings all the northern movement on the interstate to a halt. There's no getting around. No backing up. Jammed in there. And then the dead start to move from the trees.

Now it was time to open the lanes. If all went well, the Northeast Corridor will eventually stretch from D.C. to Boston and the precious cargo (medicine, bullets, foodstuffs, people) will travel unimpeded up and down the coast. Mark Spitz's wrecker detail was responsible for a stretch of I-95 in mephitic Connecticut and the occasional tributary, foraying from comfy Fort Golden Gate. In prelapsarian days, the base had been one of the largest retirement communities in the state, known for its facility with the latest trends and currents in Alzheimer's care. The redbrick walls encircling the property, constructed to keep the befogged safe inside, now kept those with an entirely different impairment to their mental faculties outside. Naturally, there were more gun nests.

The many-windowed campus buildings allowed the constant delectation of invigorating sunsets—indeed, it was hard for Mark Spitz to adjust to so much glass after a bunker existence—and the bungalows formerly inhabited by active, self-sufficient seniors were a serious upgrade from the communal bunks at the settlement camps. The dining hall was pastel and affirming, and no one complained when some rogue operative booted up the old sound system one day and the anodyne instrumentals scored every meal in a ceaseless loop of deracinated pop. The fort's inhabitants fluttered down the concrete paths in electric carts and every night the windows crackled with the blue glow of screens, as the extensive video library reacquainted these minions of reconstruction with the old entertainments that had meant so much to them. It was hard to believe that there had once been faces like that, the beautiful ones with their promises and lures.

Fort Golden Gate, in a suburb of Bridgeport, was a nexus of reconstruction initiatives. Mark Spitz played poker with nuclear technicians, civil engineers, and sundry gurus of infrastructure. It was from Golden Gate that the first recon teams ventured to explore the viability of a Manhattan operation. Months later, he remembered some of his hold 'em buddies had murmured about a "Zone One."

The majority of Golden Gate's inhabitants hailed from the Northeast, in keeping with the demographics of ruin. It was an interregnum quirk: people tended to stay in-region, roving in circles, bouncing back off an invisible barrier two states south. A mountain range draped in imposing shadow scared them toward the survivor community the other wanderers kept babbling about. In the chow line, Mark Spitz's fellow reconstruction drones trembled and tic'd like contestants in some deplorable PASD beauty contest. Observing them, Mark Spitz put the rebirth of civilization at even money. Even if every last skel dropped to the ground tomorrow, did these harrowed pilgrims possess the reserves to pull out of the death spiral? Will the gloomy survivors manage to reproduce, the newborns fatten up? Which of the hoary debilitations and the patient old illnesses will reap them? It was not hard to see the inhabitants of the camps devolve into demented relics too damaged to do anything more than dwindle into extinction in a generation or two.

Even money. He was glad to have his own bed, convertible from the sofa in the living room of a spacious and tastefully appointed bungalow. The owners had spent their sunset years on an assiduous circuit of the world's top cruises, and photos of the grand ships sailed the wall over his head as he slept. Once or twice, the old couple crept into his current dream narratives, and the dead played shuffleboard and carried plates to the early-bird buffets, which visited a different world cuisine each night, All You Can Eat, All-inclusive.

He shared the bungalow with the Quiet Storm and Richie, the three of them comprising half a wrecker team. The wrecker teams drove heavy-duty tows and boom trucks—imposing before the disaster, when welded and bolted and otherwise fastened to the latest fashions in anti-skel plating and grillwork, the trucks became the physical, diesel-powered manifestation of pure-blooded American bad-assery. Four guys worked the stalled vehicles, coaxing and untangling them from multifarious confusions, as the other two stood sentry on lookout-and-drop-'em duty. Mark Spitz and Richie took skel detail, popping any dead meter reader or dead weatherman that drifted in from the median, or was trapped in the backseat of, and pounding on the blood-smeared back window of, the overturned yellow cab, radio-station promo van, or hearse. You never played Solve the Wreck because the answer was obvious: It had been drive or die.

Lookout had more downtime. The dead were low density in this part of the coast, in those days—they had stopped speculating about why and merely accepted it as fact—and the ones attracted to the noise of the engines never amounted to more than one or two every couple of hours. The trapped skels—skittering Little Leaguers sans hands, bound and trussed matrons with maniac snarls on their faces—were mere target practice, and few. If those fleeing cared enough to bring their feverish, succumbing kin on the trip, they weren't going to abandon them once they had to hoof it. Most of the doors were wide open in the aftermath of escape. The refugees hastily considered the imponderables—take mama's jewelry or the tackle box, the bag of rice or the carton of vitamins—and joined their neighbors on the run, disappearing into the abject void of the interregnum.

"Probably Vanderbilt 80s, right?" Gary asked.

"What?"

"The wreckers? The tow trucks. Those guys are sweet."

"I really have no idea."

The work was straightforward. The keys were in the ignition or weren't, the master keys worked or didn't, they could push them off the road or the wreckers came into play, chains were hooked to chassis, the disabled behemoths winched over to the shoulder. Depending on the size and number of the lanes, the type of bottleneck, and the number of stalled vehicles, the vehicles were parked perpendicular or at angles to the road, or they made a new expressway wall of compacts, sports-cars hybrids, intermingled with the odd ice-cream truck whose freezers sloshed with melted sweets. In theory. The Quiet Storm followed to a different mandate.

Mark Spitz encountered parables, as usual, in the evidence

left behind. The freeway was clear for half a mile, and then the cars appeared, bumper-to-bumper, doors and hatchback wide, you tracked ahead to reconnoiter the scene and discovered the cause of the jam: a jackknifed eighteen-wheeler, collision of family vans, a barricade erected by the local county authorities out of short-sighted precaution. Half-devoured corpses slumped in the passenger seats, or were buckled in behind the wheel, final curse against traffic still discernable despite the fact that their lips had been eaten: the invective was deep in the muscle. If enough bodies were in proximity, the wreckers made a bonfire, but the elements and microbes were doing a swell job of cleaning things up on their own.

It was nice zipping home at the end of the day down a stretch of highway you'd cleared. It was measurable progress, visible mileage into the new world. The work left aches in his flesh as proof, in the way inventory lists of bottled capers did not.

"You haven't got to the Mark Spitz part yet," Gary said.

"It's soaking through again," Mark Spitz said. He ripped open another medi-patch and continued.

"I rode in the lead wrecker with the Quiet Storm," he said. The Quiet Storm was one of the new skinheads, who shaved their scalps to commemorate their deprivations. It was just then taking off in the camps—how else to recognize one such as yourself, the most harrowed of the harrowed? She was an early rescue on the part of Buffalo's recovery teams, a member of an etiolated clan that had spent a year locked in the basement jail of a small-town police station, the unlucky wards of a madman. She didn't really go into it.

She was a lean greyhound, hyperalert in the manner of those who'd suffered their refuge overrun too many times. Everyone got overrun, and then there existed those in a whole different tier of frequent-flier status. They never slept, rarely blinked. The Quiet Storm was more functional than most skinheads in that she still spoke, and occasionally permitted a smile to splinter her lips.

She'd worked in a tree nursery before the recent engrueling of the world, tending to and cultivating the hedges that prevented the hoi polloi from peeking at the aristocracy. Not very effective barrier material, Mark Spitz thought when informed of her occupation, unable to stop his immediate assessment. Everything was either a weapon or a wall, to be quantified and sorted in its utility as such.

She was their team leader and quite particular about how she liked her vehicles arranged on the asphalt, perhaps her previous job's affection for the long view shaping her wreck style. Sometimes the Quiet Storm's directives did not inspire conjecture as to her motives; equally as often her orders contravened intuition. On this segment of uneventful highway, there might be only five cars mucking up the right-of-way, and she'd order them parked perpendicular, or perhaps at a forty-five-degree angle, even though the shoulder had plenty of room for bumper-to-bumper. One school of car alignment maintained that this latter placement would, like a breaker, impede a swell of dead attracted to the noise of a convoy; Buffalo was a vocal proponent for a while. Mark Spitz noticed that the Quiet Storm favored patterns divisible by five, and grouped them by general size and occasionally by color, sometimes even towing a car for miles to fulfill her conception. The Quiet Storm consulted her tablet, skittering the stylus over the computer maps, effecting hieroglyphic notations. "Orders," she said. Mark Spitz chalked it up to pointless military micromanagement or her brand of PASD, one or the other of these steadfast debilitations. It wasn't until later that he saw the truth of it.

"What do you mean?"

"I'm getting there."

The wreckers parted the junk sea, de-gnarling, unwinding the chaos. When a mammoth pileup gave issue to a serpent of silenced vehicles uncoiling for miles, their system disassembled it. They restored order. Sometimes Mark Spitz imagined that for every inch of asphalt they cleared, they reversed an equal increment of tragedy, undid whatever misfortunes had befallen the missing occupants. He immediately mortified himself for such thinking and fixed on the next looming collision. After a month, short supply trains utilized the roads they had cleared, bearing lima beans to the west, moving the water trucks to the dry gallon containers. The alchemy of reconstruction. The mileage of the wrecker teams north and south of them would connect eventually, in the manner of the transcontinental railroad. Connect the isolated camps and forts one by one, link the independent towns just now seduced to the national bosom, bid the life-giving vital material flow once more: they secured the track, advanced the heading mile by mile.

On the freeways Mark Spitz became a marksman. With the benefit of backup, line of sight, the luxury of drawing a bead on some slow-approaching creature at his leisure, he mastered the five target points on the skull most recommended by Buffalo for skel-dropping. (They'd done tests, collected oral testimony.) Some days the wreckers were outfitted with laser sights, if the army or marines passing through Golden Gate didn't snag them, and after a time Mark Spitz articulated his own floating ruby bull's-eye over the world when he went in for a kill with a bullet or a hatchet or baseball-size hunk of granite, activating a calm computer register inside his brain that calculated distance and wind speed, compensated for the level of erraticism in the target, the distance and accessibility of escape routes. The exquisite new art of drop 'em.

He eliminated that which would destroy him. In the broken land, the manifold survival strategies honed over a lifetime of avoiding all consequences rewrote themselves for this new world, or perhaps they had finally discovered their true arena, the field of engagement they had been created for. They had been put forth, tested, amended, debugged over a lifetime of tiny trials and contests, evasions of dangers big and small, social, symbolic, and, since the plague, lethal. If he'd been able to explain the extent of what was happening in his brain that day they nicknamed him

Mark Spitz, the host of manic, overlapping processes, perhaps he'd have earned a different moniker, one suitable for the completely bloodless processes inside him.

"I was finally complete, in a way."

"Not following."

"Sorry."

Their assignment on the day in question concerned a fouled-up segment of 95. One of the generals visiting Golden Gate on a fact-finding tour of New England reconstruction efforts had sworn by this highway when visiting family over the holidays, back in the good old dead world, and thus his pet shortcut became an official leg of the corridor. The skel weather was light, one or two per mile. The wreckers had started taking the kill fields for granted, it was hard not to; their fight-or-flight impulses no longer enjoyed their daily exercise regimen. The crew discovered clear blacktop between cities. "I need some cars," the Quiet Storm told Mark Spitz. "It's coming together in my mind."

A satisfied chuckle escaped the Quiet Storm when they reached the viaduct. The choker of lost vehicles, unruly and melancholy, stretched a mile. When the wreckers tracked ahead to see what kind of jam they had on their hands, they saw that it terminated at the northern edge of the concrete span, which was completely barriered by hotel courtesy shuttles and barbed wire. Three police cruisers butted bumpers beyond them, and the wreckers hazarded that this had been some country sheriff's attempt at banishing the plague from his or her jurisdiction. They had failed, obviously, and the blockade had merely impeded these people's escape, no doubt fatefully. No judgment. Whether the plague marked these pilgrims here or miles up the road, the resolution was the same.

The wreckers split up. Martha, Jimmy, and Mel, the other half of the crew, took the southern end of the line of stillborn escape craft, and Mark Spitz's contingent nabbed the viaduct. The cloudy water produced a pleasant melody beneath the span, a reassuring whisper. Taking care of the barbed wire looked to be a hassle, so

Mark Spitz suggested they put off the barrier and start with clearing the bridge, which, it turned out, jibed with the Quiet Storm's intentions for this lot. They confronted the familiar conveyances and the predictable anecdotes of desertion: four motorcycles that had squeezed between cars to the front of the blockage and then couldn't turn around; utility vehicles that had been over-packed according to the emergency broadcast system's monotoned instructions, in order to abandon the lifesaving supplies at this roadblock; a bare sedan with all its doors open because every seat had been taken, and then every seat evacuated, no trace.

The only unusual specimen was the eighteen-wheeler athwart the span, the logo on the side of the trailer marking it as part of a box retailer's fleet. The wreckers weren't a salvage detail. Their manifest included a daily gas quota, which they siphoned once the vehicles were cleared, and they were allowed to grab for personal use any food they discovered, the energy bars and preservative-laden snack chips, but that was it. When Richie unlatched the back of the trailer, he told them later, it was to see if it was worth a later trip by a proper team. Richie was a stickler, a teenager who'd been taken in as a mascot by the first military detachment at Golden Gate. Clearing wrecks was his first detail beyond the walls of the campus.

How and why the dead had been herded inside was a mystery. The Quiet Storm offered that it was a government job, the creatures earmarked for experiments, in those early days when that was a priority; perhaps a computer in Buffalo had this shipment flagged as MIA and after the engagement the file was appropriately amended. Mark Spitz's theory was drawn from the stories of those who had kept their loved ones chained up in the rec room or the garage in hope of the cure's arrival. The erection of this viaduct barricade was contemporaneous with the heyday of such optimistic gestures: We can beat this, this is just a temporary thing, if we keep our wits. He imagined the block association of a tight-knit suburb, some planned community off the interstate—on the border of the country club's golf course, a quick drive to the outlet mall—corralling all their infected kin into the trailer, Mom and Dad, the Smiths and half of the Joneses, for a road trip. To a place where they could be cured, or set free, or exterminated with a semblance of dignity and a smidgen of religious custom. The driver of the cab was a local pillar, worked his way up from country-club caddie to master of the nabe, owning the biggest house on the cul-de-sac, a spectacular castle that seemed, on certain nights, to float on its own bourgeois cloud above the development. Didn't mind driving a load of kids to the multiplex, to boot—if anyone can get them there, it's him. "Sent to live on a farm upstate."

At the moment Richie reached for the trailer's door, the Quiet Storm was settling before the cab's dashboard, communing with the machine, and Mark Spitz crouched inside a minivan of German manufacture, opening a packet of chocolate-covered peanuts he'd found. He heard Richie shout. Richie rushed up the side of the truck toward his comrades, followed by the stupendous troop of skels he'd just released. Were there sixty or seventy or more? When they recounted the story later, they were invariably accused of exaggeration, and the anecdote stalled for a few minutes until the debate over that modern version of How Many Angels Can Dance on a Head of a Pin, How Many Dead Can Fit into a Trailer was settled. "Quite a few" was the invariable conclusion.

At any rate, the wreckers were in the middle of the bridge, cut off from land. The trio had two weapons, as they had never needed more than that on an excursion. The Quiet Storm had stopped packing her rifle; she hadn't used it in weeks, and then only when Richie was out with a stomach thing. That was the problem with progress—it made you soft. The dead shimmied and squeezed between the vehicles, the green convertible with the shredded vinyl top and the plumber's van. When Richie removed himself from his sight lines, Mark Spitz proceeded to drop the creatures, bringing down a skel that wore bloody surgical scrubs—

impossible to know if it had earned that mess on or off duty—and an urban cowgirl whose rhinestones sparkled coolly in the sunlight. He obliterated their faces and everything beneath their faces, but there was no way his team was going to get them all. The wreckers couldn't quantify the horde's numbers.

"We're not getting through this bunch," the Quiet Storm said. They were calm. They assessed. The sheriff of the local municipality and his posse had blocked off their little patch of Heaven quite efficiently; the wreckers couldn't even squeeze around on the railing past the barbed wire.

"Looks deep enough," Richie said as he jumped off the bridge and into the water.

The drop was twenty feet. Richie's head popped up ten yards downstream. He beckoned them down to the water. The Quiet Storm scratched her fingers through the bristles on her scalp, delivered a stream of invective, and followed his lead.

It was impossible. Mark Spitz counted the massing dead. The forsaken devils waded between the cars, dumb and foul, groping toward their food supply, which had dwindled by two-thirds before their devoid mentalities. They were too brainless, he thought, to be disappointed by having to share the scraps of him after that endless internment in the trailer. No way Mark Spitz was going to be able to get past them. They were too many. You ran in this situation. A simple calculation without shame.

Richie shouted from the shore. The gunfire would have alerted the other three wreckers; they'd have backup soon. Instinct should have plucked Mark Spitz from the bridge and dropped him into the current by now. But he did not move.

When he told them later that he couldn't swim, they laughed. It was perfect: from now on he was Mark Spitz. But he had no fear of the water, not with his dependable comrades down there, and his undimmed halo of luck. He knew a few strokes. No: he leaped to the hood of the late-model neo-station wagon and started firing, first taking out the grandmotherly type in the tracksuit and then the teenager wearing grimed soccer-team colors, because he knew he could not die. He vaulted onto the black sedan beside him and demolished the craniums of two more skels, who dropped and were stepped on by the replacements behind them. He had suspicions, and every day in this wasteland supplied more evidence: He could not die. This was his world now, in all its sublime crumminess, where intellect and ingenuity and talent were as equally meaningless as stubbornness, cowardice, and stupidity. He shot the one wearing green-lensed aviator glasses in the middle of the forehead, and twice shot the creature in the hunting jacket in the chest before he mortified it with a final blast. He could not die. Two more creatures tumbled to the asphalt, their craniums disintegrated. Beauty could not thrive, and the awful was too commonplace to be of consequence. Only in the middle was there safety.

He was a mediocre man. He had led a mediocre life exceptional only in the magnitude of its unexceptionality. Now the world was mediocre, rendering him perfect. He asked himself: How can I die? I was always like this. Now I am more me. He had the ammo. He took them all down.

. . .

Forlorn Tribeca. Mark Spitz tracked west on his uptown sojourn and as he passed the corner lounge where he'd met Jennifer for drinks once after work, he allowed that it was possible his subconscious steered. At ten o'clock the bouncers dragged out the velvet rope and started choosing survivors, but early evening the attitude merely simmered. (Another barricade: sorting the sick from the healthy.) Happy hour was impenetrable, as bedraggled drones convened on stools and soft, low-slung couches, whipping out the measuring tape to see who had the biggest complaint and trying to forget that the minute you bury the miserable day it rises from its coffin the next morning, this monster. Jennifer's invite text received an eager response. She was a quick drinker who bullied and heckled her comrades into keeping pace. She'd make sure he got a full dose of medicine.

His job hadn't been unduly bothersome; mostly he hated the commute from the Island and the sense of being becalmed. He worked in Customer Relationship Management, New Media Department, of a coffee multinational. A college buddy tipped him to it: "You'll be perfect. It doesn't require any skills." The coffee company started in the Pacific Northwest with a single café and a proprietary roasting process, inquiries about which never failed to bring a thin, curious smile to the owners' lips. One storefront divided into two, a dozen brick-and-mortar locations metastasized into an international franchise entity with a disposition, underdog yet indomitable, hawking paraphernalia that articulated in physical form the lifestyle philosophy the customer had unknowingly subscribed to years before, through a hundred submissions and tacit oaths, and was now fully ripened. Every package of beans brewed in the logo-dappled paraphernalia reminded you of the larger mission and the nation-state of like minds. Your home was your own personal franchise. Didn't even have to post a sign in the bathroom reminding you to wash your hands.

The enchanted beans were organically farmed and humanely picked, the marketing uncanny in its engineering and ruthless in its implementation. It was his job to monitor the web in search of opportunities to sow product mindshare and nurture feelings of brand intimacy. As his supervisor put it. This meant, he soon learned, scouting websites and social-media apparatus for mentions of the brand family, and saying hello. He dispatched bots into the electronic ether, where they mingled among the various global sites and individual feeds, and when the bots returned with a hit or blip, he sent a message: "Thanks for coming, glad you liked the joe!" or "Next time try the Mocha Burst, you'll thank me later." He perched on the high-tension wires like a binary vulture, ancient pixilated eyes peeled for scraps. When he saw meat, he pounced. Sometimes the recipient responded, sometimes not.

The denizens of the void, chewing on their tails, compulsively broadcasting the flimsy minutiae of their day-to-day on personal feeds and pages, didn't have to name the products directly. The pale, thin boys two floors down in Implementation broadened the keywords to encompass the entire matrix of coffee consumption and coffee-philic modes of being so that references to caffeine, listlessness, overexcitement, lethargy, and all manner of daily combat preparedness pinged his workstation, whereupon he dispatched a "Why don't you try our seasonal Jamaican blend next time you're in the 'hood?" or a "Sounds like you need a hearty cup of Iced Number Seven!" He rationed exclamation points, cursed them by lunch, fell in love with them anew.

The company software kept tabs on his clients, as they were called, so that if they mentioned a birthday celebration or meaningful life event months later, he transmitted a frothy "Many more!" and offered a gift card redeemable in the contiguous states. Or a "Sorry about the breakup—sounds like it wasn't going to work out anyway" and a gift card. It felt nice to send out a gift card, providing they sent him their info via secured connection. He was instructed to push the gift cards a certain number of times each day. They were a bit of a racket, when you added up the lost cards, the expirations, and the thirty cents left over here and there that was never used up.

His supervisor, strictly a tea man, and decaffeinated at that, encouraged him to cultivate an individual social-media persona. No cussing, no politics, use common sense, etc., the e-mail elaborated. He entered into artifice easily, it turned out, a natural at ersatz human connection and the postures of counterfeit empathy. He was helpful ("A sprinkle of cinnamon will add that special zing"), dispensed passive-aggressive admonishments ("Why go to our competitors when we're up at the crack of dawn trying to make you happy?"), and did not shrink from the anodyne ("Doesn't a nice cup of coffee make the world live again?"). Without that human touch, he was told, they might as well push that rudimentary artificial-intelligence algorithm the nerd-practitioners cooked up, which everyone knew was a bust even before the battery of focus groups weighed in. No soul.

Two months after he started, there was a five percent uptick in the corporate site's traffic. Whether this was due to Mark Spitz's impersonation of caring or the rollout of the new affiliate program was unclear, but he received a pretty nice e-mail from his supervisor's supervisor, the woman who had invented his job after some deep thinking at the annual retreat, along with a promise that his good work would be recognized come next quarterly review, which was actually going to be two quarters from now, as technically he was still a probationary hire.

It wasn't the worst job he'd ever had. He was working there when Last Night slammed down, scratching at his law-exam-prep notebooks at night in the rec room. The New York headquarters of the coffee company was in Chelsea, a mile and a half past the wall. He could only speculate about who had made it out and who still roamed the halls. His social-media persona probably continued to punch the clock, gossiping with the empty air and spell-checking faux-friendly compositions, hitting Send. "Nothing cures the Just Got Exsanguinated Blues like a foam mustache, IMHO." "Sucks that the funeral pyre is so early in the morning—why don't you grab a large Sumatra so you can stay awake when you toss your grandma in? Wouldn't want to sleep through that, LOL!"

By providence Mark Spitz glanced down Reade and spied the restaurant's distinctive signage two blocks ahead, instantly reassuring. He was halfway to Wonton. His stomach fluttered. In his head he heard the tumultuous community board meeting where the residents complained over the news of its opening: Not in my backyard, it'll ruin the neighborhood. Bistros and next-level gastro gizmos served Tribeca's preferred grub, not vulgar chain operations. No, Mark Spitz thought. This restaurant belonged everywhere. Living out of range of its concoctions was a tragedy. An easily avoidable tragedy, it turned out, given the many convenient locations.

He had time. He cut the bolt and rolled up the metal grate. Depending on the condition of the back exit, he was the first uninfected person inside since Last Night's grisly embrace. There were plenty other, easier places to loot. Scavengers stripped the supermarkets and groceries and bodegas first, then restaurants, but the science of higher-level foraging never achieved full flower in the city, given the skel concentration before the marines' arrival. The dead owned the island. Mark Spitz wasn't hankering for industrial-size cans of buffalo sauce and powdered potatoes, but they were back there in the freezers, doubtless, next to the rotted maple-apple sausage links and salmon patties that had been squeezed into shape and packaged in the silent factories.

He listened for the dead scraping into dumb activity at his noise: nothing. He trained his helmet light where daylight failed, scanning the brass railings circling the family-size banquets, the deep dark wood of the bar with its elbow-fretted layers of lacquer. He scanned the checkerboard tile for any creature untangling its limbs from sub-table roost. Red-and-white checks provided faithful trim on the menus and the signs and the staff uniforms as well, which were not in evidence at this moment, thank God, draping some limp-hoofed wreck bearing plates from the kitchen with a "May I take your order?" gape. The uniforms had made the waiters and waitresses into referees adjudicating obscure food-related competitions. It did get kinda rough on All-You-Can-Eat Shrimp Tuesdays. His father got into a scuffle once re: dibs on a final spoonful of Oriental Shrimp that wobbled in a bath of orange gelatin. The incident became a running joke in his house, called for duty whenever they geared up for a trip to the local franchise. "Feel like punching someone in the face today," his father said, launching into a stream of mock-trash talk, and Mark Spitz knew where they were eating that evening.

The restaurant was his family's place for the impulse visits and birthdays and random celebrations, season upon season. As a child he clambered into the booth and hid behind the gigantic menu until the first "Hello, my name is" from that evening's server, whereupon he tried to imagine what he or she looked like from their voice. The waiters had longer mustaches than he pictured, the waitresses larger breasts. Until he hit puberty anyway. In their orbits, replicas of gold and platinum records, momentous front pages, concert posters, and sports trophies tracked across the walls. He didn't recognize any of the celebrities, the historic occasions or bands or teams, the backstories of the big playoffs and names of the pop hits. But they had to mean something if they were up on the walls. Why else would they be there? He was crestfallen when he ate at another location for the first time and saw the same stuff on the walls. His introduction to the nostalgia industry. Memento factories overseas stamped out these artifacts utilizing cheap unregulated labor, his sitter explained later. She was a college junior and her eyes were open for the first time. The individual operators were free to choose their memorabilia, but the inventory sheets contained only so many boxes. Overlap was unavoidable; it was built into the mechanism. He'd taken the signed baseballs and mounted guitars as originals, strangely heartened that he ate in the establishment of a world traveler, a collector of curiosities who'd had adventures. The summer before he went off to college, he'd read in the paper how the local franchisee had been sent to jail for embezzling. A love nest, pics uploaded to an amateur porn site. The man's cousin took over and when Mark Spitz returned for winter break it was as if nothing had happened. The restaurant shambled on.

Classic rock had greeted them every time, scrabbling beneath the chatter of work deadlines nailed or ignored, unsettling confidences, the roundup on that afternoon's couples therapy, power tools. Newer artists occasionally muscled their way into the pantheon, along with risqué confections; closer to midnight the place achieved its full sour blossom as a pickup joint, and the array compressed at the bar required inspiration for their boasts and well-trod inducements. The cracked jukeboxes at the tables never worked, but he borrowed two quarters from his dad without fail. The sound of chinking metal was music enough. The place was the stage for cherished theater. Each visit his parents scrutinized the menu as if for the first time and Mark Spitz inquired if they had crayons, even though he knew they kept a whole army hospital ward of them, a whole drawer filled with bacteria-smeared, half-chewed nubs in mutilated cardboard holders. His mother always wondered aloud if they had any specials, when whatever misbegotten entrée corralled into the night's fare would surely recoil from such a designation. As he waited for his food, he'd drag a green fragment through the Kidz Circle place mat, connect the dots to de-atomize the zoo's menagerie animal by animal, undo the effects of the alien ray that had torn things apart. He ravaged the children's menu, cycling through the tenders and star-shaped recombined fish parts and syrupy seltzer concoctions, wolfing them down hideously. This was fine American fare.

Today, Mark Spitz snagged a menu from a station, his arm vibrating with pain from the previous day's assault. He had let them get a piece of him. Corporate had finally tampered with the lineup, adding a Mediterranean Festival Salad and a Lemongrass Chicken plate to the roster of cholesterol delivery systems that crowded the oversize dishes, glued in place by sauces thick and suspect. Calorie counts and government guidelines catcalled next to the selections, jeering at customers' waistlines. His father had often joked that when he had to meet his maker, he prayed for a quick heart attack in his sleep after one of their giant flame-broiled double cheeseburgers. His mother tut-tutted those statements, disapproving of this so-called humor. It wasn't a heart attack that got him.

He dragged his hand along the brass railing, roving. He had been here before and not been here before. That was the magic of the franchise. Small differences in layout aside, the mandated table-and-chair arrangements survived the Manhattan dimensions, the vermillion shades clasped the ceiling bulbs in old-timey elegance, sconces camouflaged as lanterns were nailed into the walls at prescribed intervals. He had been here in other lives that were now pushing into this one. He pressed his forehead against the glass and gazed down upon himself: a five-year-old lump of boy-matter; the slovenly tangle of him at sixteen; some vague creature attending his parents' thirtieth who pinched balloons when he thought no one was looking. He grew dizzy in his mesh. He felt like a little kid who'd split for the restroom and then forgot where his parents were sitting. Another family had replaced his own when he reached the table, no kin of his at all, they hailed from the badlands, sizing him up, suspicious and foreign. An elemental horror roiled in his skull and he swiveled his head, sweeping his light across the darkness and dust. Search as he might, this time he was not going to find them.

He was a ghost. A straggler.

The monster-movie speculations of his childhood had forced him, during many a dreary midnight, to wonder what sort of skel he'd make if the plague transformed his blood into poison. The standard-issue skel possessed no room for improvisation, of course. He'd hit his repugnant marks. But what kind of straggler would he make? What did he love, what place had been important to him? Job or home, bull's-eye of cathected energy. Yes, he loved his home. Perhaps he'd end up there, installing himself in his worn perch on the right-hand side of the sofa (right if you are facing the entertainment center, and where else would you be facing). Perhaps there.

He consulted the tattered ledger containing his employment history. He didn't see himself maundering around the cashier of that artisanal sandwich joint he worked in for two summers, that loser gig, or so emotionally imprinted on his time slinging coladas that he'd devote his existence to swabbing the bar with a gray rag until his body disintegrated into flakes. Or the American Phoenix mobilized past Zone One and the next zones and starting cleaning up the rest of the country, and some future sweeper on a future crew shot him in the head. If he got infected when alone, that is—the tacit death pact was the new next-round's-on-me. Put me down if I get bit. And he certainly wasn't going to troop up to Chelsea and pretend to type perky encomiums into the dead web. Maybe he'd come here.

One Sunday night early in his tour, he was sipping sponsored wine with Kaitlyn in the dumpling shop when the Lieutenant bounded through the door. Mark Spitz and Kaitlyn had ditched the gathering in the dim sum palace after a platoon recharging en route to Buffalo started in with the stale skel jokes endured a hundred times before. ("I told you to give me head, not eat my head.") Then the Connecticut gang, Gary included, tried to compete with the marines, enumerating baroque skel mutilations and beheadings, and it was time to go.

"This is my real office," the Lieutenant said. "Sanctum sanctorum." He waved them down when they rose. "But you may join me. I have wisdom, and I see you are seekers." Mark Spitz knew the Lieutenant was bombed come nightfall, smelled the sweetish, boozy wisping from his pores in the daytime, and now it was late in the evening. On this matter, Mark Spitz remained true to his policy of judge not the dysfunctions of others, lest ye be judged.

The Lieutenant weaseled into the booth next to Mark Spitz, across from Kaitlyn. "Irish wake," he said. The label on his whiskey was missing to hide the name of the unsponsored distillery, snotty yellow bands of glue levitating on the bottle.

Kaitlyn shivered and drew her arms to her chest.

The Lieutenant said, "Gooseflesh. The night breeze or the drifting rads?" He rubbed the corner of his mouth. "We secured our nuclear plants against mishap—secured the nuclear plants and Fort Knox and the bigwigs' bunkers—but not everyone did. Now we got all this misty meltdown stuff, flying over the Pacific. Like invisible snow."

"Or ash," Mark Spitz said.

"Or ash." The Lieutenant inquired about the Zone and they delivered upbeat reports about how unexpectedly easy the job was turning out to be. Pop this one here, that one there. Zip 'em up. Hardly any trouble at all. Kaitlyn told him they might finish ahead of Buffalo's projections. "I'm glad it's just stragglers," she said.

"We're all glad," the Lieutenant said. "Bless 'em. Imagine what the world would be if the plague made *them* ninety-nine percent of the skels, and not the other way around. That'd be some shit." Had they ever thought about that?

The sweepers admitted they hadn't. The Lieutenant grabbed two water glasses and filled them with whiskey, tinking them against the wineglasses. "Mix and match," he said. He hunched over the table. "Help me out, picture ninety-nine percent straggler. Never mind how everyone'd get bit—let's say it was airborne instead. What would we do with them? All these skels standing around. Can't cure them. Bring 'em home into 'familiar surroundings' and they'd probably just get up and walk back to where you found them. You leave them there, it seems to me. Wherever they chose. Let them sit in the cubicles, let them ride the bus all day and night and in the depot after hours. Chillin' on the beach catching some rays. They don't know what's going on—they probably think it's business as usual. Going about their day like they always did."

"That's sick," Kaitlyn said, crossing her arms. "You're sick." Kaitlyn invariably described her parents in the past tense, resisting the scenario where they walked slowly through her hometown, muddle-minded and peckish. Mark Spitz figured she imagined Mom and Dad at the backyard gas grill, frozen and damned on the slate patio.

Frenetic honks came from the street: the driver of a jeep warning Sunday-night drunks out of the way. The Lieutenant leaned back into the vinyl banquette with his customary sluggishness. "No, you're right. Mustn't humanize them. The whole thing breaks down unless you are fundamentally sure that they are not you. I do not resemble that animal, you tell yourself, as you squat in the back of the convenience store, pissing in a bucket and cooking up mangy squirrel for dinner." The Lieutenant took a loud slurp. Mark Spitz couldn't tell if the man was belittling Kaitlyn or his own trodden illusions. "You're still the person you were before the plague, you tell yourself, even though you're running for dear life through the parking lot of some shitty mall, being chased by a gang of monsters. I have not been reduced. 'Hey, maybe this dead guy has some stuff in his shopping cart I can eat.' "

Kaitlyn moved her mouth and then checked herself. She had dealt with deadbeat teachers before and prevailed. "If the plague transmits through the air," she said, "you wouldn't keep them around."

"This is an abstract thought process."

Mark Spitz said, "After a while we wouldn't even notice them."

The Lieutenant worked up a mealy grimace. "That's why I like stragglers. They know what they're doing. Verve and a sense of purpose. What do we have? Fear and danger. The memories of all the ones you've lost. The regular skels, they're all messed up. But your straggler, your straggler doesn't have any of that. It's always inhabiting its perfect moment. They've found it—where they belong." He stopped. "Mark Spitz, I see you've taken to the whiskey. It's nice, right?"

They finished the bottle. The next week, the three of them wandered in one by one and it became a Sunday-night custom.

In the restaurant months later, after more contact with the creatures, grid after tedious grid, he wondered if they chose these places or if the places chose them. No telling the visions wrought by the crossed wires in their brains, that bad electricity traipsing through their blighted synapses. He thought of that first straggler, standing in the disappearing field with his stupid kite. The easy narrative held that he played there as a kid, gazing up at the sky, oblivious to the things that made him stumble. Maybe it wasn't what had happened in a specific place—favorite room or stretch of beach or green and weedy pasture—but the association permanently fixed to that place. That's where I decided to ask her to marry me, in this elevator, and now I exist in that moment of possibility again. The guy had only spent a minute in that space but it had altered his life irrevocably. So he haunts it. This is the hotel room where our daughter was conceived and being in here now it is like she is with me again. It wasn't the hotel room itself that was important, with its blotched carpet and missing room-service menu and pilfered corkscrew, but the outcome nine months later. The straggler was in thrall to Room 1410, not the long nights in the nursery making sure those diminutive lungs continued to rise and fall, or the sun-kissed infinity pool of the resort where they spent their best four days/three nights, the steps at stage left where they hugged after the school play. So she haunts it, Room 1410. Relieved of care and worry, the stragglers lived eternally and undying in their personal heavens. Where the goblin world and its assaults were banished and there was nothing but possibility.

He stripped off his poncho and dropped his pack. He laid his weapon on the bar and walked to the wall. He'd forgotten the homilies in silver frames scattered among the paraphernalia. "Love to one, friendship to many, and good will to all." "Every guest leaves happy." "To the good old days, which we are having right now." Text-size affirmations. The antecedents of his coffee-company dispatches, as communication caught up with the tried-and-true commonplaces and the benighted adopted the ways of the old sages. Keep it brief and keep on message, please. Use the symbols. It's how we speak to each other these days.

He missed the stupid stuff everyone missed, the wifi and the workhorse chromium toasters, mass transportation and gratis transfers, rubbing cheese-puff dust on his trousers and calculating which checkout line was shortest, he missed the things unconjurable in reconstruction. That which will escape. His people. His family and friends and twinkly-eyed lunchtime counterfolk. The dead. He missed the extinct. The unfit had been wiped out, how else to put it, and now all that remained were ruined like him. He missed the women he'd never get to sleep with. On the other side of the room, tantalizing at the next table, that miracle passing by the taqueria window giving serious wake. They wore too much makeup or projected complex emotions onto small animals, smiled exactly so, took his side when no one else would, listened when no one else cared to. They were old money or fretted over ludicrously improbable economic disasters, teetotaled or drank like sailors, pecked like baby birds at his lips or ate him up greedily. They carried slim vocabularies or stooped to conquer in the wordsmith board games he never got the hang of. They were all gone, these faceless unknowables his life's curator had been saving for just the right moment, to impart a lesson he'd probably never learn. He missed pussies that were raring to go when he slipped a hand beneath the elastic rim of the night-out underwear and he missed tentative but coaxable recesses, stubbled armpits and whorled ankle coins, birthmarks on the ass shaped like Ohio, said resemblance he had to be informed of because he didn't know what Ohio looked like. The sighs. They were sweet-eyed or sad-eyed or so successful in commanding their inner turbulence so that he could not see the shadows. Flaking toenail polish and the passing remark about the scent of a nouveau cream that initiated a monologue about its provenance, special ingredients, magic powers, and dominance over all the other creams. The alien dent impressed by a freshly removed bra strap, a garment fancy or not fancy but unleashing big or small breasts either way. He liked big breasts and he liked small breasts; small breasts were just another way of doing breasts. Brains a plus but negotiable. Especially at 3:00 a.m., downtown. A fine fur tracing an earlobe, moles in exactly the right spot, imperfections in their divine coordination. He missed the dead he'd never lose himself in, be surprised by, disappointed in.

He missed shame and guilt and a time when something higher than dumb instinct directed his actions.

He dropped two quarters into the nearest tabletop jukebox. He didn't have two quarters but that was okay. The jukebox started up without complaint and he listened to the concert of secret levers shifting the 45 into its berth above the dust. The lights in the machine blinked on sprightly, the ones in the corner sconce by the bathrooms, over the bar, in the booths one by one, and then all the lights vocalized.

His machine trembled to life. The speakers picked up the song in the third verse, blaring at the preferred deafening setting marked by a notch of tape. A quarter of the occupants proceeded to hum and bop their heads; it had been a powerhouse single twelve summers ago. No room at the bar. The regulars at their posts groused about when management was going to fix the wobbly stool, they'd been suffering for weeks. The bartender's girlfriend tried to get his attention but he practiced his trade's skill of selective vision, which he employed all too often when he was not behind the bar. Then he saw her and grinned. It was their anniversary. Three months. Smeared plates marched up the busboy's arm; he pretended to drop one, joshing with the elderly couple grabbing a bite before bridge. Same day every week, same dishes, same lousy tip. In the corner, the rambunctious party of eight started in with "Happy Birthday" and customers in the vicinity were shamed into joining in or at least mouthing the words. The hostess directed the termite specialists to a two-top underneath the high-def and they asked for another table. The game was on in half an hour and they hated the pregame announcer so ferociously that they'd been looking forward to heckling him all day. The hostess's new diet was doing the trick for a change, everyone kept telling her so and it seemed like they really meant it. Indeed her uniform was too big. Fortunately she still had her old one somewhere, or had she thrown it out? Then another table cooked up a drunken "Happy Birthday," even though no one in their party was having a birthday, for they were under the mistaken impression that it earned them a free round. They confused this chain for that other chain. The new waitress bore the tepid meat loaf back into the kitchen. Every week her apologies would diminish in sincerity.

His parents were right where he left them, his dad unbuckling his belt one notch and his mom grinning, eyes bright at the sight of him, sipping from the oversize green straw in her banana daiquiri. The red vinyl was still warm. It was their night out.

. . .

"Want a lift?"

Now the world was muck. But systems die hard—they outlive their creators and unlike plagues do not require individual hosts—and thus it was a well-organized muck with a hierarchy, accountability, and, increasingly, paperwork. Bozeman's appointment in the current order was as Wonton's top military clerk, principal caretaker of the camp's holistic integrity in all aspects. Every night, Bozeman held the garrison over his shoulder and burped it, cooing work-order lullabies. He knew the secret contents of the parcels in the bellies of the choppers crisscrossing the seaboard, he ensured that designated calibers reached the waiting chambers, he slept nights with the key to the fridge that held the brass's grass-fed porterhouse on a chain around his puffy neck. Mark Spitz was surprised to see their steward at the wheel of the jeep, as the man rarely strayed from the second-floor offices of the bank. Surely the farther he strayed from ground zero, the more he shriveled.

In the passenger seat, a civilian wrapped in a black pencil skirt and white blouse sized up Mark Spitz over the rim of her blue-tinted sunglasses. She was a meteor crashed from another part of the solar system, or a place even more remote, life before the agony, strutting from a magazine catering to the contemporary professional woman. The cover lines were scrubbed of compatibility tests and dispatches from the frontiers of How to Please Your Man research, and teased instead testimonials to self-sufficiency, the virtues of a contained existence, the holy grail of complete actualization. She threatened a fly with a glossy white folder and smiled at Mark Spitz, the first bona fide citizen he'd seen since the Zone. "Plenty of room," she said. It was, in addition, the first time he'd seen someone wearing pearls since he started running.

Mark Spitz did as he was told. Bozeman informed him they were headed to HQ after a brief pit stop on West Broadway. "This is Ms. Macy," he said. "She's here from Buffalo doing some recon." Bozeman put a bit of spin on this last word, what Mark Spitz would have called ironic if the world hadn't rendered such a thing into scarcity. Irony was an ore buried too deep in the crust and the machine did not exist on Earth that was capable of reaching it. The clerk kept his eyes on the road, swerving around mammoth scorched patches of asphalt where the marines roasted dead skels before Disposal's implementation. The black spots of buckled tar were no threat to the vehicle. Mark Spitz chalked it up to superstition.

They jetted past a row of upscale clothing stores, the final displays and markdowns pouting in the jaundiced light. Ms. Macy said "Oh!" and then "Never mind" as she realized that her current escorts would not be simpatico with an impromptu raid. Mark Spitz smiled. It was like being on a long road trip, moving through the city, whether on foot or in a car, with Kaitlyn and Gary or anyone else. Your fancy dangled coyly through a shopwindow and the old consumer electrons agitated with purpose. Then you squashed the impulse at the reality that you were not stopping, it was too late to stop, there were other passengers besides you and your whim. The moment disappeared. You'd be disappointed anyway. The store at the side of the road was not so eccentric now that you got a good look at it, that authentic mom-and-pop fare curdled on the tines, and the oldest roller coaster in the state closed down years before and the rat-poison warnings prevented even a quick look-see of the dilapidated premises. Like all mirages, they evaporated up close.

Anti-looting regs kept the world-renowned shopping of New York City off-limits, but he suspected Ms. Macy had enough pull to arrange an after-hours spree, for a price. Four juice boxes.

She turned to Mark Spitz. "Let me take this opportunity to thank you on behalf of Buffalo for all the great work you men and women are doing," she said. She tucked a sprig of hair behind her ear. "You have a lot of supporters up there."

"Thanks."

The jeep shot left and Ms. Macy clutched her seat, perfect nails pinioning the cushion. He'd call the nail polish light blue but a more fanciful appellation no doubt decorated the bottle. "It's not often I'm out in the trenches," she said. "Mostly we sit around our little conference table with our sad little plant and our wipe board and come up with our grand plans. But that's changing." Grit infiltrated her eyes and she twisted around to massage them in the cracked mirror of her compact, tilting it to find a workable angle.

Bozeman pulled up in front of a boutique hotel, caressing the curb as he parked. The army had cleared the cars from this side of the street since the last time Mark Spitz was here. The dark metal sheeting of the façade was artificially stressed, striated and pocked with calculated imperfection that in this depleted era implied foresightedness. Surely this was the forward-looking architecture they had all been waiting for. Mark Spitz recognized the humble inn from its regular invocations by the extinct gossip pages. It was home to premiere parties of dud movies and the desperate pell-mell drug binges of celebrities and rich children who had never been hugged properly. Ms. Macy and her escort stepped to the sidewalk, the young woman scampering ahead for the glass awning that kept the rain at bay with bone-white glass and stainless-steel ribbing. "Why don't you come with," Ms. Macy said, bowing to see Mark Spitz's face. "I could use your expertise."

He didn't know what she meant, as his only expertise was his cockroach impersonation, the infinite resilience of said critter he had down cold. A continuous grumble of gunfire from the wall uptown murdered the silence. They walked over the sparkling cubes of glass that had once been the front doors, Ms. Macy tentative in her pumps and frowning and making clucking sounds. Bozeman tracked ahead to scout the first-floor lounge, that dim sac nestled into Reception like a tumor. Mark Spitz made a quick survey of the hallway feeding into the restrooms and hidden employee preserves. He sensed the three of them were alone but beat it back to the lobby just in case. The place was clear of skels, but it wouldn't make anyone happy if he were wrong and one of Buffalo's own got her face eaten, in such beautiful shoes.

Ms. Macy paced the cold tile, slow and pensive. He liked the sound of her heels on the floor. They echoed with enticing glamour, like the growling of a promising party behind the door at the end of the hall. She said, "Five blocks." It was five blocks to the wall, he calculated, and twenty-plus floors above before they ran out of rooms. She was looking for housing.

Bozeman emerged from the lounge and shrugged when Mark Spitz looked at him for an explanation.

"I thought you said the doors were fixed," Ms. Macy said. "We don't want squirrels and rats and God knows what else moving in here."

"We're working on finding a proper glazier, ma'am," Bozeman said.

"Glazier?"

"Window-makers, dealers in glass. So far the only ones we've turned up are in the far camps. They're really cracking down on nonessential air travel lately, what with the operation gearing up."

She shook her head. "Don't get caught up in the deprivation game. That's the old days." She appeared vexed, and dumbfounded as to the source of her vexation. Then she looked up at the ceiling, where a crude map of old Dutch New York unscrolled in slapdash yellow strokes. The amateur nature of the rendering was intentional, to ameliorate the bloodless deliberation on display everywhere else. Her shoulders sank. "How are the rooms?"

"Fine. Apart from what's in the folder." He added, "As far as I know. I wasn't here during the inspection. But they're very good at their jobs."

"In Buffalo all we have to go on is what you tell us."

"Evacuated in the first wave. Whole place locked up." He paused. Locked up except for the front doors. "But we can go upstairs and conduct a personal inspection if you like."

"With the elevators out?" She made some notes. "Those will have to go," she said, pointing to the wall art. Two monstrous canvases hulked above the black leather couches, depicting the metropolis at night from a vulture's vantage. In the first, fires burned at intersections, faint but unsettling in their even dispersal through the grid, while the companion piece maintained the angle but captured the rapacious fires gnawing their way up the buildings, the inhabitants curled over windowsills watching the progress of the flames. The hungry catastrophe, creeping apace. Wall art.

"They are a bit gloomy," Mark Spitz said. He wasn't sure if he was supposed to speak, if he was employing his expertise, but he wanted to let Bozeman off the hook. During their first weeks in the Zone, the sweepers hit the grids without the new mesh fatigues. An indispensable bit of gear, to say the least, but the sweepers were not at the top of the list. When the shipment was finally en route, Bozeman tipped Mark Spitz and he was first in line at distribution. "You're a Long Island boy," he explained later, "like me."

"The thing about these boutique hotels is that you can be anywhere in the world," Ms. Macy said. "They really had it down before the plague—the international language of hospitality."

"Ever been to Barcelona?" Bozeman asked. "They stay up all night."

"I'm thinking kids," Ms. Macy said. She slashed a red marker across her mental wipe board: Let's put our heads together, team. "Pictures of pheenie kids in the camps, cavorting and pitching in. Pressing seeds into the soil and sharpening machetes. No machetes—kid stuff. Smiling and laughing and doing kid stuff. They're the future, after all. That's what this whole thing is about, the future."

The future required many things, but it had not occurred to Mark Spitz that it needed interior decorating. Yes, kids would really tie the room together. He hadn't been aware that he missed the sleek argot of the urban professional class. It was like a favorite sweater pulled out at the first autumn chill, tested and reassuring and cozy. The future was what formerly had been called a transitional neighborhood. Essential services in short supply, the poodle-grooming salons and scruffy cafés, but if you got in at the right time it didn't matter that the building next door was writhing with skels. Eventually they'll be displaced three subway stops away by rising rents and you'll never see them again. The boîtes are coming, be patient, my pet. "Why are you here, Ms. Macy?" Mark Spitz asked.

The visitor deliberated. "I'm not supposed to say anything yet," she said, "but you guys are safe. We've been lobbying for it, and we just got word last week that Manhattan is going to be the site of the next summit. Great news, right?"

Mark Spitz and Bozeman marshaled an appropriate response.

"New York City is the greatest city in the world. Imagine what all those heads of state and ambassadors will feel when they see what we've accomplished. You've accomplished. We brought this place back from the dead. The symbolism alone. If we can do that, we can do anything."

"We might even be in Zone Two at that point, if we stay on schedule," Bozeman said, taking the advantage.

"This is America."

"Shoot."

"I know," she said. She had a halo, trick lighting. "Isn't it great?" She ran her fingers along the top of the reception desk, fiddling the dust between her fingers. "An oasis, as soon as they set foot in the Zone. I can sign off on this place, I think. They'll enjoy their stay. As they used to say."

They returned to the jeep. Ms. Macy walked backward, pinning the details into her mind's scrapbook. "Rip up the carpet and put in something red," she ordered her invisible assistant. "Some kids losing their baby teeth, grinning and doing what they do." She slapped the pages of her notebook until she found a fresh page. "First thing at Wonton I'm going to get on the comm and have them send a photographer to Happy Acres and Rainbow Village to snag some head shots. There must be some good kids somewhere."

On the short ride uptown the Zone stirred around Mark Spitz. After two blocks, a soldier bent to tie her sneakers, black goggles following the civilian as the jeep purred by. After three blocks a pair of soldiers humped a leather club chair down the sidewalk toward a hideout they'd scoped, like sophomores beguiled by a vision of the coolest dorm room. After four blocks they were firmly in Wonton's domain, painlessly assimilated into the combine. Mark Spitz remembered his first ride in a military transport, the armored behemoth that retrieved him from the great out there. When he clambered out of the hatch and blinked at the perimeter lights and sentry nests, order in its accumulated manifestations, he knew he had been cast in a new production. This was no jerry-rigged fortification of depleted wanderers, bolted together by blood and self-delusion, this was government. This was reconstruction. The end in abeyance.

. . .

His final night in the wastes transpired on the outskirts of Northampton, Massachusetts, neighbor to loathsome Connecticut but an entirely different beast. For weeks, Mark Spitz had avoided all but the smallest towns, as he'd come to perceive, correctly or incorrectly, that lately the dead gravitated to the former population centers. Or were repopulating the former population centers, to look at it another way. That's where the complications awaited, time after time. For so many months there had existed an equivalency of peril between rural areas and cities. Now, out in the countryside, the density was lower. Few sightings, few attacks, fewer withdrawals from his reservoir of last-minute escapes. No one he hooked up with seconded his observations, but he was unswayed. They were clotting together, the dead; he spied idiot cliques or duos rather than singletons, and they stuck to the roads and man-made routes feeding into towns. When he came upon the Northampton farmhouse, he was convinced of his new travel method, circling around anything on his latest map that resembled a town as he tracked north. His theory was no more worthless than those offered by other survivors.

The farmhouse was prim and elegant, sticking up out of the overgrown lawn and companion acres, jutting from the industrious wildflowers and grasses like an iceberg. It was getting dark and he needed to bunk down, either inside or out atop the porch, depending on how he felt once he cased the property. He was feeling devil-may-care today, the weather was nice and he hadn't tired of the constellations. Halfway to the front door and two feet above the ground, cans and rusting metal strips twisted on a wire that snaked around wooden stakes, encircling the house. A line of magic powder that kept out evil spirits. The alarm system was intact. Planks from a disassembled shed or other outdoor construction, weather-beaten on one side and unblemished on the other, lay fast and even across both floors' windows, so evenly that if they had been painted white he'd have taken it for an aesthetic choice. No light emerged from the cracks in the boards, the blacked-out windows allowing those inside to move around at night.

This was not a refuge assembled in haste but a sedulously executed bunker. Its architects intended to outlast the disaster here. Mark Spitz saw no indication that the castle had failed, the tangle of boards before the broken window where the hordes exploited a chink. The front door was secure and not splayed in the universal sign of harried evacuation. Soon it would be dark. Mark Spitz jerked the wire twice and slowly made his way up the front steps to the wraparound porch, hands up at his shoulders.

He called out. They'd had time to assess him from their spy hole, which he hadn't sniffed out yet. Good for them. He knocked. He backed away, chose the side of the house without the porch, and prowled to the back. It was only polite to give them more time to deliberate. For later reference, he noted the location and number of the windows on both floors, and the drop to the ground. A gravel path curved toward a small barn out back and as he approached the structure, he waved back at the boarded windows, as innocent a gesture as he could manage. The barn's windows were unfortified. It had been converted into a smart office, the walls a multicolored stream of book spines, with a small kitchenette and probably a bathroom behind the one door. Crimson-bound library books and squared piles of notes covered the antique desk in the middle of the room. Dead flowers slumped out of a turquoise vase on a wooden stand bearing an open volume of the *OED*. He was staring at a diorama. Maybe they'd let him spend the night in the studio unmolested and he'd be on his way in the morning. The sofa looked perfect.

The wild grasses behind the studio rasped a warning. The tree line shook out two skels moving in tandem, matching each other's laborious steps. The tallest one had been male, its stained overalls hanging from still-muscular shoulders. A recent inductee to the horrors. Its companion was of an earlier vintage, old school and Last Night from the extent of the winnowing, shuddering forth in a canary-yellow apron bearing the slogan "Hot Pot o' Love" in puffy red letters. From the residue on the apron, tonight's recent menu was home-made strawberry jam, or something decidedly less wholesome. The skels waded through the thistles in eerie synchronization. It was a trick of perspective, but he squinted nonetheless at this new wonder of parallel skellery.

Mark Spitz drew his pistol—he was in a pistol phase, despite the ammo hassle. The back door of the farmhouse creaked. A woman dashed toward him, brandishing an ax, clad in the leather padded suiting favored by motocross racers, bent low like a defensive lineman. The helmet covering her face prevented a read of her disposition. Another figure crouched in the kitchen doorway with a shotgun. The barrels glared at him. Mark Spitz called out softly: yes, my brain works, synapses still firing in all the important ways we've come to cherish. As the lady with the ax hurtled past him, tramping through goldenrod, she said, "Don't shoot, dummy." She reached the skels and decapitated them with two swift chops as they slowly raised their arms. Their bodies swayed, dark liquid burbling from tubes in their necks, then collapsed into a clump of foxtail at the same time.

"Get inside," she said. "You've been out here too long already."

He hadn't gazed upon a kitchen that immaculate and decked out with appliances since the afternoon he'd tumbled into the quicksand of a marathon of that cooking show his mother used to like. Devices for pulping, fizzing, julienning, and caffeinating gleamed on the counters, making a case for themselves despite their incongruity with the dark pine floors and weathered cabinetry. Rusty cooking implements hung from the joists in manicured decay. A tidy galley was one of the first things to go in a hideout, for obvious reasons. But the three residents maintained a heroic level of cleanliness. "The place was so nice when we found it," Margie explained later, "seemed a shame to wreck it."

Mark Spitz remained a guest long enough to get the recent history of the property. The absent owners had moved out here to flee the city, advance guard of a wave of upper-middle-class pioneers boldly striking out for the hinterlands in wagons of reclaimed wood covered in eco-friendly bamboo fiber. A photograph in the front hall captured the farmhouse in the flaking throes of neglect; in their renovations the newcomers had devoted countless hours and no small measure of love to the hulk, every inch of modern insulation and plumbing a prayer. The studio out back belonged to the professor. She taught literary theory at one of the local colleges, after making her mark with an evidently groundbreaking collection of essays about "The Body." (Each attempt at the introduction gave Mark Spitz an ice-cream headache.) Her partner worked in steel. A line of pictures adorned the wall along the stairs, confirming that her own workspace was elsewhere. An airplane hangar would not have fit on the property, and there were probably zoning issues.

Jerry, the man wielding the shotgun, had sold them the house. He was a tall, ruddy-faced man with a county-sheriff scowl, his buzz cut glowing an unnatural orange from salvaged dye. Mark Spitz would have taken him for the leader of the group, had the others paid his protestations any mind. Jerry was the most antagonistic to granting Mark Spitz sanctuary for the night, let alone five minutes. "He led them here," he said, eyeing their visitor's pack. "Haven't been any around for ten days."

"I told you to let him in the second we spotted him," Margie said. Underneath the helmet, hers was a minuscule, almost pixie face, although the livid gash stretching from her tiny earlobes to her jaw belied the sylvan cast to her features. She pulled a cylinder of antibacterial wipes from the cupboard beneath the sink and wiped the ax blade. "Leave him out there to poke around and he's a dinner bell," she said. "You can see he's harmless." She looked at Mark Spitz. "No offense."

"I haven't seen a skel since the airport," Mark Spitz said, referring to the commuter airport south. He'd dared a raid on the vending machines and loaded up on power bars before being forced to make a break for it. The dead were a risible sight on the geometry of the runway, taxiing this way and that with their scrambled guidance systems.

"Dag," Tad said. "Ten days—that was a new record." The final member of their group, Tad, was a slender young man who wore a faded green T-shirt that portrayed the zodiac in silver glitz. He sat at the barn-wood table in the middle of the kitchen when Mark Spitz came inside, assault rifle flat across his knobby knees. Backup in case the other two ran into trouble. His spectacles were thin wire frames held together by fraying black tape. He was Mark Spitz's age, but his long ponytail was completely gray, which Mark Spitz took as a recent development.

Jerry lost the argument for expulsion quickly. The man's objections seemed a performance for Mark Spitz's benefit, to show him this wasn't as slapdash an operation as it appeared. Mark Spitz promised to move on at first light and contributed his canned clams as an appetizer to that night's repast of venison curry and mushrooms. He hated the tinny taste of canned clams but had carried them in his pack for three months for a day such as this, when he met an aficionado. Jerry was his man. In turn, Mark Spitz was grateful for the variation on deer, after the numbing rotation of venison stew, venison kebabs, and venison jerky he'd endured in the previous months. He'd met folks who carried around their favorite hot sauce in their pack, sure, drizzling it onto a rabbit drumstick or unidentifiable fowl, but few wanderers had the luxury or inclination to grind their own spice blends, and Mark Spitz appreciated this gustatory verve.

"Do you have any food allergies?" Tad asked.

"No."

"I've been trying to perfect my peanut curry."

They ate at the dining-room table, candlelight bestowing dramatic shadows to their movements as they forked morsels out of bowls decorated with pale green triangles, which looked to have been purchased at a neighbor's yard sale for the nostalgia they invoked for visits at grandma's house. It was still light outside, but behind the occluded windows it was always midnight. The house had probably been a no-shoes preserve before the catastrophe and now that edict kept the noise to the necessary minimum, and the dead walking on by.

He gave them the Anecdote and he listened to their stories in turn. Last Night swooped down on Margie as she visited a small island off Cape Cod, where she remained for the entire first year of the ruination. She'd been a houseguest at the beach compound of a college friend, bodysurfing and munching on clam rolls, and if she hadn't decided to leave Monday morning instead of Sunday afternoon as planned, she might not have made it through. There were five houses on the island; two were unoccupied that weekend and one family decided to brave it to one of the shelters announced on the radio, in those early days of frantic transmissions and haven roll calls. They never returned. That left ten people on the tiny lump of sand, and they struggled and fretted together. They rowed to the mainland for foraging excursions in their little dinghy but mostly stuck to their island dunes, fishing and waiting for news. Bandits razed the community, creeping ashore one day in their ruinous morality. They raped, they pillaged, sparing nothing, not even the lobster traps, which they dragged ashore with glee. Margie was the only one to escape—she had ever prided herself on her swimming—and her placid stay left her ill-prepared for life in the wasteland.

"I caught up," she said. They were playing hearts in the parlor. Mark Spitz didn't know if her memories or her cards were responsible for her rueful expression. She tried to hoof it back to Vermont, where she worked for an outfit that sold artisanal pickles—"We were really huge at all the big farmers' markets"—but never made it out of the state. She hooked up with Tad in a high-school cafeteria, and together they returned to the farmhouse, lugging big plastic bags of powdered eggs. Tad was born the same year as Mark Spitz, but unlike Mark Spitz he'd found his vocation before the upheaval, scripting interstitial narrative sequences for a video-game company that specialized in first-person shooters. In between levels, Tad's cutscenes on how the aliens came to be split into two adversarial species, or the magic amulet was lost in the volcano, allowed the players to rest their thumbs. A respite in their quest through the carnage.

Tad had attended college in town on the six-year plan, and returned after steady promotions at the game company, e-mailing his scripts from the group house he shared with his old buddies. He made a breathtaking wage compared to his peers, who wafted through the local service industries, pressing veggie sandwiches for coeds and hollowed-eyed dissertation jockeys, or selling gently used Adirondack chairs and a previous generation's musty ball gowns and leisure suits to weekenders and summer people. Tad designed the house's barricades, after he "just fell in love with the place." The walk to the creek was a relatively secure jog with nice sight lines, and after he lucked out in a round of raids on the neighboring premises, he gathered a hearty store of rations. Before he found this place he was holed up on a marijuana farm with fellows of like-minded spiritual outlook. He wouldn't talk about how that particular situation fell apart.

Tad fancied himself a hearts guru, not without cause. He shot the moon with irritating frequency that night as Mark Spitz maintained his standard B-grade execution, consistently in second or third place. As Tad tallied the last game of the night, stifling a grin, he told their visitor how when Jerry showed up at the door with fresh meat, he was immediately invited to stay after the pro forma examination. Jerry hooked up with the Massachusetts National Guard when the plague rolled in, touting his extensive knowledge of the area—"I've been helping people find their dream homes in Hampshire County for fifteen years, damn it"—and his two tours of duty in one of the Middle East wars. The local search-and-destroy posse outlasted many in the country, a whole three weeks, although by the final day, Jerry had to admit, it was only him and a former greeter at one of the local big-box stores, a man who suffered from senile dementia and kept pestering Jerry about their trip to the zoo. After the man died in his sleep, Jerry hunted solo, scraping by until he joined a caravan of six RVs headed to Canada. "The intel seemed good on that one," he said, still disappointed. They had become a backward people, stunted and medieval: the world is flat, the Sun revolves around the Earth, everything is better in Canada. The travelers made it to Niagara Falls before things disintegrated in their predicable course, "over a woman of all things." He returned to his hometown after spending the winter in Buffalo, only two miles from the fledgling HQ of reconstruction, although no one in the house knew this.

The trio was staying. Until the skels died off for real or were exterminated by a revivified government and galvanized citizenry sick of living in caves and eating ramen. "This is a war we can win," Jerry said. The hunting was good, the water supply accessible, and their complementary talents and temperaments made for a convivial household, as such things go. "It's nice to have a fourth for hearts," Jerry admitted after the final game that evening, and Margie seconded. Mark Spitz stretched out on the parlor sofa and slept with his pistol under a frilly white pillow. He dreamed of Mim.

He asked, but no one knew what had happened to the owners.

He woke up in the middle of the night. Each night, before he went to sleep, he repeated to himself his current location, to ward off the morning vertigo, the disorientation that affirmed his utter unmooring from all things. He had murmured to himself: the projection booth of the discount theater that showed indie films, an elm tree off the overpass. A farmhouse in New England. He had no confusion over his whereabouts when he woke, and he listened for the thing that had punctured his rest. It called again: metal on metal. Tad appeared on the landing, the candle's light on his white pajamas making him into a ghost.

"Too dark to see what it is," Tad said. They waited. The alarm tinkled anew, then was silenced. "That's the wire breaking. Raccoons will do that," he said. "Sometimes."

"You're not going anywhere," Margie told him the next morning. She placed a cup of chamomile tea on the coffee table. "Not until they wander off." Peel-away spy-hole slits were set into the tar-papered windows. This morning each window confirmed that the dead infiltrated the yard on all sides, ten or so having wandered onto the grounds in their misbegotten mission. A hard-luck ballerina and a kid with a green Mohawk roved in figure eights. They remained, not drifting away like dandelion seeds as they should have but tarrying on the property.

As the hours passed, the residents worked over the problem. Mark Spitz hadn't drawn them because the dead appeared hours later. And they hadn't given any indication to the skels that there might be dinner inside; they were sure of their precautions. "We're goddamned ninjas in here." They whispered, they padded in socks, they startled at the slightest noise, a kitchen drawer too hastily shut or unexpectedly brisant flatulence. Nonetheless, the creatures didn't slink away in their infamous habit, and by lunch twice as many roamed the weeds. Margie wished she'd made a water run the day before, the first of their band to vocalize the fear they might be besieged for an unknowable length of time.

By dinner there were fifty. Mark Spitz was confounded: They lingered over an empty plate. Happened all the time that a skel might seem to sense someone quivering behind a door, inside the cellar or guest bedroom, but if you kept still, you waited them out. None of them had witnessed this before, a convocation this inexorable and unlikely, given the absence of aural or visual stimuli to attract or keep the skels interested. Insofar as their febrile brains could be said to be interested in anything. Mark Spitz and his hosts played hearts until late and prayed the gruesome assembly would adjourn by morning. Tad, preoccupied, did not repeat the previous night's championship.

The next two days the dead roamed the drizzle in gloomy addition. The creatures displayed no curiosity about the house. They didn't dig their blackened fingers between the planks to wrench the barricade, tug the gutters, collect around the doors, or scrabble at the walls. If it had been accursed Connecticut, the place would be a pile of timber by now, naked chimney poking up like a bone. Mark Spitz recalled an animation in high-school physics, where the red molecules inside a balloon recoiled from the skin in random vectors, ever in motion, ever directionless, ever bound. Why did this motley remain in the skin of the property line, and why did more of them keep coming? They counted a hundred by next night's supper, the same ones from the first morning—a priest oozing from every visible orifice, a paunchy woman dressed for the gym, the cop—and their silently recruited companions.

"Maybe they're locavores," Tad said.

"They blew in, they'll blow out," Jerry said. He was bent over the mail slot, under a black hood. The monsters were a kind of weather after all; Mark Spitz noticed that they'd started being described as such, among wanderers who had never met, in spontaneous linguistic consensus. They could have terminated the first ones, but now there were too many. All they could do was wait. Mark Spitz reconstructed the grounds and local topography in his mind, a disembodied presence gyring over Hampshire County. If the dead started ripping the house apart: Jump out one of the back windows and head for the creek, or break for the road? Solo, what he knew best, or take one of the others with him? He hadn't the opportunity that first evening to stash one of Mim's emergency packs. No one side of the house offered better escape prospects than another. The dead diffused evenly in the flowers and drab grasses, just another species of weed carried in by the wind.

"I wish they'd hurry up and take their heads off, already," Tad said. The *they* in question were whatever new authorities emerged out of the darkness with guns and slogans and fresh vegetables. At Tad's sentiment, Mark Spitz's hosts began to air their post-plague plans and schemes. This was a rare pastime, at least in his vicinity, not easily indulged in, and Mark Spitz was surprised to hear perfectly (relatively) sane people partake. More than a jinx on deliverance, this was straddling reality with a pillow while it was sleeping and pressing down while it bucked and kicked. Especially with the invaders out in the yard, waiting for an invitation. From the nodding and encouraging affirmations, it was a regular diversion of theirs, like hearts. He told himself: Hope is a gateway drug, don't do it.

Tad was working on a new video game. He had it all mapped out. One level would take place in a fortified farmhouse in the middle of the country, then it switches to towns, cities, each step more complicated and deadly than the last. "It'll move a million copies," he said. "Those old World War II games still sell. Vietnam, realistic Middle East shooters. It's catharsis. Whether you were on the front lines or at home. And here we're all on the front lines at home. If you did what we're doing, it's therapy. How are you going to kill the nightmares when this is all over? It's a healthy outlet for aggression. And the babies who aren't even born yet—it'll teach them about what Mommy did in the war. I won't even have to make it up this time."

"Don't put me in it," Jerry said. "Hard enough meeting a good woman. And now everybody's dead, to boot."

"I'll have them work up a Crusty Old Guy avatar. If they can do space aliens, they can do you, Jerry."

Jerry said he'd resume selling real estate. Surplus inventory will be a tough nut in every market, but once rightful owners and heirs are sorted out, business will start up again. "Not to be morbid," he said, "but that's facts. In a time of national despair—like a recession—you have to hustle for clients because people don't know what they're capable of if they really put their minds to it. Buyers won't need convincing this time around." Northampton will appeal for all the reasons it has always appealed, he told them, but there will be even larger numbers of people trying to move out of the cities and start fresh. Too many memories in their old neighborhoods. "Take a house like this—you don't see another in any direction. It's a healing thing," he said, too forcefully, as if mentally imprinting the new slogan onto business cards.

Margie shushed him. She jerked her thumb over her shoulder toward the congregation outside.

"Sorry, dear."

"Still pickles, Margie?" Tad asked.

"If they make it through," she said, referring to her former employers. "Maybe I'll start it up again myself."

"Another brine mess you're getting yourself into," Tad teased. She punched him in the arm. They were a family. Mark Spitz was at his girlfriend's house for the holidays, stuck on the sofa with her kin while she took a nap upstairs. They passed his test, and he theirs. What were the chances of this raggedy bunch finding one another in the ruins, he wondered. Drawn together by the magic of this place the same way the missing owners were, inspired to make a new start. The toy store. He'd had something like this, briefly, in the toy store. The accident that outlives its circumstance and blossoms. All over the country survivors formed ill-fated tribes that the dead inevitably tore to shreds. Desperate latecomers asked for asylum from those inside and were turned away at the barrel of a semiauto: This is our house. He'd slept in the dead trees and now here he was with this family. He could've spent the night inside the studio and awakened to a property full of skels. Would he have made it out? As before, home was a beloved barricade. When school, work, the many-headed beast of strangers and villains comprising the world threatened to destroy, home remained, family remained, and the locks would hold, the lullabies would ward off all bogeymen. He was trapped in this house and he couldn't think of where else he'd rather be.

Margie asked Mark Spitz what his plans were. She'd scratched at the wound on her face all night, and a clear bead of fluid appeared at the edge of the scab. They each wanted to resume where they left off. Go back to the place where they were safe, he thought. Early notes in his unified theory of stragglers.

"Move to the city," he said.

They offered to let him stay after the siege, if he liked. He said yes.

It ended quickly three days later. Mark Spitz could have kept his wits a good deal longer, but his companions were fashioned of less durable alloys. Mark Spitz pegged Jerry to be the first to crack. Mark Spitz was from Long Island and maintained the suburban boy's suspicion of the pastoral, and here was a man who hunted, gutted, and dressed big game. Mark Spitz cast Jerry as the cowboy right-winger who was going to show this vermin who was boss, blast one of the front windows into splinters and start sending these cretins to their God. Firing into the agitated horde until one of the monsters got ahold of his gun barrel, wrestled it away, and the rest started picking at all the boards. It always happened quick. One part of the barricade failed, and then it was as if the refuge sighed and everything disintegrated at once. The spell of protection sputtered, all out of eldritch juice, and the mighty stronghold was made of straw again. All it took was one flaw in the system, a bug roosting deep in the code, to initiate the cascade of failure.

Tad, when he snapped, was the type to unlatch the front door and run screaming into the mess of them. Suicide by skel. There was a limit to what the human mind, born into that sweet and safe and lost world, could endure. He hadn't suspected Margie, whom he had decided to save if possible. Bring her with him out the second-floor window, then on the top of the porch, jump and roll and keep moving. In retrospect, the fact that she wore her motocross gear for the final forty-eight hours might have been a hint.

Yes, Margie beat him to the porch roof. In the parlor, Mark Spitz read a spy thriller on the orange shag rug by the fireplace and the other two men were deep in quiet rounds of rummy. They didn't hear her ease the boards from her bedroom window, but they could not overlook the explosion of glass outside. Margie screamed, "This is our island! Get your filthy hands off of me!" Tad and Mark Spitz broke for the spy holes, but Jerry understood and sprinted upstairs, yelling her name. In the middle of the yard three skels twisted in the blaze of the Molotov cocktail, the dry barnyard grass and sow thistle crackling into sparks and sheaves of flame. The burning security guard, whom Mark Spitz had watched for a whole hour the previous afternoon in a fit of impregnable boredom, staggered and fell on his face as the other dead twisted toward the house, half their ghoulish faces upturned to the commotion on the second story, and the rest to the bottom floor and its suddenly intriguing fortifications. They moved on the house, the mob of them constricting with purpose. Finally the things knew why they had gathered there, as if there had ever been any other reason.

Margie screamed again and the next bomb detonated among the creatures. The bottle was one of those that had held the concoctions of French seltzer and fruit juice, with the elegant label describing the manufacturer's legend, the commitment to quality, and the ancestral springs. It was a direct hit on the ballerina. The thing collided with another skel, one of the local hippie varietals, and that one went up in flames. The nights had been so dark, moonless and dead, and now the fires livened it all to exuberant performance, embers pirouetting in the air. The wrestling upstairs continued. Glass shattered, and he saw flaming liquid pour over the lip of the porch's roof and onto the front steps. Not long now.

His mechanism clicked and stuttered. Once again in a stranger's house, the next residence in the endless neighborhood that snared him his first night on the run. Their different layouts and constructions did not fool him; chimney or no chimney, English basement or cinder-block sump-pumped storeroom, he moved through a single infernal subdivision without outlet, serried cul-de-sacs and dead-ends overlooking broken land. He invited himself in to spend the night and the houses were empty or filled with the dead. It was as simple as that. He couldn't save these strangers any more than they could save him. His hosts were as alien to him as the soiled rabble mustered outside, now clawing at the windows and doors, ravenous for access. The creatures would find it. The house sighed around him, submitting to the business of dying.

Mark Spitz went for his gun and pack. Tad paused at the landing. He translated the expression on Mark Spitz's face and bolted upstairs to help his housemates. The ground growled and shook. Hell dropping pretense at last and opening up to claim them. No time to ponder that. He computed: The noise will draw most of the skels out front, but a number will head for the nearest point of entry. The backyard would still be rife with them. Upstairs was a no-go. One of the dining-room windows shattered. The teeming porch. He fought the urge to reinforce the perimeter there. Useless to try and save it. They'd be at the other windows even if he did get that table up there. He couldn't do it by himself. They were taking on water. Upstairs they were fighting. One plan: Fall back to a bedroom on the second floor and barricade as the first floor filled with skels. They're on the stairs in minutes and then he is locked in the tiny room. Even if most of them came inside, enough would remain in the yard to be a problem if he jumped. Think: The porch is on fire. For a second he pictured himself underneath the news copter as the folks in more fortunate weather watched from home. He was on the roof, the brown floodwaters pouring around the house. Why do these yokels build a house there when they know it's a flood zone, why do they keep rebuilding? He says, Because this disaster is our home. I was born here.

The line of ceramic teapots above the fireplace hopped to the floor at the tremors. They don't have earthquakes in Massachusetts. In goddamned Connecticut, either, but Mark Spitz didn't put it past that territory to figure out a way to outwit geological process, out of spite. No, the monster vehicles approached. The vibrations surged into him through his feet. He reached the kitchen and the barrage started. The bullets penetrated from every direction, shredding the wainscoting and knickknacks, the hard-won bounty of a hundred internet auctions, casting splinters and shards into the air like the confetti guts of firecrackers. A pebbled-glass lampshade jigsawed, the chandelier's dead bulbs popped, and the wooden doors of the media center finally revealed the vulgar flat-screen TV hidden inside, that lost treasure. He hit the floor. Beyond the walls, a woman spat orders. She was authority. The gunfire halted. Resumed. Mark Spitz rolled over on his back. Debris and glass roiled in the air, the long three-tined forks and oversize ladles hopped from their hooks. The kitchen was ruined, he thought. He mourned the kitchen, its stolid German cappuccino maker, the retro-style juicer with its cool mercury lines, the stainless-steel fridge's long-barren ice dispenser. Bit of a fixer-upper, needs TLC.

One of the dead bumped open the swinging doors. Some ex-kid in a denim vest festooned with buttons detailing the slogans of doomed causes and the unphotogenic candidates stumping for esoteric platforms. The doors bounced back and clocked it in the face. Mark Spitz fired, missed, and then his bullet smeared away the top of the thing's cranium as three high-caliber bullets burst through its chest. The artillery paused again. Boots pummeled the stairs and kicked in the front door, not that there was much of it left, he reckoned. Isolated shots crackled in the yard—picking off the remainders. How many of them were there? Bandits? He'd dealt with bandits. The scenarios impelling bandits toward their ill works were nothing compared to the visions slithering in his head. Bandits were a restaurant out of tonight's special and late trains and undependable wifi. He could handle bandits. He said,

"I'm alive in here! I'm alive in here!" The kitchen doors swung open again. He looked up.

He never got to ask Margie what finally made her crack. If she pushed Jerry off the roof into their hungry arms or if he slipped. She disappeared into the woods when the convoy took a piss break. Captain Childs wasn't going to wait. "Those are the kind that get you into trouble," she said before ordering them to move out. The caravan continued north for another two hours. Mark Spitz and Tad slumped in the bucket seats of the armored vehicle, eavesdropping on the young men muttering into their headsets. He pictured himself laid out on a gurney in the back of an ambulance, plugged into machines and bottles. They're not using the siren because he is going to make it. They are specialists. They will not let him perish.

He climbed up the ladder into the crisp daylight. A corporal helped him out of the hatch and off the transport and he was inside Camp Screaming Eagle.

Safe.

. . .

Saturday's visit to the local military installation was not as auspicious. Mark Spitz registered the manic vibe the moment he left the jeep. Bozeman had parked over on Hudson, per Ms. Macy's interest in seeing the Coakleys, and because "parking is a bitch" over by Wonton Main. Same old, same old. The local blizzard was under way, and the machine gunners up and down Canal shuddered over their weapons in neurotic fervor, rending the bodies of the things beyond the barrier with a profusion of high-velocity projectiles. The thunder the soldiers made had reverberated between the buildings all day, so much so that it had scurried beneath his attention until he got close. The fallen skels were hidden by the wall, and from the amount of artillery expended Mark Spitz imagined the hostiles changed into some new variety of monster, a second transformation that would induct the survivors into the next devastating ring of hell. Wide scaly wings, rapier-length fangs, a ridge of spikes popping out of their spines. You thought you knew the plague? It was just getting started. Act II of the End of the World following the intermission, let's wrap this up, folks.

"I apologize for the noise, Ms. Macy," Bozeman said as they walked to the corner. "A lot of them showing up for Lunch today, as we say around here. Breakfast, too. Beaucoup activity the last few days, I'm sure you've been briefed."

She didn't hear him, distracted by the evanescent currents of white flakes. "It looks like snow."

They turned onto Canal, where the incinerators waited at the curb like lunch trucks competing for the noon rush, although in this case the machines waited to be fed. The two rigs were the size of shipping containers, perched on trailers that had dragged them through the Zone after they had been deposited by aerial crane. Who knew which military installation's thighs they had slithered from, what manner of other devices gestated in the neighboring R & D lab. As far as Mark Spitz determined, technological innovation since the advent of the plague had been limited to two major inventions and one minor one. The neo-aramid wonder fabric of their fatigues and combat gear was major; Gary's Lasso resided at the other end of utility. Word was the principals behind the mesh had, before the plague, impinged on the body-armor patents of a big-time weapons manufacturer, and they'd been ordered to cease and desist production of the miracle garment. The exigencies of reconstruction erased all legal arguments, however: one company's factory was in a cleared zone, and one was not. They'd sort it all out once doomsday went into remission.

The Coakley was the other prize. Although named after its creator, it was a government asset from ignition switch to heat sensor. The incinerator had been jerry-rigged for mobility, and the rear loader was obviously a late addition—the rough metal in coarse contrast to the gleaming silver body—but its original purpose remained. It burned things. Here, it burned the bodies of the dead with uncanny efficiency, swallowing what the soldiers fed into it and converting it to smoke, fly ash, and a shovelful of hard material too stubborn to be entirely consumed. Hearts, mostly. That thick muscle. The machine's purpose was clear; why it had been invented and its intended deployment before the plague was a mystery. Whatever the case, the Coakley had proven itself a most worthy recruit. The kerosene savings alone.

Mark Spitz had never seen Disposal without their biohazard suits on, but by now he recognized Annie and Lily by their voices and gait. They were in the middle of a burn, the geyser of white smoke and ash issuing violently from the stack atop the incinerator. The stack periscoped three stories, and from there the canyon vortices scattered the particles. It could not be said the others in Zone One shared Mark Spitz's perception of the ash, its constancy and pervasiveness. The ash did swirl in a radius around the incinerators, it landed as dandruff on their shoulders, and, yes, perhaps a small percentage was conscripted by rain on its way down. Certainly the downdrafts and eddies created by high-rises, the suction currents and zephyrs generated by the smaller buildings, gusted the flakes in turbulent jets across downtown. Certainly when the machine fired, it generated a localized atmosphere. But the ash did not shroud the metropolis, it did not taint the air in any sickening measure. A skel bonfire or kerosene party probably sent more toxic stuff into the air. But for Mark Spitz it was everywhere. In every raindrop on his skin and the pavement, sullying every edifice and muting the blue sky: the dust of the dead. It was in his lungs, becoming assimilated into his body, and he despised it.

He kept it to himself, this particular face of his PASD, although he did slip from time to time. It was a low-level hallucination as such things went, no real impairment. No need to share it, even if Mark Spitz couldn't help being disturbed that for the most part his symptoms appeared after he was rescued in Northampton, accumulating manifestations. His new brand of skel dream, his

ID-duty nausea, the fantastic visions of ash. He'd been healthier, more kink-free, in the lost days. Vertigo seized him now, at the edge of the wall. Where was he? He told himself, I am in New York City, I am in New York City on the street where I used to buy cheap headphones. He looked past the roaring, belching machine to traffic signs that had directed drivers to the sluice leading to New Jersey. These blocks had been so busy, so feverish, compressing the vehicles into the tunnel that would take them under the water to the other side. Moving the little bodies into a channel the same way the smokestack directed the little flakes through its insides and out into the air. The dead continued to commute, so hardwired was the custom.

Bozeman introduced the Disposal techs to the visitor from Buffalo. Annie and Lily swung the sagging body bag into the machine's rear loader. "We can't shake hands," Annie said, bowing. The tough plastic creaked at every movement.

"Charmed, I'm sure," Lily said. She leaned against one of the red biohazard bins used to ferry corpses up and down Canal. The grab cranes picked up the bodies, lifted them over the wall, and dropped them into the bins, but so much blood and infectious murk leaked from the mangled bodies that finally they had reserved one traffic lane at the foot of the barrier for corpse transport. Too much gore and ichor splatter, too many soldiers frantically gobbling megadoses of anticiprant when it splashed on them, depleting the medics' stash. The carts were filled with the bodies of the uptown skels and, intermittently, the bagged skels retrieved from the sweepers, and then they were rolled over here to this final place.

The cart before Mark Spitz overflowed, arms and legs hanging over the rim as if attached to boaters enjoying cool lake waters on a summer afternoon. Given this grisly abundance, and the constant barrage from the machine guns, he had his explanation of why they were busy feeding the second Coakley while the first was still firing. They were having serious dead weather up here at the wall.

"So this ash is—" Ms. Macy said.

"Yes—particulate by-product of high-temperature combustion," Lily said.

Ms. Macy nodded as if agreeing with the choice of red her boss had ordered for the table. "You guys got the prototype. A lot of camps would kill to get one of these babies."

"We need them the most," Annie said.

"Everybody needs them. We're all in this together."

"Tell Buffalo we're very grateful for the new unit," Bozeman said. "I know there have been a lot of supply troubles, this last week especially, with all the—"

"You got lucky," Ms. Macy interrupted. She turned to Mark Spitz and the two Disposal techs. "There have been some reversals."

"What kind of reversals?"

"Reversals. Complications. There are always complications in business. The client changes their mind. The teamsters won't unload the booth and hump it to the convention hall. You have to think on your feet. May I?"

Annie offered her the control pad, the cable connecting it to the incinerator sweeping across the asphalt. "Usually we like to stuff as many as we can in there before we fire it, but you're the guest."

Ms. Macy removed a latex glove from her purse and pressed the controller's oversize red button. The machine emitted a warning and the rear loader tumbled the four corpses into the compactor. They disappeared into the belly of the thing. The bucket slid back with a hydraulic grumbling to receive the next load. "How many do you do per load?" she asked.

"We don't keep count," Annie said. There may have been a note of derision, but the inflection was hard to discern.

"A lot," Lily said. "Enough. Heavy days like this, lotta skels coming in, we keep both going pretty steady."

"I hate these heavy-flow days," Annie said.

"I'm sure we can get those numbers for you, ma'am," Bozeman said. He passed the compactor keypad back to Annie.

"We should really recycle those," Ms. Macy said, pointing to the biohazard bin. It took Mark Spitz a second to realize she referred to the body bags intermingled with the wall corpses.

"I know, it's terrible," Lily said.

"It's what?"

"It's terrible," Lily repeated, louder this time to account for her helmet, and the renewed volley down the street. "The environment." They all turned at the approaching scraping noise. Mark Spitz identified Chip as the inhabitant of the white suit steering the fresh load of bodies. Chip reminded him of the old workers in the fashion district who shoved their clothes racks up the sidewalk and cursed the idiot cattle impeding their progress. The old New York. Mark Spitz rubbed his tongue against his teeth. That was ash he tasted. Whether it was actually there was another question.

"Told you to hold off for a while," Annie said. "Still got this whole batch."

"These are from down-Zone," Chip said. "We're not picking up anything from the wall until they get the crane fixed."

"Complications," Bozeman said to Ms. Macy. He smiled. "Shall we continue our tour?"

Mark Spitz had wasted enough time. He'd had his diversions, in the restaurant, the hotel, and now this tourist leisure cruise. The guys waited for him downtown. This excursion would tide him over until they returned for R & R tomorrow. He was about to take his leave when Lily said, "Hey, lady."

"Yes?"

"There have been rumors."

"Of?" Ms. Macy clasped her folder to her breast and pressed her lips shut, her chin slightly upturned to brunt the surf.

"Ms. Macy—is it true we lost Vista Del Mar?"

Bozeman sighed. "Bubbling Brooks."

"No, that's okay," Ms. Macy said. She was prepared. "It was bound to get out. No shame in telling the truth. We're still sorting it out, but it looks like they'd been having a density problem outside and somehow the gates were breached. Human error, most likely."

"How many—"

"They're still surveying."

"What about the Triplets?"

"I know one got out."

"Cheyenne?"

"I don't know which one."

Annie placed her hand on her partner's shoulder. It was pathetic, the sight of the two of them moving in their white hazmat suits in a dumb show of consolation. The sabotaged connection. They looked like mascots of a brand of cookie dough, meant to hypnotize the kids between cartoons. Did Annie know someone in Bubbling Brooks, or just the Triplets? In all likelihood they each knew someone there, whether they were aware of it or not: the appallingly friendly security guard from the office complex three jobs ago, or the freckled best friend from summer camp you hadn't thought of in years. He heard Ms. Macy say the words "isolated incident."

"You get back upstate," Chip said, "you tell them we need another crane down here. Maybe two. You can see what kind of volume we get here sometimes."

Ms. Macy's fingers trundled to a fresh page in her notebook. She smiled. "From your lips to Buffalo's ears."

They left Disposal to matters of immolation and started for the bank. Ms. Macy asked Mark Spitz where Fort Wonton had found him, and he started to describe the operation on I-95 but was interrupted by one of the rooftop snipers, who shouted directions to a machine gunner on the wall. "Over there, dude—the priest!" The gunner swiveled and divested himself of twenty rounds. The sniper cheered and did a jig.

"It's so quiet in Buffalo," she said.

Bozeman caught the brief flicker in Ms. Macy's eyes and said, "The more the merrier, way I see it. It'll be awhile before Buffalo sends down the manpower we need to finally cap the island, but in the meantime, the more tourists we have streaming in from the burbs, the less we have to neutralize later." He tucked her elbow into his palm to steer her around the trio of mechanics squatting before the open plate at the base of the grab crane. The machine's mammoth claw dangled three stories above, stalled over the wall and dripping on the corpses piled on the other side. Pools of blood gathered at the seams in the concrete wall where the brackets held the segments together, a wrinkled skin developing at the edges where they dried. The pools were becoming giant scabs.

"I hope you'll convey how smoothly things are running," Bozeman continued. "That we are a vital installation, even if the next summit is far off."

"You needn't worry."

"Though Chip may be right that we might need another crane. Or two."

It's different, Mark Spitz thought. Wonton was off-kilter. A vibration insinuated itself, a disquieting under-tremor to every movement and sound. Perhaps it was a higher-than-normal flood of skels at the wall. Had the fusillade paused since his arrival? More likely the loss of Bubbling Brooks. Bubbling Brooks was one of the bigger camps, fifteen thousand people last he heard. What was their sideline, besides the Triplets? Munitions? Pills? It escaped him. Some of these soldiers had worked there, dropped off survivors there. Had family there, maybe. Buffalo will be upset, of course, with this interruption of their timetables. There had to be survivors, he thought. Had to be. But a loss like that, after the recent run of good news, would certainly cripple morale. Above him the snipers trained the scopes, aimed, dropped their targets, moved to the next target in robotic sequence. The soldiers had no other course in Wonton but to avenge themselves on the dead before them, the ones they can see. Do it for Cheyenne.

Bubbling Brooks was bad news. Mark Spitz felt terrible, of course, but he knew that the refuge had done what all refuges do eventually: It failed. What else could you expect from despicable Connecticut? Precisely this kind of tribulation.

They paused at the shiny, worn steps of the bank and held the doors for three passing soldiers engaged in a lively a cappella version of "Stop! Can You Hear the Eagle Roar? (Theme from *Reconstruction*)." Bozeman told Ms. Macy he'd meet her in the conference room. "You'll be fine on your own?"

She winked. "This is the American Phoenix. You're never on your own."

Bozeman appraised her ass as she went inside. "Wouldn't mind some of those Buffalo wings," he said. He dropped his hand on Mark Spitz's shoulder and switched to his majordomo voice. "I haven't seen you since it happened. Sorry about your man."

"What do you mean?"

"Was I not supposed to say anything? I'm such an asshole."

. . .

They stayed in the toy store for months. That other, less flamboyant, more deliberate ruination altering the planet's climate had been under way for more than a hundred years, squeezing milder winters into the Northeast. People got used to it, the unopened bags of sodium chloride gathering cobwebs next to the kids' boogie boards in the garage, the nightly news footage of the venerable ice shelf splashing into the frigid seas, squeezed in if there were no more pressing outrages, or a celebrity death. The first winter of the plague was a throwback to how they used to do it in the good old days: early, unmerciful, endless. The survivors endured the tandem disasters in their refuges, without the solace of warmer days. Warm weather meant you had to go outside again.

"Kinda retro," Mim said, surveying the unlikely drifts on Main Street.

"I know," Mark Spitz said. "Come back. I'm cold."

It was the healthiest relationship he'd ever had, and not because they had a lot in common, such as a need for food, water, and fire. In the time before the flood, Mark Spitz had a habit of making his girlfriends into things that were less than human. There was always a point, sooner or later, when they crossed a line and became creatures: following a lachrymose display while waiting in line for admission to the avant-garde performance; halfway into a silent rebuke when he underplayed his enthusiasm about attending her friend's wedding. Once it was only a look, a transit of anxiety across her eyes in which he glimpsed some irremediable flaw or future betrayal. And like that, the person he had fallen in love with was gone. They had been replaced by this familiar abomination, this thing that shared the same face, same voice, same familiar mannerisms that had once comforted him. To anyone else, the simulation was perfect. If he tried to make his case, as in his horror movies, the world would indulge his theory, even participate in a reasonable-sounding test, one that would not succeed in convincing them. But he would know. He knew where they failed in their humanity. He would leave.

Over time he learned how to isolate those last nights and say, That's when they broke through the barrier. In the middle of the argument over the meaning of the foreign film they had been forced to see as members of an educated class: there. When they ran out of gas en route to the weekend at the friend's cabin and sat in the car for half an hour under the bleak moon: right there. When the last nights became identifiable, the lag time between the incident and the leave-taking diminished. He suffered no appeal. There was no way they could convince him they were human. He was dragging a corpse out of a laundry joint on Chambers Street down in the Zone when he realized that the voice admonishing him to ditch the survivors he'd hooked up with, warning him away from others, was an echo of his relationship-snuffing voice. They are lost, they are the dead, it is time to leave.

Mim did not change. Horns didn't pop out of her head or matted fur sprout on her hindquarters. Perhaps it would have happened to her in time. They were safe in the toy store. Granted asylum. To look at the lunar surface outside the shop, perhaps they were not on Earth at all, and subject to a different sort of gravity, new rules. No dead moved in the snow; Mim reckoned they were holed up in cellars, the abandoned gymnasiums of run-down high schools, caves and sewers and wherever else these monsters hibernated. No other survivors happened by; they were holed up, too, slowly rubbing their hands over the books they burned for heat, the novels devoted to the codes of the dead world, the histories, the poetry that went up so easily. Perhaps he and Mim were the last ones left. An entire society in a toy store on Main Street.

They furnished their pad in a series of forays, as if it were their first one, everything secondhand or at unbeatable prices—i.e., free. They hit all the local stores, affixing on objects in unison, disagreeing and deferring over placement with magnanimity: books; batteries; milk-crate accent tables; low-sodium ramen; lightweight portable stove; various buckets and plastic containers full of melted snow and purified water; the hyssop- and sandalwood-scented aromatherapy candles; lamps with adjustable arms capable of reducing their cones of illumination to the size of one six-point letter if needed; inflatable mattress with multiple comfort settings and heat massage; plastic boxes of antibacterial baby wipes that made them redolent of artificial lemons and lent their skin, when touched by the other's lips or tongue, a metallic tang. They read and played games. The place was lousy with board games, of course, the childhood stalwarts and the modern abstrusities with mind-bending premises and loopy procedures. Every week or two they passed whipped-cream canisters back and forth and huffed until they felt their brain cells pop like soap bubbles.

They stashed emergency go-packs at either end of town, his and hers. They were not so deluded.

When the snows ebbed, it emerged that Main Street was a sort of dead highway for some reason. "How the roads are laid out around here, I guess," Mim said, but it made for a lot of traffic. They nested in the reliquary on the second floor, where they could leave the shades open in daylight without fear. At the end of the spiral staircase the store's owner, Manny ("Good Old" as they came to call him), displayed his prized commodities: the collectible defectives, limited editions, the whispered-about rarities. Anyone born after World War I could have found intersection with their secret or not-so-secret nostalgia in that trove of Depression-era rag dolls, atomic-age ray guns and scale-model fighter jets, intricate military play sets of quaint lethality, and action figures of cameo characters who had been inserted into the sequel for the express purpose of action-figure production. In the original packaging or an accomplished facsimile, and behind locked glass cabinets.

"This stuff is really valuable," he said. His childish excitement flickering.

"Where? To whom? For what? That's the old world."

She was right, but he had hoped she'd play along, if only for a moment. The boy that wandered the cellar of his personality still nursed the naïve hunger for a life of adventure. As a kid he'd invented scenarios for adulthood: to outrun a fireball, swing across the air shaft on a wire, dismember the gargoyle army with the enchanted blade that only he could wield. Now he was grown up and the plague had granted him his wish and rendered it a silly grotesque. It was not so glamorous to spend two days doubled over, shitting your guts out because you'd gambled on the expired bottle of kiwi juice. All the other kids turned out to be postal workers, roofers, beloved teachers, and died. Mark Spitz was living the dream! Take a bow, Mark Spitz.

The key to the cabinet was downstairs, probably, but he let the treasures be. The generations had fixated on their lost toys, added to their already regrettable debt loads to obtain these tokens because the fantasies sustained them, the stories of the hand-shy orphans who discover their stolen birthright and rescue the kingdom or planetary system, the subgenre of misunderstood aliens and mechanical men who yearned to love. He'd always seen himself in them, the robots who roved the galaxy in search of the emotion chip, the tentacled things that were, beneath their mottled, puckered membranes, more human than the murderous villagers who hunted them for their difference.

The townspeople, of course, were the real monsters. It was the business of the plague to reveal our family members, friends, and neighbors as the creatures they had always been. And what had the plague exposed him to be? Mark Spitz endured as the race was killed off one by one. A part of him thrived on the end of the world. How else to explain it: He had a knack for apocalypse. The plague touched them all, blood contact or no. The secret murderers, dormant rapists, and latent fascists were now free to express their ruthless natures. The congenitally timid, those who had been stingy with their dreams for themselves, those who came out of the womb scared and remained so: These, too, found a final stage for their weakness and in their last breaths were fulfilled. I've always been like this. Now I'm more me.

They passed the time, made the nights as lovely as they could. When they discovered they were out of condoms, she told him to pull out and they came otherwise. "Enough babies," she said. Before the plague, he'd always thought it weird when people said that, as they croaked about overpopulation, the millions of kids in want of a good home, ever-shrinking planetary resources of manifold aspect. Now Mark Spitz understood plainly what they had meant by "What kind of person would bring a child into this world" and then recited statistics about polluted water tables on the other side of the world, the asphyxiated ecosphere.

The answer was, "Only a monster would bring a child into this world."

The last snows were a month behind them. They were lying on the roof looking at the stars. He'd grown up after the time when they taught the constellations, but he knew a handful. Mim was acquainted with a few more. They kept their voices down. The reality: if it was warm enough for them to stargaze, it was warm enough to start moving.

"I'll say one thing about the world today, it really keeps the pounds off," she said.

"Starvation will do that."

"I think it was all the running. I haven't been in this kind of shape since college." She brought up Buffalo. Mim still believed in Buffalo.

"By the time you hear about a place, it's gone," Mark Spitz said. "I think the very act of hearing about a place seems to will its disappearance."

"This place is different. Someplace has to be." His head was on her stomach. Her fingertips drew letters on his scalp. Words? A name? Her kids' names? "Or else we should just end it now."

"Buffalo."

"If there's nothing out there, what's the point?"

"There's here."

"Have to keep on moving, honey. You stay in one spot, you're just another straggler."

In the old joke, the intransigent father goes out for cigarettes and never comes back. The family is bereft. These days your companion in oblivion went out on a routine foraging run and never came back. One warm day, Mim left to scare up some pepper for the lentil soup and did not return. Gone, like that. He searched their neighborhood haunts, and the Main Street businesses they had put off raiding until a rainy-day need. Her various go-packs remained in their stashes. He discovered no indication of where it had happened, and it didn't matter anyway, did it? He waited a week. And then he moved on. *If there's nothing out there, what's the point?* He didn't have the answer. He laced his boots.

People disappeared. You never knew it was the last time you'd see them. For a long time, he retained most of their names. Before Northampton, he sometimes indulged visions of coming back one day to all the towns he'd stayed in during the catastrophe, in an electric car driven by his surly grandson. Meet the kids or spouses of the kindred he'd met out in the land, sit for a spell and drink a cup of tea on the plastic-covered sofa downstairs in the split-level. As if anyone they had loved would make it through.

Ever since the soldiers rescued him, he started losing them, the names. They were dust in his pocket. Their eccentricities, the moronic advice vis-à-vis food safety, the locations of the rescue centers they'd obsessed over lasted longer than their names. One night he got the urge to record what he remembered in one of the kiddie armadillo notebooks. It passed. He didn't stir from his sleeping bag. Let them go, he thought. Except her.

Unlike Mim, the Lieutenant commanded a full complement of mourners. Omega and Bravo held the wake in a Brazilian restaurant on Pearl following a quick survey of the nabe. They'd gone out looking for the other sweeper teams to no avail. The comms were useless, unleashing a metallic howling that kindled dread even in their veteran bones. Their comrades would hear about it tomorrow, and the customary Sunday-night hang out would become a second, boozy memorial.

"He'd want it that way," Carl said.

"Of that I am sure," Mark Spitz said.

Work was over once Mark Spitz returned with the news. Angela reconfirmed their choice of venue after doing recon on the liquor inventory. She'd become partial to cachaça after a six-month thing with a Brazilian guy whose constant referencing of his nationality was a cornerstone of his personality, and the drink's foreign provenance meant it was not subject to the looting regs. Unless the powers had changed the rules these last two weeks they'd been in the field—apparently all sorts of stuff was happening in the world while they roamed the bruises of this necropolis. Camps collapsing, imperiled triplets. The Lieutenant's troops would produce a worthy memorial. Reggae issued from some dead busboy's digital music dock, courtesy of Carl's playlists, and went quite well with the caipirinhas, which didn't taste half bad, chilled by chem cold packs and infused with the proper measure of lime juice and sugar. At the festivities' kickoff, Angela was scrounging behind the bar when Kaitlyn started to speak. "Don't," Angela said.

"I was going to say, take two bottles," Kaitlyn said.

Black silhouettes of blade-leafed jungle plants were painted on the walls, more goofy than exotic as they shape-shifted in the frothy light of their lamps and candles. They toasted the Lieutenant. They swapped remembrances of their first day in the Zone, their initial meetings with their eccentric superior officer, each taking a turn at the canvas. The instant Mark Spitz drained his second drink, No Mas grabbed the glass from his hand and mixed another. No Mas had been smiling at Mark Spitz and overchuckling at his jokes since Mark Spitz walked in on him and Gary in the bathroom. From their furtive expressions, Mark Spitz assumed he'd interrupted some nouveau hand-job ritual, possibly of wretched Connecticut derivation.

"Don't worry," Gary told No Mas. "He's cool."

Gary explained their side enterprise. Scavengers plundered the pharmacies of the famous painkillers first, the good stuff, and then the proven downers, the tranquilizers road-tested by generations of glum moms. Entrepreneurial salvage and distribution of the numbing agents didn't begin in earnest until the universal diagnosis of PASD exposed the unfortunate gap in Buffalo's roster of pharmaceutical sponsors—for those willing to go on the hunt for the indispensable medley of benzodiazepines and selective serotonin reuptake inhibitors, this was a primo market opportunity.

Pain could be killed. Sadness could not, but the drugs did shut its mouth for a time. It was unwise to take a pill out in the wastes, as you might not wake up when you were supposed to, at the sound of the dead multitude clawing against the barn door, for example, but in Happy Acres and its ilk one was unburdened of the curse of eternal vigil. Miss a day here and there, zonked out on this or that—they'd earned it. "Someone's got to step in," No Mas said. "People are hurting."

"What do you charge?" Mark Spitz said.

"Sliding scale, needs-based. Juice boxes accepted."

The pharmacies and residential medicine cabinets were empty of narcotics and antibiotics, but the antidepressants in their plastic cylinders sprouted like orange mushrooms behind the mirrored doors, ready for harvest. Gary and some dependable players in other sweeper units delivered their booty to No Mas, and on Sunday No Mas rendezvoused with his Wonton connection, who got the pills out on choppers to the camps. A shadow Buffalo executing course corrections for reconstruction.

Mark Spitz told them he'd keep his mouth shut. Yes, it was a necessary service. Perhaps the Lieutenant could have benefited from the cutting-edge mood stabilizers. Perhaps not.

"You're sure he wasn't bit?" Carl asked for the third time.

"No," Mark Spitz said.

"Leave a note?"

"No."

"Damn."

They suicided themselves in the homes they loved, surrounded by their beloved objects, or out in the wasteland they despised, alone in the cold dirt. Some arrived at the decision when they were safe in the camps, the semblance of normalcy permitting the first true accounting of the horror, its scope and unabating adversities. The unforgivable in all its faces. The suicides accepted, finally, what the world had become and acted logically. Buffalo was not enamored of the statistics, and ordered Dr. Herkimer to add a longer Prevention/Understanding Ideation unit to the PASD seminars. Killing yourself in the interregnum was understandable. Killing yourself in the age of the American Phoenix was a rebuke to its principles. "We Make Tomorrow!"—if we can get that far, Mark Spitz thought—so tomorrow needs a marketing rollout, hope, psychopharmacology, a rigorous policing of bad thinking, anything to stoke the delusion that we'll make it through.

Now and again, Mark Spitz held desultory debates with his own forbidden thought, most recently the previous afternoon on Duane Street. He wished the fallen a safe journey.

"Maybe he was bored."

One of the snipers observed the Lieutenant walk out to the helipad atop the bank. It was a quiet evening, sparse with the dead all day, one of the last quiet evenings before the devils started accumulating in their recent density. The sniper waved at the Lieutenant. The Lieutenant waved back and jammed a grenade into his mouth.

"Can you even fit a grenade into your mouth?" Carl asked.

"Gag reflex," No Mas said.

"One of those little thermite jobs, sure," Gary said.

"It's sad," Kaitlyn said.

Fabio had installed himself at the man's desk. Fabio knew himself to be a pretender, from the way he started and almost knocked over his coffee when Mark Spitz showed up. He looked terrible, as if he'd been living in a hamper. He spoke fast, on high rev, as he apologized for not informing the sweepers earlier. With the whole eastern seaboard lit up and scrambling the last two weeks to cover the recent blips, Buffalo thought it best if the sweepers kept to their timetables.

"Blips?" Mark Spitz asked.

"Reversals, complications," Fabio told him. "Blips." Fabio was in command until they sent down a replacement. Buffalo had already missed the last two food drops.

The office's digital player, enthroned on a doily in the microwave/coffeemaker nexus by the watercooler, had been playing a set of old pop and Mark Spitz was startled by the DJ's sudden bluster: "Hey! All you out there. Hope you're getting a chance to enjoy this sunshine today!" Surely there were no radio stations up yet. The DJ forecast fair skies for the rest of the afternoon, and Mark Spitz realized it was a recording of a radio block from some random afternoon before the disaster, a ghost transmission of yesterday's deals on teeth bleaching, ads for movies playing in dead theaters, and last-minute invitations to join class-action suits.

A new recruit Mark Spitz hadn't seen before, one of the teenagers from the camps, entered the office and dropped himself at Fabio's old desk. Distribution may be a mess right now, but Buffalo had a lot of spare parts lying around.

"We can't believe Fabio's been our man up there and we didn't even know it," Gary said.

"It's disgraceful," Kaitlyn said.

They quickly ran out of remembrances. Honestly, they didn't know him that well. "Pretty cool boss," Carl said. They waded into deep, frigid silences and drank. Carl changed the mix on the digital music player, saying, "This one's remixes." It had been rare to memorialize someone's passing. You were on the run; you left the bodies behind to leak fluids in the sun. This was the first time since the world ended that most of them had the luxury to do things in the old style. They had little to say.

The drinks executed their mission. No Mas saluted the silhouettes on the wall, slow, catching on his gears, and Mark Spitz guessed the man was performing his Lieutenant impression for his inner audience. No Mas smiled faintly. Kaitlyn strangled a loop of hair on her index finger. She caught Mark Spitz looking at her and said, "The subway."

Seven weeks into their mission, the Lieutenant had Fabio summon them from the field. This was unprecedented, as they only returned to Wonton on Sundays and were now deep in the rhythms of their work flow, replete with Monday-morning despair, hump-day torpor, and a fragile strain of muted Friday-afternoon euphoria. The comms still worked back then, providing a tether to a mending civilization. For his part, Mark Spitz appreciated the interruption of that week's grid. Omega wormed through the intestines of a starter-apartment rental tower, and floor after floor of beige carpet, noise-permeable walls, and fingerprint-smudged doorways soured his disposition. His friends in the city lived in buildings like that, and the hallways reeked of the dead ambitions decomping behind the doors. They'd had hopes. Now the cheap, emptied construction signified the complete eradication of aspiration, all luminous notions.

In the dumpling house, the Lieutenant told them that Buffalo wanted them to sweep out the subway tunnels.

"I thought the marines already did that," Metz said.

"Mostly," the Lieutenant explained. When the marines landed, they'd locked up the black gates and turnstiles to the platforms. The thinking was, they'd clear out the tunnels later. But once they cottoned to the fact that the top of the island was uncapped and the northward rails were wide open, the brass grew apprehensive. Even though skel migration patterns didn't work that way, everyone started having nightmares of miles and miles of tunnels brimming and bursting with the dead, envisioning the uptown lines as umbral channels rerouting these very, very sick passengers to right beneath their tamed Zone boulevards. Ghoulish faces smeared into the bars and verminous mitts clawed through the metal grating in a hellish rendition of the worst rush hour ever, gates wrenching free from the concrete platforms . . . In their final mission before redeployment to the latest, more fashionable instability up or down the coast, the marines blocked the underground tunnels at the northern edge of the Zone, as if the Great Wall of Canal extended through the asphalt and deep into the Earth's crust. Then the marines swept through the downtown shadows after the trapped skels.

It was the Lieutenant's first week in the Zone. Buffalo was all paperwork; he wanted a proper posting. He led a platoon down the Lexington Avenue line. "Sketchy is the word I'd use. We'd tamed aboveground. Put them down. Underground was skel territory—as if it still belonged to the interregnum, even though it was just under our feet. Even with the subways blocked off, there was this feeling that the other end of the tunnel, its terminus, was in the dead land. Claustrophobic as hell, despite the trolleys we had on the tracks carrying the spots—the brass had reallocated our night-vision gear for some op up north, so we had to bring our own light. You're not in the city anymore down there. It's medieval. Water streaming down the wall like a catacomb, rats running around, and then you're lurching in the pits between the tracks. The third rail's dead, but it's still creepy, like it could come on any second and zap you.

"But the main thing was never knowing what was around the next bend or how many were going to come pouring out of the dark. Guys pissing themselves in fear, even after all they'd seen in the wasteland. To make it extra hellish, the general had the bright idea to make us bring flamethrowers, which was fine for making human—or subhuman—torches, but there was no ventilation. When the subway's running, they got superfans going to keep the air in circulation. Halfway in, it's full of dead air down there, eyes burning from the smoke, can't breathe, skels crashing at us through the flames—"

The Lieutenant paused. He wasn't selling the sweepers on their temporary reassignment very well. He poured a glass of water from the plastic pitcher on the podium. "But we pulled it off. Elbow grease, American Phoenix, rah rah. Now they want you to finish it so it's a hundred percent. Do what you're doing now, pop 'n' drop whatever skels have wandered in from some maintenance conduit over the last weeks, or that one random fellow in the supply room. If any. The hard stuff has been taken care of," he said. The Lieutenant's face sketched a look of bravado Mark Spitz had not seen on the man before, so he took it to be fake.

Omega and Gamma were assigned the Seventh Avenue line, Canal to South Ferry. The most noble of subway routes in Mark Spitz's estimation, hallowed meridian of Manhattan Island. When the two sweeper units arrived at the uptown side of Canal, the yellow tile of the station entrance generated a familiar calm in him. During his first teenage missions in the New York City underground, the steps leading to a subway platform offered refuge from the madness of the streets above, sparing him the skyscrapers' indictment of his shabby suburban self and the constant jostling of strangers, who cut him off, scowled at his tentative steps, tried to puncture his eyeballs with their umbrella spokes and render him defenseless so they could devour him. He caught his breath on the platforms and furtively checked the transit-authority app on his phone so that no one would know he didn't have a clue of where he was going. He was a rube, but he was no tourist. One day he'd live here and be one of their tribe. Mark Spitz got out at his stop, at some part of the city he'd never been before, to complete the assignment given by a website—in search of imported sneakers or limited-edition hoodies—eager to school himself in this new cranny of the city.

Back then, if the worst happened, his phone would transmit the coordinates of his murdered body to the satellite and back down to the authorities and eventually to his parents on Long Island. What a quaint notion, to die while looking for cool T-shirts.

The sweepers unlocked the gates and gained the platform. They did not speak. They tightened the straps of their night-vision goggles and waited for their eyes to recalibrate to a new, murky-green modality that made them into scrabbling things at the bottom of a deep-sea chasm. It was as the Lieutenant described it: a decrepit dungeon, with a slow, miasmal atmosphere and secret topography. Trevor said, "Looks like we just missed the train," and they laughed and walked over to the hooked ladder at the south end of the platform.

Gamma was a unit of mellow bandwidth, third-generation

potheads to a man, who couldn't wait for the new era of marijuana tolerance sure to come in reconstruction, the legislative nobrainers and utopian buds. "When we put it all back together, we will institutionalize joy," Foreskin said, "for the medicinal toke is the balm of oblivion." Richard Cowl, a.k.a. Dick Cowl, a.k.a. Foreskin, was Gamma's leader and a former sommelier at a high-end novelty eatery in Cambridge that specialized in offal. "Which is sort of amusing, given the skel's yen for human entrails. They're my regulars!" Even in these times of scarcity he was a vegetarian. He never sampled the exotic delicacies on his employer's menu but accomplished a mean pairing nonetheless. According to him, at any rate—pre-plague triumphs were often exaggerated, given the lack of contradicting witnesses.

Joshua and Trevor were the other two Gammas. The only description Joshua gave of his former life was that "I was an alcoholic, and I'm still an alcoholic." One Sunday at Wonton, Josh related how his mother flipped on Last Night and Mark Spitz almost shared his similar tale but declined. Josh didn't have the bearing of one who was going to make it to the other side; there was something taffy to him, despite the fact he'd survived this long, and to tell him the story would be like pouring coffee into a broken saucer. As for Trevor, he had been a mall security guard in the bright, prelapsarian days of shopping abundance. When they met, Gary teased that Trevor must be glad to "finally have a real gun" after his stint as a fake cop, and Trevor had replied evenly that he hadn't needed a gun in his mall rounds. He had everything he needed in his hands—Trevor was a master-level practitioner of a branch of martial arts Mark Spitz had never heard of but, after an impromptu demonstration, had become convinced of its lethal pedigree. Gamma got high every night, the minute they bivouacked for the night, "In police stations if one is handy," Foreskin said.

One of the most solemn rounds of rock-paper-scissors in human history ruled in favor of Omega: Gamma was on point.

"It's all right," Foreskin said. To draw the skels out, Josh started playing an old heavy metal song on a kazoo. The title eluded Mark Spitz. In the video the band played a bar mitzvah dressed in thick biker leather. Top-notch anti-skel gear in retrospect, save for the exposed neck. Soon they were all humming the song, then giddily crooning it at the top their voices.

The Franklin Street station hove into sight when they heard a holler, back from Canal. Safeties clicked. The dead did not speak. Was it some misbegotten freak who'd been eking it out down here, hiding? Mark Spitz had never come across a true homesteader, but the marines had rounded up a few on their first rounds through the Zone. Citizens who'd locked themselves in insubstantial one-bedrooms and unlikely studios and somehow made it through until the soldiers came to take back the city. What must it have been like, to see the choppers after all that time, after they'd emptied the larder of hope and had only mealy, unleavened stubbornness to chew on? Marines sliding down cables, grinding up the bodies of the dead with their .50-.50s, those devils that had besieged them for so long. They were insane, most of them, and had to be pried out screaming before being taken to the Wonton medics, where the top-shelf antipsychotics awaited. One or two attacked their rescuers, shooting the soldiers in the head, unable to believe in their deliverance—and some homesteaders were no doubt mistaken for skels in turn, palsying in their PASD. There weren't many, but they did exist. Some homesteaders were still immured north of the barrier; a few managed to signal choppers and were plucked from the roofs. Perhaps others shrank from view when they heard a helicopter, content in whatever doomsday theater played out in their traumatized heads.

Omega and Gamma readied their weapons. Gary lit a cigarette. Mark Spitz thought of the old sign in the token booths: I AM THE STATION MANAGER. I AM ASSISTING OTHER CUSTOMERS. YOU WILL RECOGNIZE ME BY MY BURGUNDY VEST. The man identified himself, and when he got close enough Mark Spitz saw he was not wearing a burgundy vest. It wasn't some transit authority rep or bearded subterranean hermit who hailed them, but the Lieutenant, in full combat gear, the first time they'd seen him so outfitted. Their laconic boss was aboveground in Wonton; down here he was a real soldier, veteran of the calamity. Shamed, the sweepers assumed their idiosyncratic versions of combat stances. "Thought I'd tag along and get some exercise," the Lieutenant said.

He hadn't geared up in months, "But it's like riding a bike. A hell-bike, made out of hell." Over whiskey the following Sunday, he confided to Mark Spitz and Kaitlyn that he'd had a bad feeling about Broadway, ever since Buffalo gave the green light.

Mark Spitz kept tripping over the crossties. He didn't like walking in the rut, where the bilge seeped into his boots, so he jumped from tie to tie like a kid in a hopscotch grid. He was paranoid about the niches cut into the wall, where a track worker might duck if caught in front of a train. Each black hole harbored a skel, each maintenance corridor was full of hostiles about to spill onto the track, the native population bursting from their shadow habitat to rout the invaders.

"We've never been on the subway before," Gary said.

"Usually you ride in train cars," Mark Spitz said.

"Do you think they'll start it up again?"

"Have to get around somehow. Zone One, Zone Two. Once they get the juice on." The subway will be reduced in the next world, stripped of its powers like some punished god. Forced to recapitulate childhood stages, when it extended through the savage city neighborhood by neighborhood, line by line.

"Queens?"

"I don't think we're sweeping Queens anytime soon," the Lieutenant said. "It's Queens. But yeah, there will be power."

"It will be nice to watch TV again," Kaitlyn said.

"Certainly," the Lieutenant said. "There's some idiot in Bubbling Brooks right now thinking up a plague sitcom." He whirled at a scurrying sound, then resumed his march. "Filmed in front of a live studio audience. Half filled."

Mark Spitz imagined the hunchback in the cement-block chamber a mile beneath the city, sweating through a yellowed wifebeater, who hit the switch. A hundred thousand refrigerators hum-to at once, 12:00 blinks on the displays of a million microwave ovens and digital video players, all the sad machines that had shut off in the middle of their humble duties, waiting for orders. The hallway lights of tenements and corporate towers snap on, and in the underground, the red and green signal indicators. The magic third rail in deadly awareness. The machines wake to a new world where their old routines are void. As if they were human beings powered down by the plague and then reinitialized for an alternative purpose.

He acclimated to the underneath world, the echoes of their voices and boots that fluttered from wall to wall like bats, the spitting and streaming water that pushed through every crack. An eerie tranquillity settled in his chest. There had been a lot of ash swirling in the air that day, oppressive in its steady, mindless assault on his personal zone, settling in drifts on his barriers. The black stations were an asylum again, the platform a sturdy rock to cling to, as it had been when he was a teenage explorer in the city and the vast human current was attacking him, plucking at him. Before the unwinding of the world, he could always catch his breath here, beneath the uncountable tonnage of the city, the mass of strivers' aspirations and evanescent hopes, and prepare himself for the next engagement. So it was again.

Everything was copacetic until Chambers, when that eternal question confronted them: local or express. "What do you think, Lieutenant, South Ferry or Brooklyn?" Joshua asked. He snapped his sponsor chewing gum like a bored teen being shuttled to the family reunion. They'd seen rats, dried blood puddles, dust, and chips of bullet-lacerated subway tile, but not a single skel. The marine operation had been so noisy that any plague-blind galoot skulking in the tunnels had been drawn out and cut down. When Disposal came for the bodies, they'd terminated the one or two laggards that wandered out like the unpopular kids no one had told about the end of hide-and-seek two hours prior. It was becoming apparent to Gamma and Omega that underground was as straightforward as their aboveground sweep. Actually, easier, for any stragglers—the odd, befuddled straphanger waiting for the train that would never pull in, or the token clerk hovering over a stack of two-day passes—had already been wiped out. The darkness did not squeeze so tightly now.

"We'll do South Ferry first, get to the end of the line, and then double back," the Lieutenant said.

"Then we have to come back tomorrow to finish," Foreskin said.

"Then we come back tomorrow."

"How about we take the express and Omega takes the local?" Foreskin suggested. Split up, rendezvous here, and call it a day.

The Lieutenant glared at the two southbound tunnels, the dead black eyes of them. Gary raised his eyebrows, clowning.

"We're up in the Zone day and night," Trevor said. "This is just another basement, if you ask me. We've been in some serious basements the last few weeks."

"Serious basements," Joshua said. They all nodded at the sage assessment, and Mark Spitz chuckled. Nobody knows the basements we've seen . . .

The Lieutenant stalled in the loop of one of his trademark hesitations and relented. Gamma chose the express tracks, which sloped down south of the station, and Omega took the local. Foreskin resumed Gary's heavy metal song and the two units proceeded to their fates. During a later Sunday-night confab in the dumpling house, the Lieutenant regretted not riding with Gamma. "The bad feeling I got was an express-track bad feeling, not a local-track feeling, but this escaped me when we split up. I fucked up." He had brought a present: ice cubes. They clicked and tocked in their glasses. Kaitlyn crunched them in her teeth. That's the express all over, Mark Spitz thought: It gets you to your final destination quicker. He decided the Lieutenant's bad feeling told him that the express was a preordained clusterfuck, and that's why he posse'd with Omega. To save those who could be saved.

"Bzzzz bzzzz," Gary said. He tapped the third rail with his sneaker.

Mark Spitz was on point. Kaitlyn diligently retraced Gary's footsteps, as if they were in a minefield. It was getting on his nerves. "For luck," she told him when he complained. He told her to back up. She didn't. The Lieutenant pulled up the rear, dawdling for a reason, trying to figure out what detail eluded him.

"What's next?" Gary asked.

The old World Trade Center station, Mark Spitz thought. That was a long time ago, but he remembered.

The reports of Gamma's assault rifles churned through the tunnel as if on slick steel wheels. Mark Spitz looked uptown and downtown to fix the origin of the gunfire, and he was back on a platform in the old days, trying to figure out if that was his train approaching or the opposite track's. They ran back to Chambers. Their night vision atomized the beams and struts into grains, flimsy pixels, that rose and submerged from shadow. The world dissolved into and re-formed out of darkness with each step, and the barrage continued. Three weapons firing, shouts, then a lesser volley. One weapon silenced. The Lieutenant hollered commonsense rules of engagement, but between the gunfire and the military jargon, Mark Spitz found it hard to make out. He relied on his standard translation of mayhem, which had served him well so far.

When the downtown tracks merged, and Omega leaped between the columns to the express, the shooting had stopped. The Lieutenant cursed. One man shrieked and then the man's cries sputtered to a wet gurgle. They recognized the sound of people being eaten. Gamma's flashlights were on now, reflecting from around the bend in the tunnel as if the first train of the reborn metropolis were approaching the station. The Lieutenant tracked ahead. The lights jiggled. The screams sputtered. The Lieutenant motioned for them to slow down as the crouching skels appeared in the lights, pieces of their bodies moving in and out of illumination, so engrimed by the underworld that as they fed, they were gargoyles glistening with blood.

"Heads!" The Lieutenant didn't need to remind Gamma, as there was little chance of them being hit by friendly fire, prostrate on the tracks, pinned beneath monsters. The bullets detonating in the craniums of the skels interrupted the feast. One looked into Mark Spitz's eyes, face decorated with gore, and then resumed eating Trevor. Other dead on the edge of the feeding huddle were more interested in the prospect of a deeper menu, and wafted clumsily toward Omega, stumbling between the tracks.

The four survivors intended to continue their march through the dead world, as they had since Last Night. They terminated the skels, draping their disparate masks over the faces of the damned so they could be certain of who and what they were killing.

They each saw something different as they dropped the creatures. Mark Spitz knew Gary's appraisal of the dead. They were the proper citizens who had stymied and condemned him and his brothers all his life, excluding them from the festivities—the homeroom teachers and assistant principals, the neighbors across the street who called the cops to bitch about the noise and the trash in their yard. Where were their rules now, their judgments, condescending smiles? Gary rid the squares of their heads with gusto, perforated them redundantly to emphasize his contempt.

To Kaitlyn, this scourge came from a different population. She aimed at the rabble who nibbled at the edge of her dream: the weak-willed smokers, deadbeat dads and welfare cheats, single moms incessantly breeding, the flouters of speed laws, and those who only had themselves to blame for their ridiculous credit-card debt.

These empty-headed fiends between Chambers and Park Place did not vote or attend parent-teacher conferences, they ate fast food more than twice a week and required special plus-size stores for clothing to hide their hideous bodies from the healthy. Her assembled underclass who simultaneously undermined and justified her lifestyle choices. They needed to be terminated, and they tumbled into the dirty water beside Gary's dead without differentiation.

If the beings they destroyed were their own creations, and not the degraded remnants of the people described on the things' driver's licenses, so be it. We never see other people anyway, only the monsters we make of them. To Mark Spitz, the dead were his neighbors, the people he saw every day, as he might on a subway car, the fantastic metropolitan array. The subway was the great leveler—underground, the Wall Street titans stood in the shuddering car and clutched the same poles as the junior IT guys to create a totem of fists, the executive vice presidents in charge of new product marketing pressed thighs with the luckless and the dreamers, who got off at their stations when instructed by the computer's voice and were replaced by devisers of theoretical financial instruments of unreckoned power, who vacated their seats and were replaced in turn by unemployable homunculi clutching yesterday's tabloids. They jostled one another, competed for space below as they did above, in a minuet of ruin and triumph. In the subway, down in the dark, no citizen was more significant or more decrepit than another. All were smeared into a common average of existence, the A's and the C's tumbling or rising to settle into a ruthless mediocrity. No escape. This was the plane where Mark Spitz lived. They were all him. Middling talents who got by, barnacles on humanity's hull, survivors who had not yet been extinguished. Perhaps it was only a matter of time. Perhaps he would live until he chose not to. Mark Spitz aimed at the place where the spine met the cranium. They fell without a sound. He'd had practice.

They fired until all that needed to be killed had been killed, and they stood numbly looking into the darkness for more, the next apparitions hiding in the wings, for surely they were not finished. They were human beings, after all, and full of things that needed to be put down.

Mark Spitz didn't know what monsters the Lieutenant saw, but his system must have worked, for the man dispatched them with brisk proficiency.

From what they could reconstruct, the dead had been trapped inside a transit-authority control booth that the marines had missed in the first sweep of the tunnels. Gamma freed them. Mark Spitz pictured them splashing forth from the room, as if from the burst membranes of a cyst. No, not liquid, something electric—the banks of quiet machines, the neglected, pining keys and blank screens coordinating the subway system were full of frustrated energy and those bottled-up forces finally exploded in recrudescent fury. Released at the first indication that the people might return, the people from above, the riders who gave these tunnels purpose. Trevor, Joshua, and Richard Cowl had made it ten meters back up the tunnel before they were overcome, or one was pinned and his brothers failed in their rescue. In the light of their helmets, the blood was very dark against the rails, mixing with the black water trapped in the ruts. No one said "Name That Bloodstain!" because you didn't play Name That Bloodstain! with people you knew. Mark Spitz told himself, I can Name That Bloodstain! in five seconds: It looks like the future.

That was the end of sweepers in the subway. The Lieutenant informed Buffalo the tunnels could wait until the next detachment of marines arrived, when they initiated Zone Two. He wasn't going to send his people back down there. "One of my unit leaders majored in communications, for God's sake."

Bravo and Omega drained their glasses in the Brazilian churrascaria. No one talked. The digital musical player chirped uplifting verses about summer love. Mark Spitz realized he hadn't told them about Bubbling Brooks yet.

"Oh my God," Angela said.

"Those poor people."

"The Triplets! What about the Triplets?"

"They say one made it out," Mark Spitz said.

"Which one? Was it Finn?"

"I don't know."

"I hope it was Finn," No Mas said. "He's my favorite. That little motherfucker got heart."

"Poor Cheyenne," Kaitlyn said.

Gary closed his eyes and nodded, communing with the world's most hardscrabble triplet.

They set up the motion detectors and bunked, nestling gamey rims of sleeping bags under their noses. Kaitlyn propped herself on her elbows, flossing. She said, "Bright and early, back to work." The matter of who owned the disputed grid, with its walk-ups and cherished parking lot, had been settled in Omega's favor. One final gift from the Lieutenant.

Mark Spitz closed his eyes to the jungle shadows on the wall. The last time he saw the Lieutenant had been in the dumpling house, as their Sunday-night confab was winding down. Kaitlyn was asleep, leaning against the wall in a full-on snore session. Greater Wonton was in a jovial mood. Italy's prime minister had released Gina Spens pinups, for the sake of global morale, wherein the bikini-clad warrior woman posed with a machine gun on a beach, draped herself coyly on a radar panel, and the like. There had been another three kill fields reported, even though one turned out not to be a bona fide kill field but the dumping ground of some master-level skel slaughterer, identity unknown. (Buffalo was keen to find him for a profile.) Good news, although the Lieutenant's features argued otherwise. Mark Spitz said, "You resist?"

"I'm not immune. I sleep poorly, but I nap rich. The plague is the plague, though. I don't see a reason to believe it's finished."

"Didn't take you for a divine-justice whacko."

"Not God. Nature, if you have to call it something. Correcting an imbalance. It kicks us out of our robotic routine, what they called my dad before we pulled the plug: persistent vegetative state. Comeuppance for a flatlined culture."

"Maybe it's corrected now," Mark Spitz said. He'd had a lot of whiskey for a tint of optimism to leak into his words. "Got rid of the extra population and now it's done." He was immediately disgusted with himself for phrasing it that way and checked to make sure Kaitlyn, his externalized conscience, hadn't heard. She snored.

"Maybe Buffalo is right and we're done with the plague and this is a vital enterprise we're doing here. Maybe we're merely butchers scraping off the gone-bad bits off the meat and putting it back under the glass."

"Then why are you here, if it's doomed?"

"I apologize again for not bringing ice."

"It's fine."

"I was trying to make it into a weekly thing, but I forgot." He took a big sip. "You know why they walk around? They walk around because they're too stupid to know they're dead."

"I'm here because there's something worth bringing back."

"That's straggler thinking." He smiled. It was the faintest of disturbances on his face, as if a black eel miles below on the ocean floor had turned in its sleep and left this slim reverberation on the surface. "I'm grateful. Buffalo has given us some busywork to keep our minds off things. Dig a drainage ditch for the camp, shuck the fucking corn." He raised his glass to his friends across the table. "Clear some buildings. You have to admit, it passes the time."

SUNDAY

"Move as a team, never move alone:
Welcome to the Terrordome."

When the wall fell, it fell quickly, as if it had been waiting for this moment, as if it had been created for the very instant of its failure. Barricades collapsed with haste once exposed for the riddled and rotten things they had always been. Beneath that façade of stability they were as ethereal as the society that created them. All the feverish subroutines of his survival programs booted up, for the first time in so long, and he located the flaw the instant before it expressed itself: there.

The morning the Zone died Omega slept in, murk-mouthed in hangover. Normally the unit would have punched out at 3:00 p.m. and hit Wonton, but Kaitlyn reminded them that they'd knocked off early yesterday. She "didn't want to let them down," *them* being that many-headed pheenie hydra, whether it quivered in a bauxite mine waiting for the dead weather to clear or was clutched tight to the happy bosom of a settlement camp and at this very moment scooping Sunday brunch out of aluminum tins in the mess hall. Mark Spitz registered Kaitlyn's response to the news of the Tromanhauser Triplets, and interpreted this morning's dedication as a sacrifice toward their welfare, zipping out across the miles: May it keep those tiny hearts pumping. In her action sequence, Kaitlyn emerged from the burning shed in slow motion, outrunning a covey of skels, one triplet under each arm and the last in a sling on her chest.

The two sweeper units wished each other swift recovery from dehydration and alcohol-wrung melancholy. Hair of the dog once they got back to Wonton, no question. Then it was back to work. Fulton x Gold. Yes, Omega savored their hard-won parking lot row by row, that void in their work detail, every blessed cubic foot of it and the fallow air rights to boot. The line of four-story tenements were devoid of demons, save for two suicides they bagged at 42 Gold. The pair killed themselves in identically laid-out junior one-bedrooms two floors apart. The elderly occupant of 2R hung herself from a stained-glass chandelier in the living room. Once the fixture tore away from the ceiling, the plaster bits mixed with the decomp sludge and lent her corpse a unique, lumpy texture that reminded Mark Spitz of the things lurking in old takeout. She had mutated, stranded in her cardboard carton at the back of the fridge. He recognized the ottoman on which she'd steadied herself; he had impulse-bought the same one online, on sale, the spring he moved into his parents' rec room. Stainproof, one of the new miracle weaves, machine washable. He'd used it to change the recessed energy-saver bulbs in the track lighting, whose pallid light he accused of draining him of vitality and cheer.

The neighboring suicide upstairs blew his brains out on his sofa. The man in 4R was owl-faced with thin straw hair and shrunken limbs that poked from clothes a size too big. He'd starved before offing himself, noshing on the doomsday stock he gathered for his market-rate bunker: the bathroom tub was full of licked-clean cans and neatly flattened boxes, tied up and bagged in preparation for recycling day. Gary observed that his stench didn't jibe with that of your average putrefying New Yorker, and indeed inspection of the hatbox next to the body revealed it to be the tomb of the fuzzy, deflated form of the calico recognizable from numerous photographs adorning the apartment. The suicide note mentioned this roommate prominently, conjecturing about a mingled animal and human afterlife that did not discriminate between species, or possession of a brain big enough to conceive of an afterlife. Neither resident was bitten; they acceded to their particular forbidden thoughts.

Omega bagged the two neighbors and left them in the street for Disposal. They zipped up the calico with its owner.

The fortune-teller was their final sweep of the day. It was almost six o'clock. Kaitlyn suggested they pick up here tomorrow, but Gary said, "I want to get my palm read."

Mark Spitz could not fathom how this deathless codger of a storefront had endured the relentless metropolitan renovations. The only answer was that the city itself was as bewitched by the past as the little creatures who skittered on its back. The city refused to let them go: How else to explain the holdout establishments on block after block, in sentimental pockets across the grid? These stores had opened every morning to serve a clientele extinct even before the plague's rampage, displaying objects of zero utility on felt behind smudged glass, dangling them on steel hooks where dust clung and colonized. Discontinued products, exterminated desires. The city protected them, Mark Spitz thought. The typewriter-repair shop, the shoe-repair joint with its antiquated neon calligraphy and palpable incompetence that warned away the curious, the family deli with its germ-herding griddle: They stuck to the block with their faded signage and ninety-nine-year leases, murmuring among themselves in a dying vernacular of nostalgia. Businesses north and south, to either side of them, sold the new things, the chromium gizmos that people needed, while the city blocks nursed these old places, held them close like secrets or tumors.

The fortune-teller's was precisely such an atavistic enterprise, a straggler in the current argot, with disintegrating tinsel sparking dully beyond the tacky exhortations stenciled on the window. Garlands of Christmas lights and black necklaces of dead insects beaded at the bottom of the window display. Every other store on the block ministered to some yuppie lack, bent toward the local demographic sun and absorbing into its capillaries imported kitchen implements and upscale children's accoutrements. Yet here was the fortune-teller's. Could events have transpired differently? If Bravo had won Fulton x Gold, Mixed Residential/Business, that other unit's blend of personalities might have shepherded events in a different direction. If it hadn't been Omega's last stop before R & R, perhaps Gary wouldn't have been in such a jovial mood and played the fool. Later Mark Spitz untangled the string of inevitabilities. It looked like a choker of dead black flies.

Gary snipped the bolt and Mark Spitz helped him slide up the shop's recalcitrant gate. The dark brass doorknob and lock were relics, smoothed to an otherworldly luster by the caress of generations' hands. Mark Spitz didn't see this tacky shop attracting a high volume of seekers, but who knew what vital shops operated here before the clairvoyant unpacked her arcana, the clandestine line of utility and desire terminating at this address. Real estate agents, butchers, antique jewelers, and cell providers stood behind the counter, tending customers who wore fedoras, then loops of metal in soft tissue. Hoop skirts, panty hose, then blue ink where the symbology of the upstart faiths and outsider iconography were carved into their skin. The sole page in this address's photo album he could see was the one before him now.

The proprietor sat at the table in the center of the room. Eschewing the traditional finery of her profession, this straggler was dressed in the all-black uniform of a downtown punk. She was around Mark Spitz's age, not yet thirty when the plague dropped her in its amber, with green streaks entwined in her ebony-dyed hair and smudged mascara deepening the plague bruises circling her eyes. The signs on the wall provided a menu of services in a popular computer font: Astrological Charts, Numerology, Aura Manipulation, and the enigmatic "Recalibration." Small jars and bowls of herbs, rainbow powders, and bone-white charms perched on tiny metal shelves, props acquired from an internet retail site. Red and brown earth tones dominated the tapestries, pillows, and rugs, bestowing the aura of a lair. Omega stood before a medium's sanctum as portrayed in pop culture, the demeanor of the clairvoyant herself bestowing a small, necessary tweak. The fortune-teller in the modern city, plying the Old World enchantments and scrying trade of her ancestors. Her parents probably thought she'd forsaken her heritage when she came home with that loop of metal in her nose, but it was an adjustment that allowed the family biz to keep up with the protean city. Everybody needs a shtick to keep competitive, Mark Spitz thought.

A hunk of the fortune-teller's neck beneath her right ear was absent. The exposed meat resembled torn-up pavement tinted crimson, a scabbed hollow of gaping gristle, tubes, and pipes: the city's skin ripped back. She haunted her old workstation, hands flat on the ruby-red cloth adorning the small round table. There were two chairs, her messages intended for one soul at a time.

Kaitlyn said, "I got the back" and retreated into the recesses of the shop, parting the curtain of red beads with her assault rifle.

Gary snickered mischievously.

Mark Spitz said, "For fuck's sake." His new policy announced itself: The sooner you take the stragglers down, the better. They weren't the Lieutenant's sentimentalized angels, dispensing obscure lessons through the simple fact of their existence, and Mark Spitz's impulse to leave Ned the Copy Boy at his post in the empty office was no mercy. These things were not kin to their perished resemblances but vermin that needed to be put down. Why had he faltered?

Gary dropped his pack and ensconced himself in the seeker's

chair, removing his mesh gloves with a theatrical flourish. He arranged the proprietor's pale and faintly gray hand on his open palm. "Just a quick reading, Mark Spitz," Gary said. "There are things we need to know."

"It's disrespectful," Mark Spitz said. He raised his rifle; Gary waved it away. Gary wasn't inclined to abuse on the caliber of his old bandit cronies, but that didn't mean Mark Spitz wanted to be a witness, and there was no point in mocking a skel unless you had a witness. Mark Spitz couldn't isolate the origin of his distaste, and was disinclined to associate it with the previous afternoon's solicitude toward Ned. He was too tired to take on the added freight of new symptoms.

His hand nestled in hers, Gary's black fingernails found analogue in the red grit beneath their host's. Soothseeker and soothsayer alike had clawed through their respective cemetery dirt. Gary winched his eyebrows. "Anyone you want to talk to in the Great Beyond, Mark Spitz?"

A few blocks past the wall, his uncle's apartment hovered nineteen stories above the street, a pulsing presence. Mark Spitz didn't need a medium; signal flares and semaphore would have sufficed. What revelation would Uncle Lloyd have delivered? What did his uncle know now that he hadn't known before the cataclysm? Nothing. Nothing Mark Spitz hadn't already discovered in the wasteland.

At Mark Spitz's demurral, Gary attached an invisible headset to his ear and radioed, "Lieutenant, do you copy? We need our orders. Don't leave us to Fabio, bruh."

Gary could have addressed his brothers, had he been able to evade and outwit his denial over their deaths. Any séance was doomed, in Mark Spitz's estimation, even if the young psychic had functioned properly, if she had still owned her talents. He'd sifted through the failed proofs of an afterlife many a cold night. There was a barrier at the end of one's life, yes, but nothing on the other side. How could there be? The plague stopped the heart, one's essence sloughed off the pathetic human meat and dog-paddled through the ectoplasm or whatever, and then the plague restarted the heart. What kind of cruel deity granted a glimpse of the angelic sphere, only to yank it away and condemn you to a monster's vantage? Sentenced you to observe the world through the sad aperture of the dead, suffer the gross parody of your existence. Outside Zone One, the souls sat trapped in the bleachers, spectators to the travesties committed by their alienated hands.

The death of the afterlife was not without its perks, however, sparing Mark Spitz the prospect of an eternity reliving his mistakes and seeing their effects ripple, however briefly and uselessly, through history.

"This Gypsy's missing a few screws," Gary said. He lifted the slab of her hand and dropped its dead weight on the table.

Kaitlyn rejoined them. "Looks like she started living back there once it went down." She shook her head at the tableau before her but was unable to be authentically appalled. It had been a long day. "You're sick, Gary."

"Nothing you'd like to ask, Kaitlyn?" Gary gripped the fortune-teller's hand again. "Don't you want to know when you meet Mr. Right?"

"Okay, I'll bite—"

"Wrong word."

His comrades settled into Solve the Skel joviality, Mark Spitz told himself to relax. It had been a rough two days, between Human Resources and the Lieutenant's execution of the forbidden thought. In half an hour they'd be at Wonton and another week closer to the remaking of the world. He felt something in his skin, though, the faintest of vibrations.

Kaitlyn asked, "Will the Triplets make it through?"

"What's the matter, plague got your tongue? . . . Hold on, I'm getting something . . ." Gary vamped, eyes clenched. "Three brave souls . . ."

"Cheyenne, fool. Is Cheyenne okay?"

"The answer is . . . Yes!"

"Sweet lord."

Mark Spitz asked, "Will we make it through?"

Gary opened one eye and grinned. "Let me check, hold on a sec . . . Madame Gypsy, can you help us see the future?"

We make the future, Mark Spitz thought. That's why we're here.

"It's hazy," Gary said. He concentrated harder, hand trembling. "What you really want to know is, will you make it through?"

"Yes."

"Hold on a sec . . ." Gary's body convulsed, a ferocious psychic current entering at that intersection of his skin and that of the fortune-teller. The mechanic couldn't keep a straight face as he combated the forces of the spirit world, frail conduit. For the first time Mark Spitz noticed the tiny smile engraved into the fortune-teller's black lips, as if she enjoyed the joke as well, or an altogether different amusement, the exact grain and texture of which only she could appreciate. Gary collapsed on the table, milked the moment, and then wearily raised his head. "They say everything is going to be all right, Mark Spitz. You don't have to worry about a thing."

To be a good sport, Mark Spitz made a show of relief. On the street, his ash had begun to fall, his vanguard flakes.

"Okay, up, up, Gary," Kaitlyn said, "let's finish this off."

"Don't sulk," Gary said. He lifted his fingers from the fortune-teller's hand and the instant he broke contact she grabbed his hand and chomped deep into the meat between the index finger and thumb. Blood sprayed, paused, sprayed again with the exertions of his heart. The Gypsy's mouth ground back and forth, ripping and chewing, and she gobbled up his thumb.

Kaitlyn's bullets disintegrated her head and she slumped to the floor, spewing the dark fluid in her veins onto the shelves of a home-assembly particle-board bookcase filled with her occult troves. Before her face was liquefied, her smile returned to her blood-splashed lips: a broad, satisfied crescent of teeth. Or so Mark Spitz imagined.

He ministered to Gary's wound while Kaitlyn shot the fortune-teller four more times, cursing. Gary's shrieks of shock and agony turned into a command for anticiprant. "Gimme the shit, where's the shit, gimme the shit," he cried, hands roving over his vest. Mark Spitz found his friend's supply of antibiotic, in the same pocket that held this week's hoard of mood stabilizers. Gary gobbled up the anticiprant, and then Mark Spitz's stash and Kaitlyn's. He howled.

It was folklore, the megadose of drugs that snuffed out the plague if you swallowed it quickly enough. Anticiprant had been a second-tier antibiotic in the previous world; no telling how it had been cast as the cavalry repelling the invading spirochetes of the plague. Poll a random mess table at a resettlement camp and you'd find one or two pheenies who claimed to know someone who knew someone who had been saved by this prophylaxis. When pressed, of course, no one could claim firsthand knowledge. Mark Spitz didn't believe in its powers. More likely, the original carriers of this doomsday folklore hadn't received a proper wallop of the plague, enough to infect. But it didn't hurt to carry some pills in your pocket. People carried crucifixes and holy books. Why not an easy-to-swallow caplet of faith, in a new fast-acting formula.

Kaitlyn stabbed Gary's arm with a morphine ampoule and finished dressing the wound. She wiped the blood off with a fuchsia hand towel from the back bathroom. He moaned and glared at his Gypsy as if to cut her open and fish around for his thumb and sew it back on. "Gypsy curse," he said, spitting a ruby to the dusty carpet. The white mitt at the end of his wrist was pricked with red specks that bloomed into red petals, became a bouquet. Mark Spitz opened another dressing.

They didn't have to get into the heavy stuff yet. There was

time. It was faster now, after generations and mutations, but there was time.

"I want more pills," Gary said.

"I'll see if Bravo is still up the block," Kaitlyn said. Given their temperament, the unit was long back at Wonton, but Mark Spitz knew she wanted a chance to try and get a signal out to report the situation. Get a higher-up to weigh in, even if it was lowly Fabio.

They settled in the back room. The fortune-teller had dug out a meager alcove in the interregnum, for a few weeks at least. The apartment bore the telltale markers of siege life, in the goo mounds of candle wax, the ziggurat of cans of beans and soup. The couch and its cocoon of blankets was the nest where she plotted her unsuccessful escape. Mark Spitz helped Gary over to it, the wounded man traducing their dead host with every step.

Kaitlyn will be right back, Mark Spitz reassured. She's dependable.

Gary dragged a fistful of quilt to his chin, like an old lady vexed by an ineradicable draft. "Why do they call you Mark Spitz?" he asked.

He told him about the wreckers, the Northeast Corridor, and the jokes when they got back to Fort Golden Gate from the viaduct. He'd laughed along with everyone else, but later he had to look up Mark Spitz, in a surreptitious mission for an old paper encyclopedia. First he had to find one, which took time. Finally he was saved by movie night at the bungalow of one of the infrastructure guys; the previous inhabitants owned a big fat dictionary, old school, with pictures, even. His nicknamesake had been an Olympic swimmer in the previous century, a real thoroughbred who'd held the world record for the most gold medals in one game: freestyle, butterfly. The Munich Games—Munich, where the scientists had made biohaz soup of the infected, in the early days of the plague, as they worked toward a vaccine. The word "soup" had stayed with him, after one of the denizens of the wasteland had told him the story. People were becoming less than people everywhere, he had thought: monsters, soup.

Seven gold medals? Eight? Here was one of the subordinate ironies in the nickname: He was anything but an Olympian. The medals awarded this Mark Spitz were stamped from discarded slag. Mark Spitz explained the reference of his sobriquet to Gary, adding, "Plus the black-people-can't-swim thing."

"They can't? You can't?"

"I can. A lot of us can. Could. It's a stereotype."

"I hadn't heard that. But you have to learn how to swim sometime."

"I tread water perfectly."

He found it unlikely that Gary was not in ownership of a master list of racial, gender, and religious stereotypes, cross-indexed with corresponding punch lines as well as meta-textual dissection of those punch lines, but he did not press his friend. Chalk it up to morphine. There was a single Us now, reviling a single Them. Would the old bigotries be reborn as well, when they cleared out this Zone, and the next, and so on, and they were packed together again, tight and suffocating on top of each other? Or was that particular bramble of animosities, fears, and envies impossible to recreate? If they could bring back paperwork, Mark Spitz thought, they could certainly reanimate prejudice, parking tickets, and reruns.

There were plenty of things in the world that deserved to stay dead, yet they walked.

Gary had ceased speaking in his fraternal we. Were the weevils munching through even now, gnawing canals in his brainstuff? He heard Kaitlyn reenter the shop. He recognized her walk, but he had to double-check. With Gary's attack, he was one foot in the wasteland again, and nothing could be taken for granted. He felt energized, a reptilian knob at the base of his skull throbbing.

Kaitlyn dropped into the morass of the orange beanbag chair, sinking deeper than she expected, and told them she saw no sign of Bravo. Still only a squall of feedback on the comm. Gary closed his eyes. Mark Spitz said, "Stay awake. Stay awake. There's one more thing about the highway I want to tell you. You'll think it's cool."

He told his unit how he'd discovered the clandestine heart of the Quiet Storm's maneuvers. He was aboard the chopper on his way to the Zone. The other wreckers had opted to stay on the corridor. Richie didn't like "the big city" as he called it, although like many who uttered these words, he had never been. Mark Spitz didn't point out that what he most likely despised about the city was gone: the people. The Quiet Storm told him she still had work to do, in her weird affect, which he didn't pay attention to at the time. He finally saw it from above, what she had carved into the interstate. While the other wreckers, indeed all the other survivors, could only perceive the wasteland on its edge, the Quiet Storm was in the sky, inventing her alphabet and making declarations in a row of five green hatchbacks parked perpendicular to the median, in a sequence of black-and-white luxury sedans arranged nose to nose two miles down the road, in a burst of ten minivans in glinting enamel tilted at an acute angle half a mile farther north. The grammar lurked in the numbers and colors, the meaning encoded in the spaces between the vehicular syllables, half a mile, quarter mile. Five jeeps lined up south by southwest on a north–south stretch of highway: This was one volley of energy, uncontained by the routes carved out by settlers two hundred years before, or reified by urban planners steering the populace toward the developers' shopping centers. Ten sport-utility vehicles arranged one-eighth of a mile apart east–west were the fins of an eel slipping through silty depths, or the fletching on an arrow aimed at—what? Tomorrow? What readers? Then his chopper was over a midsize city in botched

Connecticut, beyond the margins of her manuscript, and he was halfway to Zone One.

"What's that supposed to mean?"

"We don't know how to read it yet. All we can do right now is pay witness."

She wrote her way into the future. Buffalo huffed over its machinations and narratives of replenishment, and the wretched pheenies stabbed their bloody knees and elbows into the sand as they slunk toward their mirages. And then there were people like the Quiet Storm, who carved their own pawns and rooks out of the weak clay and deployed them across their board, engaged in their own strategic reconstructions. Mark Spitz saw her mosaic, in its immense tonnage, outlasting all of Buffalo's schemes, the operations under way and the ones yet to be articulated. What readership did she address? Gods and aliens, anyone who looks down at the right time, from the right perspective. To Anyone Who Can Read This: Stay Away. Please Help. Remember Me.

"Maybe it says: It's safe now, we're gone. Maybe it says: I'm still here." She had told him when she declined to leave the corridor that she wasn't finished yet.

"Sounds like PASD to me," Gary said. "In Rainbow Village this one guy wrote Bible verses in his own shit." He tapped his vest after his sponsor cigarettes, drowsy. "Who's going to go up and get me more penicillin?"

"I'll go," Mark Spitz said.

"Try not to fuck around, going on about how the ash is falling," Gary said. "You're not going to mention the ash, right?"

"Yes."

"I see you looking out the window," he said. "It's best to keep it to yourself, I think." Like a parent telling a kid to lay off the nostril-mining, just for an hour. People might talk.

"You're not on your deathbed. Death-futon."

"How am I supposed to light a cigarette with this?"

Mark Spitz waited for Kaitlyn to join him outside. Up the street, Disposal had tossed the bodies of the suicides into the back of their cart. The overcast sky ushered in premature evening and he wondered if it was going to rain, even though the thunder he heard wasn't meteorological but martial. Kaitlyn emerged from the shop, wiping her fingers with antibacterial wipes. "He says he wants to stay here," she said. "He doesn't want to see anyone."

"I'll check in with Fabio, hit up the medic for something to make him more comfortable." The euphemism came easily. "What if he turns quick?"

"I'm ready. I won't leave him alone. I only came out here in case he wanted a minute to off himself."

"Okay."

"Run."

He beat it uptown. Two blocks uptown he realized he'd forgotten his pack; he decided not to go back for it. The thunder of the artillery intensified, cleaved from the lightning that might have, for an instant, lit his passage through the worsening gloom, livened his ash into brief fireflies. The thunder has lost his brother, he thought. When was the last time they enjoyed a proper dinner as a family? Done it right, without griping about the brass at Wonton, complaining about blisters, had a dinner devoid of one person's brooding or sullen reverie about the time before the flood. Omega had taken it for granted, the family meal. It came to him as he skidded onto Broadway: Kaitlyn's birthday. They were yo-yoing up and down the stairwells of a corporate megalith and she'd dropped no less than three anecdotes detailing some of the key birthday parties of her youth: the educational visit to the eco-friendly ranch where alpacas nibbled gray pellets from her tiny palm, their rough tongues tickling; the excursion to the mad scientist's laboratory where her third-grade friends had spun filaments of cotton candy; the surprise party it seemed the whole town was in on, so elaborately did the charade about the "visit to the dentist" unfold. Eventually Gary had no choice but to ask when her big day was. "Today," she said, as the body bag in her hands spontaneously unzipped, loosing chunky gallons of fluids and innards.

Omega cut their biscuits in half for buns, lit a ball of C-4 to make a fire, and grilled up some spamburgers, which they consumed happily in the private room of an upscale Italian restaurant off Laight. "Fancy," Gary said, belching. A pinch of cumin and coriander made all the difference, it was unanimous. Omega drank some of the Long Island cabernet that had been circulating around Wonton, after one of the generals dispatched a search-and-rescue team to the Bridgehampton vineyard. The vintners were ensconced at Camp El Dorado, became sponsors, patriots.

It was after they opened the cellophane on the coconut cupcakes and crooned the mandatory song that Kaitlyn told them the Last Night story she had held back for so long. Hers was no numb recital; she did not tell them out of compulsion to indulge in the cheap catharsis of the Big Share. She told them to eulogize to the disaster. She said, "Let me tell you about the night I started running, and make a toast to the end of that race."

He ran. Uncle Lloyd's building reared up as he turned the corner, one of the garrison's spotlights fixed on the sheer blue metal of its midsection. He flagged: What was it trying to tell him? He'd pressed his nose to the thick glass of airliner portholes for a glimpse of the building when he returned from a trip, sought its profile in the rows of skyscrapers when he was caught on one of the expressways that fed the metropolis, and when he finally rescued it from the crowd, its blue skin soaring over the bores never failed to cheer him. Each time he thought: One day I will live in a place like that, be a man of the city. Now the shimmering blue moon the spotlight punched out of the night sky was alien and unnerving. It was not the same building. It had been replaced. He ran through the ash, which was really coming down now, in his mind or everywhere, in slow, thick flakes that eased to the sidewalk in implacable surety. He was close enough to the incinerators that it was possible it was real ash. The Lieutenant was in that stuff, smithereened by the Coakleys.

The night of her birthday, in the Italian eatery, Kaitlyn explained that she booked the train even though it was more expensive than flying because there was so much of the country she had never seen. The invigorating virtues of the scenic route. While the world outside the windows was inspiring, the one inside the car was less so. Erratic shooting pains traversed her calves after three hours in her stiff seat, and the wifi whispered in and out so capriciously that she gave up on the half season of the lawyer show she'd intended to stream. The final queasy indignity occurred when a person or persons three rows back unleashed a sort of casserole salute to cheese that filled the car with a reluctant-to-dissipate stench, almost corporeal, another passenger. But her friends were waiting for her on the platform when she arrived for their reunion weekend, beckoning from beyond the metal barriers, where the steel-eyed German shepherds of the security teams chafed on their chains. Kaitlyn forgot the train's farrago of torments until her pals returned her to the station three days later.

Her homebound train stopped outside Crawfordsville. The name of the town lilted in her brain all this time later, singsongy, the locale in a country-and-western song where the singer met her unexpected love, or lost it. The Sunset Dayliner did not budge, the lights stuttered, the circulated air loudly chugged on and off—a moment of turbulence, as if they had passed through a bad pocket. On the other side of this disturbance, one of the conductors hustled between the seats toward the front of the train, ignoring questions, eschewing eye contact, and mumbling in code to his crackling handset. A pair of Concerned Passengers huddled by the handicapped-access bathroom in consternation, and she heard the time-honored threat of the impotent consumer: *I'm going to get to the bottom of this.* They had God-given rights as paying customers, the phone numbers of corporate hotlines awaited in their smartphones, beckoned from the internet, consumer-protection apparatus listed helpful e-mail addresses to capture their appeals and apply remedies.

The woman in the window seat, a birdlike thing who hadn't removed her beak from her tablet's screen since boarding, looked at Kaitlyn for the first time as the static-y voice hit the intercom: We are being held here momentarily. The woman tugged the earbuds from their inputs in the sides of her skull. "Where are we, anyway?" she asked. Later, a national guardsman shot her six times in the back with a machine gun as she tried to make a break for the woods.

After the announcement, the first person on his feet was a fifty-something man garbed in a blue denim suit, his beard mashed through red-and-green beads. He tried to transfer to the next car; the door did not budge. They were locked in. An hour passed. The bars on Kaitlyn's cell dropped one by one and the wifi shut off for good. Before the other passengers lost reception with their personal networks (in one sinister moment, a cascade of disappointment), the news blogs filled in what the conductor withheld: The train was under quarantine. A passenger had been "acting strangely" in the café car, attracting the attention of train personnel. After a scuffle, the terrorist barricaded himself in a bathroom and threatened to release a biological agent. "They have to let us out," someone wailed. A woman shouted, and everyone in the car looked out the windows at the military trucks and jeeps, the soldiers spilling onto the gravel shoulder of the right-of-way in their white hazmat suits. Kaitlyn couldn't see their faces.

The terror plot remained the cover story for the first couple of hours, plausible and self-organizing. Later, when Kaitlyn was on the run, she discovered what the rest of the country heard from the news media, before the news media was reduced to a numb scroll of rescue stations and an evanescent list of contradictory infection procedures. Before the media sighed into the depths, senescent, dumb. The train's Patient Zero had turned feral in his seat—dropped out of humanity's codes and into the solemn directives of the plague—and bit three people before being restrained; the conductor's call for aid triggered a local military response. The authorities were on alert for certain keywords on the emergency channels, as it was early in the death of the world and the military still mobilized to distress calls. Some calls, anyway.

No one was getting off that train. On that Eve of Last Night, some of the passengers in Kaitlyn's car tried to make a break for it—chute out the emergency window and sprint through a perceived weakness in the cordon. Thus did Kaitlyn first encounter that interregnum cliché, wherein the alpha male or female recruits support for a nutty plan and organizes the doomed sortie: pell-mell out of the surrounded Victorian; bursting from the collapsible door of the trapped school bus in a whirlwind of ad hoc truncheons, ladles, and chimney pokers. Out of the quarantined train car that had been plucked from its steadfast route and deposited forty-eight hours in the future, into the collapse. On the last night before the Last Night, the machine guns dispatched these intrepid; after that, it would be teeth.

When the soldiers suddenly bugged out the following evening—the armored vehicles spinning out into AWOL missions after loved ones or vain ops intended to keep it all from flying apart—Kaitlyn started running. She and the other passengers extricated themselves from the dead mass transit to master the new lessons, or else perished in their scattered elementaries. Eventually her run took her to Zone One, to Gary and Mark Spitz, the birthday celebration in the function room of an Italian restaurant, where on panels of dark wood the caricatures of the deceased regulars promenaded, famous and not famous, distended chins and knob noses protuberant and gross. Kaitlyn told them her Last

Night story not to enter into ritualized mourning but to say: This is a story of how it used to be. When we didn't know what was happening and were defenseless. Kaitlyn made a toast to Zone One and the new world they chipped from the stone, building by building, room by room, skel by skel. The intent of the caricature, Mark Spitz thought as he listened to her story, is to capture the monstrous we overlook every day. Maybe, she said, we can unsee the monsters again.

Mark Spitz cradled this memory of their last celebration as he entered Wonton's corona. It had been a lovely night, that time they tried to kid one another that the world was not ending. Listening to the gunfire from uptown, he knew what was happening. The barrier was about to fail. It was falling down, as it always did.

It started like this: On White Street he flagged down Lester, one of the Alpha Unit guys and self-appointed party wrangler for Sunday R & R ever since their first week in the Zone. Lester carried a case of Long Island red, and a huge plastic bag of popcorn dangled from the fingers of his left hand. He nodded toward the wall, rolling his eyes at the barrage, as if vexed by the neighbor's leaf blower during his annual barbecue. "Skels been coming for dinner all day, nonstop." Had Mark Spitz heard about the Lieutenant? Yes, he had. Lester was scrounging supplies for the next wake, bound for the dumpling house.

Mark Spitz told him he'd see them there, declining to tell him about Gary's bite, per his friend's wishes. Plus, Gary hated Lester.

It never ceased to be an odd sight, the approach to Wonton at night. The unnatural glare of the op lights bleached the buildings bone-white as the shadows gathered the potsherds of the dead world. This night he noticed the dead bargains: the handwritten EVERYTHING MUST GO sign in the second-floor window of a shop of no decipherable purpose, a banner proclaiming the specialty sandwich at the fast-food chain. At the corner of Broadway and Canal, the scale of the engagement shocked him. The anxious overture of the previous afternoon had evolved into a lush, neurotic symphony. The machine guns fired without cessation. He'd become so accustomed to the gunfire, the steady escalation of its bluster, that he hadn't considered how many men and women such an onslaught entailed. In the lairs atop the key structures overlooking the wall, twice as many snipers trained their scopes, muzzles crackling next to the squatting cornice gargoyles and the shells hopping on the rooftop tar. On the catwalk girding the human side of the wall, the troops were doubled up as well, strafing, reloading, zeroing in on a new target cluster up the avenue that was hidden from view by the wall, and then on to the next.

He couldn't see what the soldiers aimed at, but he could smell it. From the magnitude of the stench, the bodies putrefied in vast dunes on the other side of the barrier. West, toward the incinerators, the stack vented its puff of smoke and ash, but the fuel must have been sweeper deliveries, as Wonton had ceased scooping corpses from beyond the wall. The grab-crane duo, drenched in the rank fluids of the dead, were motionless, gigantic praying mantises caught in an inscrutable pose. Perhaps they hadn't repaired the machines yet or had diverted those on crane detail to the perimeter to knock down skels. Yesterday's pools of blood and gore had expanded into lakes fed by the mass of leaking corpses.

The vicinity of the wall bristled and bucked with activity, but a few feet away, beyond the combat lines, the Sunday-evening routines puttered as usual, inconceivably: Engineers strolled in an insouciant haze as they planned the evening's diversions, poker or a movie in one of the rec spaces; couples snuck off to their rendezvous before the new workweek implicated them; the guys and gals from the other sweeper teams waved at him to hurry up and join them at the dumpling house. After all this time in the abattoir, the survivors were completely inured to the agenda of catastrophe.

They didn't feel what he felt. Mark Spitz relished the cadence in his veins, the way his senses had ticked up into a state of uncanny alert. The rusty wasteland systems were powered up, the algorithms sorting input. As the door of the bank closed behind him, the muffling of the guns underscored the ferocious disposition of the street. HQ was tranquil, even for a Sunday night. Was the regular army on an op right now? No time to guess: He had a mission. The second-floor hall, so hectic as it channeled Buffalo's whims toward actuality, was empty now.

The Lieutenant's—correction—Fabio's office was locked. Mark Spitz rattled the door. Two cartons were stacked at his feet, the top one sliced open. He picked up one of the items inside: a combat helmet, the back of which had been branded with a butched-up drawing of the famous kid-show armadillo. The varmint made a muscle, bicep curving formidably, as he chomped a cigar butt between square white teeth. A cigar in this day and age, smoked by a kiddie icon: somebody was going to get fired. Mark Spitz had to give respect to reconstruction's new mascot, who was more prepared for what was coming than anyone at Wonton. Except for him.

Fabio let Mark Spitz in, tentatively, chary of the sweeper's bad news, whatever its stripe. When Mark Spitz briefed him, Fabio mumbled a curse and his glance drifted to the windows overlooking the wall. The man was in a fog. He said, "Gonna have to fill out a special T-12 casualty form. I think I have one somewhere." He hassled the top drawer of his desk, perplexed, fiddled in his pockets for keys.

Mark Spitz yanked the man forward by his shirt. He laid out the situation in more emphatic terms.

Fabio looked into Mark Spitz's face, only recognizing him in that moment. He apologized. "I thought you said it was a straggler."

"What we thought."

"That doesn't sound good."

"It's not," Mark Spitz said. Fabio wasn't partial to original thinking, but yes, Gary's Gypsy curse was a problem. This mutiny broke the rules. If one skel broke the rules, there were more. It was survivor's logic: If Mark Spitz was alive, there had to be others. Until the day it was not true. The fortune-teller must be a mistake, an errant bad comet loping into their solar system, the malfunctioning one percent of the malfunctioning one percent. Or else the world was resuming its decomp after these months of tenuous integrity, those stalwart membranes and harassed cell walls finally dissolving into a black spume.

"Where's Tammy?" Mark Spitz said. "He'll need morphine."

"You think he has the time for that?" Fabio stared, blank as a midtown sidewalk. He said, "However you want to handle it. You can have access to her meds, but Tammy's on a chopper to Happy Acres."

Mark Spitz asked why.

"We lost contact three hours ago. Sent some army guys to check it out."

"What is it?"

"The last transmission was hard to decipher."

"What Fabio is trying to say is that we've lost contact with everyone." It was Bozeman, his puffy round face harassed by worry. He had ditched his clerk's khakis for full combat gear, and Mark Spitz was surprised to see the RPG launcher slung over the man's back.

"It's the comms," Fabio said. "You know they're on the fritz."

"It's not the comms," Bozeman said. "I came here to tell you to bring the sweepers in. It's all hands on the wall now."

Fabio inclined his head toward the window. "It doesn't seem that bad from here."

"Come to the roof."

As they hustled to the helipad, the remaining army guys tromped down the halls, weapons ready, anti-skel helmets fastened to their heads. Mark Spitz hadn't seen a mobilization this big in ages. He regretted leaving his pack downtown.

The artillery battered his eardrums again once they gained the roof. The military spots were trained on the wall below; unlocking one's wheels, Bozeman groaned as he steered it to the eastern edge of the building. He adjusted the angle. The light joined those from other rooftops to unveil the horror of Broadway.

The ocean had overtaken the streets, as if the news programs' global warming simulations had finally come to pass and the computer-generated swells mounted to drown the great metropolis. Except it was not water that flooded the grid but the dead. It was the most mammoth convocation of their kind Mark Spitz had ever had the misfortune to see. The things were shoulder to shoulder across the entire width of the avenue, squeezed up against the buildings, an abhorrent parade that writhed and palsied up Broadway until the light failed. The damned bubbled and frothed on the most famous street in the world, the dead things still proudly indicating, despite their grime and wounds and panoply of leaking orifices, the tribes to which they had belonged, in gray pinstriped suits, classic rock T-shirts, cowboy boots, dashikis, striped cashmere cardigans, fringed suede vests, plush jogging suits. What they had died in. All the misery of the world channeled through this concrete canyon, the lament into which the human race was being transformed person by person. Every race, color, and creed was represented in this congregation that funneled down the avenue. As it had been before, per the myth of this melting-pot city. The city did not care for your story, the particular narrative of your reinvention; it took them all in, every immigrant in their strivings, regardless of bloodline, the identity of their homeland, the number of coins in their pocket. Nor did this plague discriminate; your blood fell instantly or your blood held out longer, but your blood always failed in the end.

They had been young and old, natives and newcomers. No matter the hue of their skins, dark or light, no matter the names of their gods or the absences they countenanced, they had all strived, struggled, and loved in their small, human fashion. Now they were mostly mouths and fingers, fingers for extracting entrails from soft cavities, and mouths to rend and devour in pieces the distinct human faces they captured, that these faces might become less distinct, de-individuated flaps of masticated flesh, rendered anonymous like them, the dead. Their mouths could no longer manage speech yet they spoke nonetheless, saying what the city had always told its citizens, from the first settlers hundreds of years ago, to the shattered survivors of the garrison. What the plague had always told its hosts, from the first human being to have its blood invaded, to the latest victim out in the wasteland: I am going to eat you up.

Mark Spitz's idea of what lay beyond the Zone, the portrait created by the incessant gunfire, was dwarfed by the spectacle before him. The wall had kept this reality from him. It would not hold, it was obvious. He had to get back to Kaitlyn and Gary, and they needed to make a plan. The dead leaked in massive piles on the other side of the wall, mounting between the barrier and the buildings on the north side of Canal. It would have been impossible for the cranes to keep up, even in working condition. The dead clambered up the bodies of the fallen and were rent by the artillery, contributing to the heap, and these latest were trampled by the next wave, which was cut down in turn. The corpses entwined and tangled in a mutilated pile half as high as the wall, and dark fluids from their wounds sprayed and gurgled through the seams in the concrete where the broad sections met, the weight of the corpses compressing the interior murk from the carcasses as if they were overripe fruit. The barrier was a dam now, suppressing the roiling torrent of the wasteland. It would not hold.

He saw the flaw, where it would break. The marines had maneuvered the concrete T segments into the heart of Canal, and once they stabilized the Zone, they secured them with redoubtable steel brackets two feet wide and two inches thick. The metal scaffolding of the catwalk assembly provided additional support on the Zone side against the malevolent forces of uptown. But Mark Spitz saw the chink through now-wastelanded eyes: the brackets were as flimsy as plywood boards nailed into a window frame, in that elemental image of the barricade. That's where every fortification splintered: where the nail pierced the wood, the rivet penetrated the concrete. The prayer met the truth. There is always a place for the dead to find purchase.

This night it was not a ravaged, skeletal hand that tore the plank away but the unholy mass of all the mobilized agony brimming Broadway. There was a furious blast of machine-gun fire, and more dead fell to the fleshy heap. The bracket at the western edge of the T section athwart the famous boulevard wrenched out of joint, and its brother connecting the next section east ejected from its moorings. It flew across the intersection and pulverized the face of an army clerk who had been gesturing to one of the snipers in her aerie. The tumbling concrete section ripped the catwalk free, and the metal armature halted the descent of the wall for a moment while hurling soldiers into the street; then it gave way. The soldier with the obliterated face fell to his knees at the same time the concrete slab hit the ground, crushing the Disposal agent who had been steering a load of rotting pets toward the incinerators and a young soldier who had been climbing one of the ladders up the catwalk. The dead sloshed through the gap, clambering over the concrete ramp and the crushed bodies, losing balance on the uneven surface and spinning in ludicrous pratfalls onto Canal. They stepped on one another, impelled one another forward in a current, spread in hungry rivulets east and west and downtown after being penned in for so long. Some of the dead that had been trapped at the bottom of the pile staggered to their feet and joined the advance.

Here they came, the ambassadors of nil. Already the front door of the bank was impassable, already the dead infiltrated one block south of the shattered barrier to reclaim the Zone as their own. The soldiers on the catwalk were stranded. They fired their assault rifles down into the maelstrom of skels, but the scaffolding terminated in ramps at either end and the men and women on the wall were cornered. The time to risk a jump disappeared; there was no open space for a landing, so swiftly had the dead swept into the street. A portion of skels dallied to partake of the stunned soldiers at the foot of the wall, but most coursed down the avenue after other sustenance. The majority of the abominations did not stop to feed, as if being loosed upon the emptied streets was meal enough, as if right now it sufficed for them to walk, to persist beyond death.

Looking down at them through the twisting ash, Mark Spitz shuddered. The dead streamed past the building like characters on an electronic ticker in Times Square, abstractions as impenetrable as the Quiet Storm's vehicles. He'd always peered from the skyscraper windows into the streets, seeking. Close to the ground, almost at their level, he read their inhuman scroll as an argument: I was here, I am here now, I have existed, I exist still. This is our town.

An explosion complicated the darkness in staggered eruptions, dispatching new quakes and tremors to replace the silenced barrage from the artillery. A truck's engine block, traversing space in a depleted, burning arc, crashed into a fast-food establishment catty-corner to the bank. Mark Spitz had eaten there seven times in his life, across the years. It had never been a destination but was a refuge in the middle of city missions, in between things, to kill time until the rain stopped, it was warm and he'd been there before. It was part of his city.

"That's the diesel going up," Bozeman said. Stray bullet, or the self-immolation of a drowning soldier taking those nibbling monsters in the blast radius with him. The snipers shrunk from their posts to secure a getaway, too late. The entrance to any building in Mark Spitz's vision was already surrounded. He heard

Fabio strategize as the three of them scrambled down the stairs to secure the front door of the bank, but Mark Spitz's brain was too embroiled in his survival schemes to comprehend. Just like old times. "Does this mean we stop referring to it as an interregnum, then?" he said. Addressing Omega. But they were not present. He supplied Gary's rejoinder: " 'Time out' is more like it." A grenade exploded outside.

When he reached the marble landing overlooking the main floor—after equipping himself in the office with an assault rifle, some clips, and, in a last-minute impulse, an armadillo helmet—the front door had been secured, the handles of the oversize brass doors swaddled in black cable. Five others remained in the building: Fabio; Bozeman; two rookie-faced army chumps named Chad and Nelson, whom Mark Spitz didn't recognize; and a furious Ms. Macy, who checked and double-checked the clip of a nine-millimeter pistol in muttering debate with herself. If pressed, with a gun to his temple or teeth to his jugular, Mark Spitz would have sworn she was saying, "Knew I should have taken that chopper."

Chad stuttered that they'd secured the south exit—the Lispenard access. Wonton had blown through the back wall of the bank to connect it with the rest of the block, which was shallow for the grid. It was Sunday night. Troops had been deployed to recon Happy Acres, and there had been more soldiers than usual manning the wall and the rooftops to tend to the dead swell, but the majority of the garrison was dispersed throughout the Zone, engaged in their R & R amusements and Sunday-night solaces. The A-list snipers and the sweepers, the indispensable clerks, and the doe-eyed engineers. With General Summers off duty, at her quarters, Bozeman was in charge. Summers lived on Greenwich, in a loft owned by a famously dissipated scion of European royalty. Great art, everyone reported. "Should we try to get to her?" Fabio asked.

Bozeman shook his head. "By now she knows the situation. Everyone's on their own." He pointed out that her quarters were half a mile south of Wonton; with luck she was on her way to the rendezvous.

"Which is?" Ms. Macy asked.

The first and last discussion of a fallback position was during the initial sweep, Bozeman explained, when Battery Park was the designated staging area for the op. The Staten Island Ferry Terminal served as the command center in those early days. "From there we can get air support. Rescue. Boats. If people remember that's where we're supposed to go," he added.

"And if there's anyone left to pick us up."

Mark Spitz patted his chest for the reassurance of his gear and was reminded that his stuff was in the back room of the fortune-teller's. Happy Acres out of contact, the other camps as well: This was not a local occurrence. Maybe this dark tsunami swallowed the entire star-crossed seaboard, camp by camp, maybe this was what was happening everywhere, all over the world. The patient stabilized for a time but now the final seizures announced themselves, the diminishing spasms conveying the body's meat to room temperature. Mark Spitz could play along with rescue talk, for the sake of the two army runts at least. The Lieutenant had designated the terminal as the fallback position at that first dumpling-house briefing, he recalled. Or was he inventing that moment, in the manner that you accomplice yourself to the shifting premises of a dream? The other sweeper units, from Alpha on up, were on the move; the wave of the dead would have swept past the dumpling joint by now. He hoped they had weapons with them, hadn't been hitting the sponsored booze all day.

"There's no time," Mark Spitz said.

"For what?"

"To sit here."

They scudded through the guts of Grid 003, Broadway x Canal, Business, passing through the termite corridors the Army Corps of Engineers had carved. Outside in the street the dead poured downtown. The wall was breached, but the bottleneck, coupled with the vagaries of skel diffusion patterns, meant they still had a chance of pushing through this local density.

"Walking is bullshit," Ms. Macy said.

"We have trucks," Bozeman said. He took point. The southern end of HQ was a Vietnamese restaurant on Lispenard. They cut the lights in the kitchen, and then Bozeman sent out one of the army guys to do the same in the main dining room. The problem being if one of the dead on the street saw the movement, attracting a covey to block their exit. Nelson made it through, and the band moved to the front of the restaurant, trying to stay out of the streetlight. The dead seeped through the east–west corridor of Lispenard but they preferred the wide avenues of Broadway, from what Mark Spitz could see from his angle. Two trucks were parked across the street, facing west. Depending on the skel distribution on Hudson, they could grind through until they outpaced the wave.

"Keys should be in there," Bozeman said.

Ms. Macy slumped by the coatroom. "I'm supposed to go in that?"

"I said we have trucks," Bozeman said.

We'll need momentum, Mark Spitz thought. These were scooting-around trucks, canvas-topped.

"I assumed armored," Ms. Macy said. "Fuck am I supposed to do, ride in the back?"

"Beats walking."

"It's useless," Nelson said. He had been weeping. He wept anew. "No one's going to pick us up."

"He's right," Ms. Macy said. "You don't know Buffalo. They're not going to send out a gunship to clean up a public relations stunt when they got camps falling right and left."

"Public relations," Fabio said.

"You have no idea how far we are from normal, do you?" She

sneered at their incomprehension, exhaled. "I'm too good at my job."

Nelson said, "I'm the last one left of my town. Everybody's dead."

"This is PR," Ms. Macy said. "It'll be years before we're able to resettle this island. We don't even have food for the winter."

Nelson said, "My own hands."

Fabio staggered as if slugged in his gut. "You said the summit."

She peered out through the glass again, taking the temperature, and shook her head. "Summit. You think he's coming back? If I had a goddamned sub, I wouldn't be coming back to this dump. Look at it out there. Those pricks are probably trying to figure out which island in the Bahamas to settle on." She checked her pistol. "Why are you smiling?"

She was talking to Mark Spitz. Shame rippled through him, the echo of a civilized self. He put it down. He was smiling because he hadn't felt this alive in months. Ever since he left the fortune-teller's, as the kinetics of the artillery hammered through his boots, shuddered into his bones, and sought synchrony with his heart's thump, he'd entered a state of tremulous euphoria. He was an old tenement radiator sheathed in chipped paint, knocking and whistling in the corner as it filled with steam heat. The sensation peaked the instant the wall collapsed and, in its ebb, he was the owner of a woeful recognition: It was not the dead that passed through the barrier but the wasteland itself, the territory he had kept at bay since the farmhouse. It embraced him; he slid inside it. Macy was correct. There would be no rescue at the terminal, no choppers dropping out of the sky at dawn after the longest night in the world. They had lost contact because the black tide had rolled in everywhere, no place was spared this deluge, everyone was drowning. Of course he was smiling. This was where he belonged.

At Bozeman's signal they made a break for it, this sad platoon, the army guys providing cover on their Broadway flank, Mark Spitz out in front with Fabio. The gunfire of the Canal engagements couldn't cover the reports as they routed the skels on Lispenard. Mark Spitz willed his rounds into the coordinates above the targets' spinal columns, as if it were possible to mentally steer them; the bullets penetrated their intended destination. Everything above the things' jawlines erupted into jelly. Nelson and Chad may have been green to Wonton but they were old hands at this brand of close fighting; they dropped five hostiles in quick succession, silent save for Nelson's blubbering.

Bozeman started the truck; Macy hopped in the passenger seat and shut the cab door. Everyone else made it into the back except for Fabio. He was halfway in when the truck lurched forward as Bozeman reacquainted himself with the mechanism. Fabio grasped for balance as if it twisted in the air before him and just as he seized it, four blood-streaked hands snatched him into the vortex. Mark Spitz trained his assault rifle on the skel in the janitor uniform as it chomped into Fabio's neck to loose a small fountain of blood. As the truck pulled away onto Hudson, he had time to put three rounds into Fabio's chest and terminate the man's screams.

The grisly tide rolled in. The truck rocked as it crunched over the dead. In the back of the truck they heard the tattoo of bodies bouncing off the hood as Bozeman managed to gather speed, the prow smashing through the breakers. Mark Spitz and Chad drew a bead on the dumb-faced skels in their wake, the ones who stood gaping, following the truck's course down the rapids. Then Mark Spitz realized he'd been cast into scarcity once more; these bullets were going to have to last. He held his fire. Outside the radius of Wonton, the streets had not been cleared of cars and trucks, and he braced himself as Bozeman zigged and zagged around obstructions. At one turn, Chad almost fell out of the back, mouth yawning in panic. Mark Spitz grabbed his arm and reeled him in.

By North Moore Street they had outpaced the inundation. Ms. Macy cursed when the truck halted. The dead surged behind them in the middle of the ave, advancing downtown. Chad and Nelson took a few down before they heard "Hold your fire!" from beyond the canvas. They made room for four soldiers, three of them hoisting an unconscious comrade into the truck. The prone figure was covered in blood, but it didn't appear to be from a bite. A new blossom of explosions colored the uptown sky orange and red, and as they receded, the lights went out. Wonton lost power. Nelson blubbered. The streets were dark. The garrison was completely submerged.

Bozeman started up the truck. Mark Spitz tried to read the street signs, eyes adjusting to the darkness. When he saw the sign he was waiting for, he grabbed Nelson's arm and said, "I have to check on my unit." He hopped out, lost his footing and rolled painfully on the pavement.

He didn't detect movement. The city here was still empty. For now, the moonlight allowed him to lay off the attention-drawing flashlight. He didn't have line of sight, but doubtless the blue moon of his uncle's building was eclipsed when the power cut off. He had seen it for the last time, he was sure. He calculated: The dead fanned from the hole in the wall, but they'd tend to splash down the big avenues. Mark Spitz's mission was a lateral move across the Zone to the fortune-teller's, before the creatures hit Chambers. He hadn't taken a step toward Broadway when he heard the truck crash. He kept moving. He'd see them at the rendezvous or he wouldn't. Halfway to Gold Street, he saw that his ash had stopped falling. Not enough memory, with his survival programs running, for his PASD. His past.

The sidewalk in front of the fortune-teller's was bereft of illumination. He hoped to find Omega in the back apartment. He crept inside and whispered their names. There was no answer. He locked the door to the shop, relieved to get off the street; he envisioned the dead as they gained velocity on these declivitous downtown streets, gravity yanking them to the bottom of the map. Once the things spread evenly through Zone One—could he call it that anymore?—it would be impossible to pass. It was probably too late to use the subway as a shortcut. They are dripping down the steps to the platforms by now.

Mark Spitz had never gamed out an escape from the island, but yes, the terminal was a good bet. Especially given the standard traffic on the bridges. The Brooklyn-bound bridges were obstructed but a person could negotiate the barriers, given time. The problem was the legions of dead invariably massed there and stretching the entire lamentable length of the span, all the way to the other borough. He'd always thought it strange, the devotion of the congregation there, as if in their fallen state they still hungered for Manhattan. Then as now, they believed the magic of the island would cure them of their sicknesses.

He swept through the shop with alacrity, in case Gary had already turned. Nothing moved. Kaitlyn had mobilized, to check out what was happening at Wonton. By now she understood the situation and he prayed she remembered to beat it to the terminal. Perhaps they'd crossed each other in the darkness, like they used to do in the old days of the living city. Happened all the time that someone you loved moved through the avenues, half a block over, one block over from you as they navigated their day, unaware how close you were. You just missed each other.

He closed the door to the back apartment to hide the light from the trickling dead. He lit a candle, in the wasted steppes once more despite the flimsy promises of architecture. Gary had bled through the blanket Kaitlyn covered him with. How long after Mark Spitz went up to Wonton? When he was a block away? After a farewell chat with Kaitlyn, then deciding after he felt something shift in his brain? In all likelihood he sent Kaitlyn on a false errand and took the opportunity.

Mark Spitz lifted the blanket. This was not a job Gary would do half-assed, but it was necessary to make sure he'd done it proper. From the looks of it Kaitlyn had put two more bullets in him for good measure. He was about to drop the blanket when he saw the paper in Gary's hand.

He pried the fingers, draped his friend again, and sank into the green armchair facing the sofa. Gary had been carrying it for a long time, from the creases and chewed edges, pocket to pocket to pocket. Since when, which asylum, consulted in the dark of how many failed refuges? Maybe he'd carried it since Last Night. It had been carefully ripped from a magazine, a level fur of fibers describing the inside edge. On one side, the island bulged from the blue waters of the Mediterranean, a knuckled lump of rock. It looked like a grenade, he thought. On the opposite, a street scene unraveled: A slim alley pullulated with men and women mid-errand, perhaps around noon. A trinket store hawked postcards on long wire racks, azure rectangles featuring more pictures of the island. A young couple enmeshed fingers at a small table outside a café, the red and white and brown logo of the espresso distributor half shadowed on a sign over the entrance. The table, aslant, jabbed its legs into cracks between cobblestones. A matchbox and a wad of napkin, the discarded shims, lay next to the woman's red sandals.

The thought of Gary smuggling a picture of Corsica, France, in his pocket through the desert all this time, while suffering through his Spanish lessons, almost made Mark Spitz chortle. Gary clearing his throat, marshaling his rehearsed patter, the greetings and sweet talk, as he walked across the gangplank off the sub to his longed-for island.

Mark Spitz snuffed the candle and checked out front. The dead teetered down Gold, southward in their hideous procession. Sparse right now. Still time to make it past them.

He returned to the back room. He retrieved his flashlight from his pack. No way to date the photograph of the alley. It might as well have been the last afternoon in the world, a scene to be inserted in the montage sequence of the disaster movie. The oblivious citizens drift on the anvil of this mundane afternoon, unaware of the bomb, the meteor, the fateful chunk of rock from outer space entering the atmosphere. In thirty seconds they will cease to exist, but for now they live in their moment of safety. Snug in sunlight, their lover's hand warm and true and solid in theirs.

The Lieutenant had asked Kaitlyn and him to picture a world where the stragglers were the dead majority, not an aberrant fraction. This photograph is what that would look like, Mark Spitz thought. The entire population snared in bygone moments, entranced by the world that no longer existed. Mesmerized by the outline of a shadow cast by a phantom that had made them happy once.

He had the forbidden thought. He didn't push it away.

It was the second time in three days, the most close together since his farmhouse rescue. It was happening again: the end of the world. The last months had been a pause, a breather before the recommitment to annihilation. This time we cannot delude ourselves that we will make it out alive.

When was the last time someone had taken his picture? Rhode Island. It was a month before he was picked up in Northampton, during a two-week stint at a hot-sheet hotel. The national budget-hotel chain had purchased an even cheaper chain and was refurbishing and renovating the universally dilapidated properties, installing the high-definition television screens on their tilting arms, tearing out the cigarette-burned and bodily-fluid-soiled carpets to replace them with the futuristic stain-impervious fibers. The franchise Mark Spitz stumbled on had been surrounded by chain-link fencing during construction, reassuringly anti-skel. One appreciated the chime of chain links these days, that perimeter-definer and alarm system.

Survivors came and went. He staked out Room 12, which was a musty box of umber and gray. The other survivors were harmless. Tired, like him, on a becalmed plateau of the interregnum. He was at a wedding, in a discounted block for members of the party. Strangers to one another but connected all this time even if they didn't know it, until thrown together in this little pocket of time outside their normal lives to bear witness. Except the ceremony kept being postponed. They extended their stays multiple times, rang the front-desk void, made the necessary excuses into the dead phones. Past complaining now, though.

Most nights, if people were up for it, they shared provisions in the tiny breakfast room off Reception, lentils or jam, and it was there he met the Simons. They were that rare thing in the wasteland, an intact family unit. Or they pretended to be. Rob and Lonnie, their kids Harold and Jennie. How they made it this far, he could not imagine. He was past curiosity, and at any rate Mom and Dad packed serious heat, ammo belts traversing their chests, tense hands never straying far from the holsters at their hips, explanation enough. Harold and Jennie were eleven and thirteen, respectively. They favored their father, especially in the eyes, and rarely spoke.

They stayed two nights. The second night they joined the small feast in Reception. Over stringy game-bird chili, Lonnie told the group they were headed to Buffalo. They had heard good things, met real soldiers who'd been there and spoke of putting it all back together. No one believed them. The Simons didn't care. They contributed five chocolate chip cookies, if he remembered correctly, which were broken into quarters and distributed around.

Before returning to their room they asked Mark Spitz to take their picture. "We like to keep a record," Rob said, placing the camera in his hands. It must have been a hassle to keep the device charged up; it was one of the last models, a buttonless cube out of Japan that did everything. The family posed by the dingy coffee machine, arranging themselves into what he took to be their standard pose, not smiling but not put out or melancholic, either. Then they asked if they could take Mark Spitz's picture.

"What for?"

"So we can remember what you look like," Lonnie said.

The Simons checked out at first light. The next day, not long after noon, bandits swept through. They executed some of the residents of the motel, tortured others in a long game they'd been working on, testing the logic of the body. Eventually an escape opportunity presented itself and most of the guests made it out intact. They knew the drill, this far into the miseries. But that was the end of the wedding party, and it was on to the next human settlement.

There was no other reality apart from this: move on to the next human settlement, until you find the final one, and that's where you die.

The parable of his journey back to the city. To keep moving, in the Mim sense. He'd always wanted to live in New York but that city didn't exist anymore. He didn't know if the world was doomed or saved, but whatever the next thing was, it would not look like what came before. There were no intersections with the avenues of Buffalo's shimmering reconstructions, its boulevards did not cross their simulations and dioramas of futurity. It refused the shapes Mark Spitz conjured in his visions of reinvention in the big city.

He dropped his new rifle and picked up his old one. It had gotten him through the Zone. It would get him out of it. Why they'd tried to fix this island in the first place, he did not see now. Best to let the broken glass be broken glass, let it splinter into smaller pieces and dust and scatter. Let the cracks between things widen until they are no longer cracks but the new places for things. That was where they were now. The world wasn't ending: it had ended and now they were in the new place. They could not recognize it because they had never seen it before.

Mark Spitz got his gear together. He stripped Gary's pack of what he could use. He tucked Corsica in his back pocket. He waved to his friend and shut the door to the apartment.

In the stream of the street the dead bobbed in their invisible current. These were not the Lieutenant's stragglers, transfixed by their perfect moments, clawing through to some long-gone version of themselves that existed only as its ghost. These were the angry dead, the ruthless chaos of existence made flesh. These were the ones who would resettle the broken city. No one else.

He was ready. He didn't like his chances of making it to the terminal. Who knew how many of the others had made it there, the band from the truck, the sundry personnel of the garrison. Officers, cooks, and clerks. He hoped the sweepers split skel heads as they beat their way downtown, or else contrived the flawless plan that eluded everyone's desperation. Kaitlyn. And if Mark Spitz did somehow blast, bludgeon, and dodge his way to the terminal, what then? It was foolish to dream of rescue.

The music sailed between the buildings, the tinkling bell and the demented melody produced at the animal's every step. Mingled with the dead, Disposal's horse drew his empty cart down the street. The animal clopped across the asphalt, mascot of ruin, without care or master. Even when it withdrew from sight, Mark Spitz heard it, the cheerful jingle insistent before the pitiless rock face of the metropolis. That's how he interpreted the melody: cheerful and undying.

On to the next human settlement, and the one after that, where the barrier holds until you don't need it anymore. He tightened the strap of the armadillo helmet. He strummed his vest pockets one last time and frowned at the density beyond the glass. They were really coming down out there. No, he didn't like his chances of making it to the terminal at all. The river was closer. Maybe he should swim for it. It was a funny notion, the most ridiculous idea, and he almost laughed aloud but for the creatures. He needed every second, regardless of his unrivaled mediocrity and the advantages this adaptation conferred in a mediocre world.

Fuck it, he thought. You have to learn how to swim sometime. He opened the door and walked into the sea of the dead.

ABOUT THE AUTHOR

Colson Whitehead is the author of the novels *The Intuitionist, John Henry Days, Apex Hides the Hurt*, and *Sag Harbor*. He has also written a book about his hometown, a collection of essays called *The Colossus of New York*. His work has appeared in the *New York Times, Granta, Harper's*, and *The New Yorker*. A recipient of a Whiting Writers' Award, a MacArthur Fellowship, and a fellowship at the Cullman Center for Scholars and Writers, he lives in New York City.